WATER TO BIND

A Jackson Flint mystery
Yellow Springs, Ohio

Scott Geisel

Fox&
Possum
PUBLISHING

scottgeisel.com

Printed and published in the United States of America.

First edition: April 2022

Cover art and book design copyright © 2022 by Pam Geisel.

ISBN 978-1-7350183-2-4

Thanks to Chuck Buster, Macy Reynolds, Roger Reynolds, Dan Rudolf, Pam Geisel, Laurie Martt, and Luan Heit. The A team.

1

SOMETHING WASN'T RIGHT. I'd only gotten a glimpse, an image in my periphery that skittered under the haze of a late-summer sun. Two teens exiting the back of the mall. But it was enough to register. Something was off.

The way they were walking? A package the taller one was carrying?

I let my head drift in their direction for a better look.

The big one saw it right away. I was the only other person in sight, and he honed in on me like he was looking for something, and like it or not, I was going to be it. He grabbed his partner's shoulders and spun them my way.

I kept my eyes casually on the two of them and leaned against the truck tailgate. It was a long way across the lot from them to where I was parked in the back row, and I had no idea why they should be interested in me.

But they kept coming. The images sharpened. Two teen boys, brownish complexions. One of them tall and with wide shoulders, the other smaller.

The thing that was wrong fell into place. The bigger guy gripped a huge stack of bills, ten or twelve inches thick, bound by big rubber bands. And he held it out like he wanted me to see it.

There couldn't have been a good explanation. Drug deal? Mistaken identity?

I should have gotten in the truck and driven away. Made a courtesy call to mall security. Let them know something was going on under their watch. Cruised down the service road that circled the mall, through the urban tangle of office buildings and medical service establishments and travelers' hotels, and out onto the back roads that would take me home to my little village beyond the suburbs.

But I was waiting for Brick. He'd come here with me to play backup while I served papers to an elusive bail jumper.

Darnell Brickman and I had gone to school together in Yellow Springs, our little haven in rural Ohio. It was a small enough village that it seemed like everyone knew everybody else, but Brick and I hadn't really gotten to know each other until long after high school. Brick disappeared into the Marines after graduation, and I mucked around for a while, enrolled in some college classes, and ended up in a job with the county sheriff.

Eventually I quit the sheriff's and traded the certainty of a paycheck and a pension for a chance to be my own man and the sole proprietor of the Jackson Flint Detective Agency, Yellow Springs, Ohio. My business cards read *Professional. Discreet.* That's all. If you wanted to know more, you had to hire me. And to do that you had to convince me that I wanted to work for you.

Eventually Brick quit the Marines and the special ops team he'd been assigned to and came home to Yellow Springs under the heavy weight of more than a little PTSD.

We reconnected on a run through the woods. I was in one of my favorite places, cruising through the thousand acres of the Glen Helen Nature Preserve. Winnie the Pooh had his Hundred Acre Wood. I had my thousand acre woods. It was quiet and cool beneath the trees, with dappled light drifting through the leaf canopy. I was out for an easy loop down the old fire road and back up along Yellow Springs Creek. Nothing too strenuous.

Brick changed that. I heard the footsteps coming fast and hard from behind me and figured it was the high school kids on the cross country team. I moved to the right of the trail to let them pass. But it was only one set of footsteps. Then a blocky, mocha-brown figure careened past me like a boat caught with its sails up in a storm.

I didn't think he'd make it very far at that pace. If he was the hare and I was the tortoise, I'd catch him well before the end of the trail. Then it got interesting. The guy looked familiar.

I kicked up my speed and came in beside the runner. The man flicked his eyes over me once and said a single word. "Jackson."

"Brickman?"

"It's just Brick now."

Our breaths came controlled and steady, the pace of our strides dictating the rhythm. I looked over. "Long time."

For an answer, he just kept running. Brick didn't burn out. He didn't keep up the wild sprint, but we set a hard pace through the trees and when we reached the boundary of the private nature preserve he pivoted onto the narrow paved road that took us into John Bryan State Park.

We sailed through the camp grounds with the tents and coolers and towels hanging from clotheslines, and Brick plunged us back into the woods on the north rim trail above the Little Miami River.

The path there was rougher and we ran single file until Brick turned onto a switchback that brought us out to the park road. From there it was a long haul side-by-side back through the state park, through Glen Helen, and up the hundred stone steps to the entrance.

It was a lot more run than I'd bargained for. I leaned over my knees in the gravel lot. "You do this very often?"

"Every day."

Sure he did. "Even your birthday?"

He didn't laugh.

"OK, so you run every day. Nothing better to do?"

There was a hard look in his eye. "Everything else is worse."

Then he turned to an old, beaten-up Jeep.

His skin glistened with sweat, and I noticed for the first time the tattooed flock of birds that rose up from beneath his t-shirt and peppered his left shoulder. I'd heard the stories about Brick and what he'd done in the service. I'd seen the reports in the *Yellow Springs News* when he'd been in a battle or been honored with a medal or an award. And I knew he hadn't been back long.

I put one hand up. "Wait. Do it again tomorrow?"

We exchanged phone numbers. Then he pulled open the door to the

Jeep. Stale air spilled out and I swear it sounded like the Jeep sighed.

"Maybe we can take it a little easier tomorrow?"

Brick nudged the vehicle to life and the transmission clunked into gear. He leaned out. "Probably not."

We ran a lot after that. And we moved on to other things, hard things. Heavy lifting, combat training he'd learned in the Marines. Brick invented crazy workouts that seemed impossibly difficult. We carried parts of an old Buick around his yard, climbed slats nailed to the side of his barn. Ran every day until we were exhausted and my dreams became filled with running.

I knew what he was doing. Leaving the military was hard for Brick, but staying in had been killing him. He had his head in the old world but his body was in a new one, and he needed a distraction as he tried to make the adjustment.

Brick had a cabin north-ish of town where he kept himself hidden in the woods. I had a house in town, a P.I. license, and a wife and daughter. Then I lost my wife Kat. And my daughter Cali and I had to adjust to a whole new world we didn't like. Brick watched it happen, and when I felt most at sea he knew exactly what that was like and stepped up to be there for Cali and me.

Life wasn't a circle, exactly, but there were twisting paths that crossed one another.

Cali and I dug out of the devastation that losing her mother and my wife had dumped on us, and now those memories were tucked somewhere in our psyches where we could manage to remember Kat but not let it debilitate us. Something like Brick had done with his PTSD.

Brick remained a recluse, and that seemed to work for him. Cali and I had a new tack on life. She was doing well in school and watching her friends go off to college and thinking about when she would make that leap too. The Jackson Flint Detective Agency was doing solid business with still just me as the only full-time employee. But lately others had been getting onto the payroll.

I used Brick for some special needs. Today his job had been easy.

I'd been trying to serve papers on a bail jumper. I wasn't a licensed bounty hunter and I couldn't arrest the guy and take him in, but I was good at finding people when others couldn't. It wasn't my favorite work, but the extra money was hard to turn down, especially with Cali's college fund looming.

The guy was slippery. Today I brought Brick for insurance.

I followed the subject to a break room where he'd been pilfering lunches at the mall. A few seconds after I entered, Brick planted himself in the doorway. There was no other way out, and I served the papers.

Easy-peasy, and easy money for Brick. The thought of it was burning a hole in his pocket and he wanted to stay and get a new pair of running shoes. I hadn't given him his cut yet, and I didn't have the stomach for a mall store, so I was leaning against the truck waiting for Brick when the two kids came.

I let my eyes slide away as they got closer. Nothing to see here, folks. Just keep walking.

The big guy wasn't having any of it. He looked maybe nineteen. Big but with rounded shoulders and a stooped frame. He had black hair and a look of the Mediterranean or the Middle East. The other kid was younger. His shoulders were wide and he had the blocky and firm look of an athlete. His skin was darker.

When I was growing up, the Black guys were always the coolest. They walked cooler, talked cooler, and laid back better. The big kid here looked like he was trying too hard at that, with a huge blunt pinched between his lips and a goofy grin on his face.

His partner didn't look cool at all. He looked like he wanted to be somewhere else.

I knew the clichés. Dark skin equals trouble. But in my experience I'd seen a whole lot more white people who shared my European descent fall into dealing weed, trafficking in opioids, beating up their girlfriends or wives or whoever they thought was weaker than them, and generally stealing and thieving. White guys with a little money were the worst, somehow believing that their lucky draw of fate put them into positions of leverage that meant they were above getting punished.

The culture had probably taught them that was true. But it also showed kids like these two that they'd been singled out and punished simply because of what they looked like.

I looked to the loop road, but Brick's green Jeep wasn't there.

The bigger kid closed the last steps between us. He plucked the blunt from his mouth and shook the fist with the block of money. "Hey, man. You see this?"

I stepped away.

He stepped around me and blocked my path to the truck cab. "You don't want to talk to me?"

I shook my head.

"Because I'm Black?"

Well, damn. No. But this was getting ugly.

"You think I don't belong here?"

"I didn't say that." Mistake. Just get in the truck and drive away. Disengage. Don't give him anything to battle with.

The guy was quick. He stuffed the money into his partner's hands and moved farther over to block my path to the truck door. He feinted a left jab that he clearly didn't know how to throw.

Ah, shit. Somebody was going to get hurt.

The eyes of the kid holding the cash said they were way off script, and he didn't like it. I knew the feeling.

The big guy rolled his shoulders. Up close he showed some muscle behind his bulk. He twisted his neck to the side and back. "Say it."

I held up both hands with my palms out. Nothing doing. I'm leaving.

I was very aware of my size, and of my background and training. I didn't know why this kid thought I'd be an easy target. Maybe it was that I was the only target, and he felt the need to go after somebody. It was a bad choice.

I was also aware of the Smith & Wesson M&P40 locked in the truck's glove compartment. I never wanted to need it, but you never knew in my line of work. One way or another I was going home to my daughter at the end of the day. If the gun was what made that possible, it would come out.

I reached around the kid to put a hand on the door handle.

He leaned into me. "Say I don't belong here because I'm Black."

"Look, if anybody doesn't belong here, it's me."

"You damn right." He pointed to his partner who still held tight to the money but was listing like he couldn't find his sea legs. "You see that? Twenty grand. Worth more than your whole truck."

True. It was worth several times over. My hand went to my pocket for my phone.

His hand went to the bottom of his shirt line.

Please, no.

I took a slow breath and let it out. Showed him that I'd reached for my phone and nothing else. "We're done here. I'm leaving."

He laughed and raised his shirt to show the butt of a handgun. "We're done when I say we're done."

Scenarios clicked rapidly through my head. Take him down now? Break his arm? How hard would I have to come at him to keep someone from getting shot?

Click click. Did the other kid have a gun too?

Click click. Was there still a chance to de-escalate?

The kid's eyes slid to his right as if he was looking at something in the distance.

I kept my eyes on the kid's hands and the pistol in his belt.

The younger kid faded back a step. I could see in his eyes that he wanted to run.

The big guy dropped his shirt back down over the gun and spun to his partner. "Deek, I will fuck you up if you run."

The guy he called Deek stopped. He cradled the money in a shaky hand like he was afraid he might drop it.

A dark green Jeep careened through the empty parking lot toward us, eating up the bright white lines like hash marks on a football field.

The kid couldn't decide where to focus, and then it was too late. The Jeep jammed to a stop and Brick jumped out and grabbed the kid, leveraged him and spun him around. Bent the kid over and pulled the pistol from his waist. "Damn, son. This ain't no toy. I could see you playing with it from way over there."

The kid grunted.

Brick twisted the arm harder and patted the kid's shirt and pants pocket. "Your partner packing?"

The other kid's hands went up, one of them still waving the thick stack of bills. I patted him down quickly, but I already knew he wasn't carrying.

Brick relaxed his hold and the kid in his grasp twisted around. "I will fucking kill you, man."

Brick tossed the gun he'd taken into the open door of the Jeep. "I don't think so." His t-shirt stretched across his pecs and announced *This Is Gonna Hurt.* Maybe so. He cut his eyes to me. "These your friends?"

"Never met them before."

"Then what the hell is happening here?"

It was a good question. "Near as I can figure, these two stopped by just to tell me their stack of money is worth more than my truck."

Brick's eyes narrowed.

"It appears somebody wanted to show off."

Brick looked at the money. "My new running shoes are worth more than your truck."

Both of the guys looked down at Brick's shoes. Another rookie mistake. Keep your eyes up on what can hurt you.

I said, "Now I think we're done here."

The kid pushed back against Brick's grip on him. "Gimme back my gun."

Brick said nothing.

"You gotta give it back. They ain't gonna like you taking it."

"Who isn't?"

The kid tried to shrug but couldn't manage it with Brick holding him. Brick released his grip. "I think the thing is that somebody's not going to like you losing it."

It hit home. The kid's eyes showed fear.

Brick said, "You really living the life, ain't you?"

"What do you know about it?"

"I know this. You're making it worse by looking for trouble with my friend here."

"I ain't looking for trouble. This guy said he don't want to talk to me because I'm Black."

Brick flicked his eyes over and back. "That right?"

"Nah."

"This kid look Black to you?"

"Well, he's some color."

"What color would you call it?"

"Hard to say. You're some kind of raspberry iced coffee." I held an arm out. "I'm pasty white." I dropped the arm. "But this guy is tougher. Something like toast that's a little too done."

"Any of that have any hoo-haw whatsoever to what's happening here?"

"Not a thing."

The big kid said, "You guys having fun?"

Brick frowned. "Son, ain't none of this any fun at all."

The kid's face puckered. "Nobody calls me son."

"I call you son."

The kid backed up. Agitated.

"Your mama and daddy ever tell you how to get by in this world?"

The kid's head went down, wagging. Like a bull that wanted to charge.

Brick pointed to the other kid. "You put that money away. It's bad enough how you probably got it. Don't be walking around showing it and make things worse."

The stack of bills went under the kid's arm.

Brick got up in the big kid's face. "And you keep your head down. Don't draw attention. You got something to be mad about, you be smart about it. This guy—" He jerked a thumb to me. "He'll take you apart. You hear me? Be smart. You just got lucky here."

The kid backed up. Head still wagging, hands shaking. Angry. "Man, I thought you'd be cool."

"You don't know nothing about it. What do you think you're doing here? How you think this is gonna play out?"

"Just give me back my gun."

Brick's eyes flicked to the money.

"Oh, hell no. You can't take that."

"You got way more trouble than you know what to do with. Who do you have to deliver the money to?"

The kid with the money bolted. Arms and legs pumping, bills flapping as he galloped away.

The bigger kid looked once to Brick, once to the open door of the Jeep where Brick had tossed his gun. Then he dropped the challenge and put his head down and ran after his partner.

Brick watched them disappearing. He looked uncertain. It wasn't something I was used to seeing on him.

I nudged Brick's elbow. "Well, that was fun. But we need to go."

He didn't move.

"Unless you want to call it in."

His head came around. "We're not calling anybody."

"Well what then? Let's go."

"It's going to be trouble for them."

"Maybe. That's something they'll have to work out."

Brick squinted at the kids. "You go home."

"I'm not—"

"Go home. To Cali. Now."

"But—"

He was already getting back into the Jeep, and before I could find the next words to say to Brick, he was gone, gunning across the hash marks, eating up the distance to the kids before they disappeared.

I didn't like it. But loyalty is a powerful thing.

I got into the truck, pushed the stick into gear, and drove away without looking back.

2

THE MALL FADED BEHIND ME, but the images in my head lingered like the malaise from a bad dream.

The big stack of bills. The big blunt and the loping smile. The gun in the waistband. The green tint to the kid holding the money.

Brick snatching the gun, holding it, the kids running away. Me standing there. I didn't like the way the images played, and I didn't like the ending.

I tried the radio for distraction. Tuned through commercials and a couple of songs and found *Queen of My Double Wide Trailer.* I tried to sing along. Even that wasn't enough to clear my head.

I didn't like leaving Brick behind, even if it was what he wanted.

My time with the sheriff's office told me this was something to call in. Don't mess around. It wasn't my case. It was just bad luck. Just call it in and get on with my day.

Running alongside that was my private experience nagging me that as a courtesy I should have alerted mall security that something was going on under their noses.

Drowning out all of that was those kids. How do they end up like that? Twenty grand and the world is their oyster. I wondered how they couldn't see that the road they were on would be a short ride.

Earlier in the summer I'd taken a case that led me to a fourteen-year-old runaway girl. When I found her she was one step in any direction away from some truly awful things, drugs and prostitution and the downward spiral of a life that collapses on itself as options become fewer and fewer. It had made me think of my daughter Cali.

Those kids now reminded me how close anyone's child was to something dark or dangerous.

The hillbilly song ended and the radio voice told me the weekend weather was going to be good. I should get out and enjoy summer while it was still with us. I imagined happy things to try to clear my head. Little birds flittering and chirping around Snow White's head. A June night with fireflies. Snow in the woods.

My daughter Cali. That did it.

Cali and I had gone through a rough stretch after we lost her mother, but somehow she had come through with enough memories of Kat intact to remind her of what her mother had been, and enough of an ability to look forward that she didn't seem to be susceptible to bouts of wallowing in grief. I was pretty sure I'd had to work harder on that than Cali had. But much of what is inside a teenager's head is a mystery, so who really knows?

When I crossed from the corn and soybean fields into the little village of Yellow Springs and neared home, I felt my mood tick up.

I pulled into the side yard under the big pine trees. When I reached the top step of the porch, Mrs. Jenkins rose from the wicker chair she'd been nestled in and set her hairy haunches down in front of the door, blocking my way.

The long-haired calico that had showed up one morning and decided she was going to live with us could be unpredictable. Sometimes she couldn't get enough people time. Other times she might disappear for a few days, or hide herself away in the weeds and wildflowers.

The one thing the cat was fairly consistent about was her special treat. Most afternoons Mrs. Jenkins would lurk underfoot, waiting for someone to get out the can of wet food that would make her purr like an Italian sports car.

I set my keys on the table. "Cali?"

Mrs. Jenkins revved the purring from first gear into second in anticipation.

"Cali?"

There was a muffled thump, then Cali's voice. "In my bedroom."

I called down the hallway. "Have you fed Mrs. Jenkins?"

"Is she following you around begging for food?"

I felt a swish at my leg as the cat tried to divert me back toward the food bowl. "She is."

"Then no, I haven't fed her."

"OK, do you want to do that?"

A quiet beat passed. "You can."

So much for gentle persuasion. I got out the can of good stuff and spooned some into Mrs. Jenkins' bowl. The purring kicked up to a high whine and then settled into a deep rumble amid the sounds of contented licking.

I went down the hall to Cali's room. The door was open a little and I could see her on the edge of her bed with her phone in her hand. I tapped some knuckles on the door. "I'm starting dinner."

She glanced up from her phone, then back. "OK." Then with one hand she twirled a strand of sandy blonde hair from her chin and tucked it behind an ear. It was a move that reminded me of her mother.

The tick up in my mood slipped into a tick back down. At that moment Kat should have been standing next to me. I should have been able to turn to her, to give her a look that said *Do you see what I see? That's what you do. That's your daughter.*

But it was just me in the door frame, and it was just Cali in her room. And she was more absorbed in her phone than her father.

I tapped my knuckles on the door again. "You need anything?"

"No." Her eyes stayed on the screen.

"How is—"

"Dad, I'm trying to get my class schedule for next week. I want to see if Jenny or Asia are in any of my classes."

Oh. Sorry. "Didn't you sign up for classes together?"

Cali's shoulders went up and down and a sigh came out with them. But she looked away from her phone. "Yes. But you don't get all the classes you want, and sometimes there's more than one section. So I don't know if we'll be together or not in all of them."

"Uh-huh."

Her thumbs moved over the screen.

"OK, I'll leave you to that."

That was like her mother too. Absorbed in something and totally unavailable until she was done with whatever was holding her attention. But that was anyone these days. Buried in their phone while the physical world spun silently past like a ghost. Add a teenager to the mix and the digital curtain could come down hard.

I slinked away to the kitchen. Mrs. Jenkins was waiting there and I bent to rub her head. She leaned an ear forward and indulged me for a second, then ducked away and pointed her nose at the door.

I held the door open for her. "You have one of these of your own."

Mrs. Jenkins showed me her hairy tail and disappeared. Why use the cat door when a human was there to open the big door for her?

I checked my messages again. Nothing from Brick. I turned the phone over and went to the pile of late-summer rattlesnake beans on the counter.

It was a lonely job cooking dinner. Cali stayed in her room. I only had the beans for conversation.

I cooked a sweet potato, a yellow pepper, and some soy sausage. They sizzled but didn't talk much either. I made rye biscuits in the iron skillet. They smelled good but didn't contribute any conversation.

I went back down the hallway and tapped a knuckle on Cali's door. "Dinner."

She looked up and smiled. The big wattage smile. Mary Tyler Moore turning the world on.

Then she sniffed. "Smells like green beans." The smile dimmed.

"If you don't want to come for the beans, then come for the sparkling conversation."

"What?"

"I haven't had anyone to talk to."

Her phone came down. "Dad, you are so weird sometimes."

"It hasn't hurt me yet. You coming?"

The phone went reluctantly into a pocket. "Well I have to eat something."

She followed me to the kitchen. "Where's Marzi?"

"What?"

"There are only two plates."

I shook my head.

"She's coming later?"

I shrugged and started filling the plates. I'd made a hash and arranged the rattlesnake beans and rye biscuits on the side.

Cali picked at the sweet potato and sausage. Little bites, around the pepper and beans.

I squeezed hot mustard over my hash.

Cali made a face.

I swished a green bean in the mustard.

Cali pushed her beans to the side of her plate.

I aimed a fork at her. "You used to like green beans."

"Maybe my tastes are refining."

"Refining?"

Her fork came down. "You wouldn't cook this if Marzi were here."

"Cook what?"

"This—" She swept a hand over the table.

"It's what we always eat. It's what's in season."

"Marzi is more of a meat eater."

"Well, sure. But she's not here tonight."

"You know she's just being nice. When you cook all this weird food for her?"

"Weird…"

But maybe it was true. Marzi O'Brien and I had been seeing each other for most of the summer. In that time I had rarely heard her say no to anything. But she could move food around on a plate without eating much of it until the remains looked like a Jackson Pollock. It was one of the things I liked about Marzi. She tried to go with the flow. Even when she didn't care much for the flow.

The awkward part had been that Marzi counseled Cali and me after we lost Kat. It was a couple of months of fairly intense sessions followed by a few more scattered meetings while Cali and I accepted the loss. Then we'd lost touch with Marzi until I found her at Tom's Market and discovered that she had moved to Yellow Springs.

It didn't take long from there. It had been hard to shake the feeling of once-a-counselor-always-a-counselor, but we were trying to make it work.

Cali had jumped in with both feet, like Marzi was the best thing since the smartphone. It was easy sailing until recently. Marzi and I had been thinking about boundaries, giving each other a little room and time while we figured out what might come next.

Cali seemed to be developing her own ideas about those things.

The cat door thumped and Mrs. Jenkins came in and broke the spell of—whatever was happening.

Cali cut the end off a rattlesnake bean and wiggled it in front of Mrs. Jenkins' nose.

"She won't eat that."

The cat meowed.

Cali lowered the bean.

Mrs. Jenkins sniffed once, took the bean, and immediately batted it away across the floor.

I pointed with my fork. "Not nearly as subtle as Marzi."

Cali didn't laugh. "When is she coming over?"

I picked up the bean from the floor. Mrs. Jenkins ambled away. I'd probably find a mouse somewhere in the house later. Payback for trying to feed the cat a bean. Felines could be spiteful like that. "Marzi and I aren't planning anything tonight."

Cali squinted a what-are-you-talking-about face at me.

It was a little unusual. Marzi and I had been spending most nights together. Many of them had been sleep-overs here.

Cali pushed her plate away. "I already invited her."

"You what?"

"We were going to watch our show."

Their show was an old TV series about a mother and daughter who lived in the fictional town of Stars Hollow, which had some small-town similarities to Yellow Springs. That was part of the attraction. Another piece of it was the mother-daughter connection in the series, which Cali couldn't get from her own mother and had been vicariously soaking up wherever she could find it.

"I thought you were watching that with Asia and Jenny."

"I am. We are. You know I've been watching some with Marzi."

I did know. I'd sat in on a few episodes, or parts of them, but mostly that had been time for Cali and Marzi.

"It's the last season. Marzi and I were going to watch it together."

"That's fine."

"But you didn't invite her over."

"But you did."

I took my plate to the sink. When I came back for Cali's, she held a hand out over the remnants of her dinner. I knew she was done eating, but I left the plate.

Cali sighed. "Why is this so hard?"

"I don't know."

But I did know. I knew it was because there were two of us when there was supposed to be three. That the loss of Kat was something Cali and I would always have to carry with us. And that the uncertainty of Marzi as the new third was not going to be an easy thing to navigate.

That, added to the mysteries of a teenaged daughter.

Cali took her plate to the counter and scraped the dregs into a left-over container. She hadn't taken another bite. "I guess you can watch with us if you want. If Marzi even comes over."

"Gee, since you put it that way." Stupid, Jackson. If I could just rewind three seconds and take that one back. I reached a hand up. "I'm sorry. I didn't mean that."

Cali shrugged. "I thought you'd want her to come over."

I thought I did too.

"Is it weird because I asked her instead of you?"

It was weird. But in that moment I heard the voice of my daughter who was much older than her years. Cali was fifteen and going into her junior year in high school. She was a little younger than most of her class, but she carried a maturity that would show when she wanted it to.

I answered with most of the truth. "I'm just a little distracted by something else tonight." That was underselling it. I'd resisted the urge several times to call Brick and ask him what the hell had happened at the mall.

Then something clicked in my head. Some little cog that moved over into a new place, telling me to let some more of the truth out. "OK, it's weird."

Cali thumped the refrigerator door closed.

"You should have asked me first."

"Marzi is my friend too."

Right. Again. "But it's different."

"What's different? I'm friends with Marzi because you were first? So I can't be friends with her on my own?"

Well, no. But there was that wisdom again, muddled and filtered by a teenager's brain and what Cali had been through. "Marzi and I are just taking a little time to see how things go."

"How much time do you need?"

It was a good question. I gave the full answer. "We won't know until we get to the other side."

It wasn't enough. Cali went down the hall to her room and closed the door.

I cleaned up the rest of dinner and went out in the yard by the garden and checked my texts, phone logs, and email messages. There was nothing from Brick.

I pulled a few weeds that taunted me in the evening light. There had been nothing. No messages from Marzi either. I knew I should call or text her, but indecision is a diabolical thing that feeds on itself. I pulled more weeds.

My phone rang. Finally.

It was a number I didn't know. "Jackson Flint Detective Agency."

"Is this Jackson Flint?"

"It is."

"I want to hire you—I mean, I think I want to hire you. I mean I have something that I need help with and I wonder if you'll let me hire you. I mean—I don't know how this works."

The voice sounded young and female. "Why don't you tell me what your situation is?"

"I bought a house—I inherited a house. In Yellow Springs. Near Yellow Springs. It's in the—It was my aunt's house. My great aunt.

She lived in the family cabin. She'd been there a long time. I just came from—I lived in New Mexico."

"All right." I'd found that if I waited long enough, people would often come to the point. I gave her some more time, but the caller didn't speak. "What is it you need help with?"

"Somebody is living in my house."

"Somebody you know?"

"No. I haven't seen them."

"You haven't seen them?"

"No. I mean I think someone is living there. Or was. Things get—moved around. Someone is coming in."

"You can call the village police for help."

"It's outside of Yellow Springs." She gave me an address and described the location. It was in a rural area toward Cedarville and Wilberforce. Both towns were small, Cedarville about the size of Yellow Springs and Wilberforce much smaller, but with a lot of interesting history. Neither was very far away. She described the house as *in the woods*.

"The Greene County Sheriff then." I knew the number. I used to work for them.

"I called. They came out. Really nice, but they said there wasn't much they could do. They looked around and told me they'd put it on the drive-by sheet."

I knew that sheet. It was what you did when there might be something going on, or there might not. You wanted to do something to make the caller feel better. A county car might drive by a couple of times during the night and stop for a few minutes and look around. Probably they wouldn't see anything. If there was something to follow up on, they would have already offered to do that.

"I could come out and look around." It would be a good distraction.

"I'm not there now. I didn't want to be out in the woods alone when I didn't know what was going on."

Good idea. "So where are you?"

"A little Airbnb down near the Grinnell Mill."

I knew the place. It was by the devil's backbone, the steep and twisting hill that Brick and I liked to race up. I would have thought she'd want to be up the hill in the village where the streets were lit and it didn't feel like you were in the wilds. "I think you'll like it there. I could come pick you up."

"How about in the morning?"

So she wasn't going to be my distraction for the night. "OK, tomorrow. Are you an early riser?"

"What do you call early?"

"Nothing in town opens until six-thirty."

There was a moment of silence. "Six-thirty is kind of early. I guess nobody gets up before that."

"Not unless you want to make your own coffee."

The caller didn't laugh. "Why don't I text you around nine?"

We agreed. "One more thing. I didn't get your name."

"Angelita Rojas Flores." There was a subtle roll in her *r*'s. "Do you need me to spell that for you?"

"No, I got it." I wrote that in my little notebook.

We ended the call and I turned and saw the flickering of the TV through the big window. Cali was in profile on the couch. The seat next to her was empty.

I took the easy way out. Or maybe the coward's way. I walked around the house to the truck under the pines and got in. Then I texted Cali that I'd gotten a call and had to go check on something for a client. I knew it was a half-truth, but my fingers moved on the phone before my brain could stop them. Cali would probably think I was going to my little office above the village, but I had another destination.

I second-guessed it while I drove. It probably would have been wiser to stay at home. To go in and talk to Cali, call Marzi and settle plans for the night. Wait until morning to get interested in work.

I almost considered calling my mother to ask for advice. It would have been the first time I'd done that. But mom was enjoying an extended trip to Europe with her new male friend. It was the first time she'd shown that much interest in anything since my father had passed nearly a decade ago.

I let the doubts drift out of my head and motored on.

The drive to the address Angelita had given me for the house she inherited took me right past the B&B where she was staying. Out of habit I slowed and looked over. Never pass up an opportunity to learn what you can.

No one was outside, but a weathered Toyota pickup peeked from behind the foliage. I assumed that was Angelita's ride, and I approved.

Angelita's house was harder to find. I crossed Massies Creek and Clark Run and twisted back over my route looking for it. Then I got my bearings and found the place in a wooded area between the farm fields and stables that dotted the area.

No other vehicles were on the narrow chip-and-gravel road. At the rusted mailbox that marked the location I pulled into brush that threatened to overtake the berm.

An old chain stretched between two fence posts and blocked the drive that disappeared into a tangle of branches.

There was evidence of some light foot traffic around the barrier. Maybe Angelita, or maybe kids who were looking for a way to get to a secluded place. It's the kind of thing I would have done when I was younger. Still would now.

Out of respect I didn't go any further. This was exactly the kind of thing Angelita had called me to try to prevent.

To take up some more time I cruised through Cedarville. For my dawdling I was rewarded with a snapshot view of small-town Americana framed through the windshield. The old opera house, coffee shops, a pizza place. Cedarville University.

Then it was back onto the rural roads and I was on the edge of dropping in at Brick's secluded cabin north of town, but that would break the code. If Brick hadn't answered my messages, he wanted to stay dark. So I kept driving.

Marzi's car was parked out front when I pulled up to the house. A flickering glow came through the window. I snapped the lights off and eased the truck in under the pines. Then I reached behind the seat and pulled out my running shoes. I laced them on and shambled out for a really long run. The symbolism didn't escape me. Running away.

When my legs were spent and my mind had slowed, I glided back home to the porch and dropped into a wicker chair. I stayed there in the dark until Mrs. Jenkins found me and curled up in my lap. Then we both got quiet and I may have nodded off.

Some time later Marzi opened the door and came out on the porch. She leaned down and spoke gently into my ear. "Jackson."

I tilted my head up.

"You OK?"

"Sure."

"You don't quite seem like it."

"Sorry."

She looked at the chair beside me. "Want to tell me about it?"

I did, but I shook my head. "It's late. I'm just thinking about a case. Did you watch your show with Cali?"

Marzi didn't take the chair. "We did. Cali thought you might want to join us."

"I had a work thing come up."

"That's what she said."

Marzi waited. I said what had to come next. "I didn't want to come in and interrupt you."

Marzi straightened and reached into her pocket for her keys. "OK. But Jackson? You're going to have to interrupt us. That's what's happening here."

She kissed me lightly on the forehead before she left. It was more than I deserved.

3

SLEEP HAD DONE ME SOME GOOD.

Things usually seem bleakest late in the day, when worries circle like vultures waiting to descend.

Sleep had cleared the vultures. I had a better feeling about Brick. That he knew what he was doing. That he could handle himself if things went sour. That he would call on me if he needed help.

That he would tell me what was going on when he was ready.

It was six and still dark, but the circuits were cleared and I was ready to go. No one else was up except Mrs. Jenkins. I was making a breakfast sandwich to leave in the fridge for Cali. Mrs. Jenkins was out on the porch eating a mouse. Neither of us offered to share.

At six-thirty I was at Dino's Cappuccinos. There are lots of reasons to like Dino's, and I was there for two of my favorites: they were open early, and they'd been making the best lattes in town for as long as I could remember.

The door jangled under the *Grazie!* sign. Dean Martin looked at me from his picture frame on the wall. Frank and Sammy looked over his shoulder. I wasn't fooled. The rat pack wouldn't have much use for a coffee shop unless there was a bar in the back.

I got a large to go.

My office is tricky to find. It's a bit like an escape room in reverse. You start in Kieth's Alley, the oddly spelled backway that runs behind downtown Yellow Springs, walk along the murals painted on the backs of the buildings, past the Black Lives Matter images, until you find the door that blends in so well it almost disappears. From there it's up a rickety set of stairs, then a winding path down twisted hallways that trace from one building to another, until you come to the door that's hung backwards so it opens to stretch across the hallway and block the entrance to my office.

Inside there's only room for a desk and filing cabinet, with a couple of folding chairs that can be crammed into the remaining space if you don't mind tucking your feet under your seat. For all that trouble, you're rewarded with a view looking down over the heart of the village.

That, and the latte, made the tiny space worth it.

I logged onto my laptop and opened my mail. Cleaned up a few things—bills, emails, inquiries, spam.

Marzi was probably on her way to work right now. Driving out of the village, her own cup of coffee in hand. I could text her. Something simple...

The something simple wasn't coming to me, so I turned back to my laptop.

I went to the county property search website and looked up the address Angelita Rojas Flores had given me for the place she inherited. The property appeared, but I didn't learn much. Angelita was listed as the owner. A link to a record for a transfer of the deed showed the previous owner's last name had been Leewold. Not a surprise.

I looked up the name Leewold in Greene County. It went way back.

Angelita's family history, or at least her aunt's on the Leewold side, was intertwined with some things from the same time period that I knew about. The Conway Colony of former slaves that had come to Yellow Springs and lived near what is now Glen Helen. The tombstone in Massie Creek Cemetery for Martin Delany, who was the first Black field major in the U.S. Army.

But I hadn't heard of Tawawa Springs, where Wilberforce University is located now, and where the Leewold name had roots. It was interesting. I kept reading. For a long time.

Tawawa had been known as a watering ground for the Native Americans who made use of the natural springs in the area. In the 1850s a lawyer and former speaker of the Ohio House of Representatives bought the land and opened a health resort he called Tawawa Springs. People came to relax, recuperate, and be healed by the miraculous powers of the mineral-rich water.

But Southerners who brought slaves and enslaved mistresses to serve them on their excursions were disdained by locals who supported the anti-slavery movement. The resort failed. In 1856 the land was purchased to found Wilberforce University, named for the British abolitionist. It was the first U.S. college owned and administered by African Americans. Tawawa House and the cottages that had been the resort were refurbished to become the college campus.

Nearly a decade later on the same night that Lincoln was fatally shot in Ford's Theatre, the main campus building mysteriously burned to the ground. Wilberforce survived and became a beacon of Black scholarship, industry, leadership, and military advancement.

The Leewold family had been entwined in all of that history. The first Leewold bought his freedom from a Southern slave owner and came north to settle in the Tawawa Springs area among other free African Americans. He worked to buy the rest of his family from slavery. Some escaped on their own and fled north to Tawawa. Later, the first Leewold to attend college had done that at Wilberforce.

The whole thing was a microcosm of what I wished I'd learned in public school. I remembered Ohio and U.S. history courses, but I didn't remember learning in them about Tawawa or Wilberforce or what a historically black college or university was. I didn't remember learning about the significance of the Civil Rights Acts or redlining. We glossed over the Fugitive Slave Law and Ohio's role in that, and how that legislation pushed the states into war.

I hadn't learned in school that Route 68, the main street that ran right through the middle of my own village, had been a major player in the Underground Railroad.

All of that knowledge came to me later. But the Leewolds would have known. Their family had lived that history for more than a hundred and seventy years, right here in Greene County. I wondered how much had passed down through the generations, from the Leewold cabin in the woods to Angelita.

There should have been a section in my schooling about local history, and how that tied to the bigger lessons. It sure would have made things more interesting. It did now as I was reading about the Leewold family.

I was still riding that wave of knowledge that the internet can be when Angelita's text interrupted me at nine. Her message was simple. *Ready.*

I replied. *Right on schedule. Be there in 10.*

I drove down the hill toward the Little Miami River and the Airbnb nestled nearby. Angelita was waiting outside, tossing a frisbee to a border collie. The dog was bringing back most of the frisbee. Some chunks of plastic had fallen by the wayside. It looked like a few may have been ingested.

Angelita gave the frisbee one more toss before she came to me. "The dog's not mine. He comes with the place."

"Looks like he'd go home with you if you kept throwing that frisbee." I held my hand out. Angelita took it and we shook.

I guessed that Angelita was in her late twenties, maybe a little older. She was slim and had a soft face that made her look young. She was tall and looked fit, like a runner or a dancer. Her last names, Rojas Flores, and the roll in her *r*s suggested Hispanic roots. Her light olive skin and long, straight, black hair completed the picture.

I gestured to my truck. "I'm happy to drive."

Angelita offered an easy smile. "Why don't you follow me?"

That, of course, was a better idea. She picked up a carry bag that was waiting beside her banged-up Toyota pickup. The border collie sat with the frisbee in his mouth, waiting for someone to come over and give it a toss.

We could have been a parade, two dented trucks bouncing down the country roads. One short of the hat trick.

The Leewold place looked less secluded in the daylight. Angelita pulled into the rutted drive and got out to unclip the chain that blocked the entry. I was surprised to see there was no lock. Angelita diligently pulled through, waved me in, and reclipped the chain behind us.

The house wasn't visible from the road, set back far enough that it would probably still be hidden in the winter when the leaves came down.

The drive was crowded on both sides by dogwoods, witch hazel, and a few young buckeye and pawpaw trees. Some dots of pale purple chicory poked through the understory. It was a nice change from the suffocating honeysuckle that usually took over.

The house had been built by hand more than a hundred and fifty years before, then expanded and kept alive through grit and determination.

Angelita unlocked the door and we went inside. She carefully tucked the key back into her pocket. "It's not much."

I turned to take in the main room.

"But it's been in my family for a long time."

"Impressively long. May I look around?"

"It would be weird if you didn't."

Indeed.

The Leewold cabin was a single story. A large hand-built chimney made of stone rose in the center of the wall on one end. On the opposite end a thick post jutted up. Between them a main beam spanned the ridgeline and supported hand-hewn joists that stretched out to the front and back of the structure.

In the front was a living room with an interior wall to one side that led to a bedroom. The back housed a country kitchen with long counters and rows of planked shelves. A single-basin sink under a window opened to a view of the woods. Opposite the counter was another bedroom that mirrored the one in front, with a cramped bathroom tucked between the two. A tightly packed utility closet held a modest furnace and water heater. It was like an archeological dig moving from the old section in the front of the house to the later additions in the back.

Outside there were woods and the swallowed-up remains of an outbuilding that had fallen long ago. The remnants of an ancient fuel oil tank groaned beside a rusty propane tank that was probably still in use.

The roof at the back of the house sloped down to a low entry with an overhang that would keep out the weather but challenge anyone over six feet to keep the top of their head in one piece.

A faded path whispered away from the house into the woods.

Angelita came out of the house and stood beside me with a what-do-you-think look on her face.

I told her. "Good construction. Held up all these years. Little messy inside."

"That's not me. I don't keep house like that."

"I believe you. Where does the footpath go?"

"Massies Creek."

"Swimming hole?"

"It was when I stayed here with my aunt when I was a teenager."

Long before that it probably meant water for the family. I turned back toward the house. "Your aunt lived here alone?"

"My great-aunt, actually. By herself for something like forty years."

I took a little notebook from my pocket and made some quick notes. "Who lived here before that?"

"Aunt Ida. She lived her whole life here."

"But not alone at first?"

"I only remember Aunt Ida. But my mother told me it was the family home for a long time. After they came up from Kentucky. It stayed in the family forever. Then eventually it was just Aunt Ida left, and she lived here alone."

"Your Aunt Ida didn't have children?

"She never married."

I left the question between us. Angelita understood my meaning. "She never had kids. It was just Aunt Ida."

I jotted that down.

"Aunt Ida was ninety-six when she passed."

"And how long ago was that?"

"June."

So a couple of months, depending on the timing. "And you inherited?"

"Uh-huh."

"There was no other family?"

"There *is* no family. It's just me. And there was Ida."

I lowered my notebook. "I'm sorry."

"My daddy is alive, but Aunt Ida didn't like him."

I raised the notebook again. Apparently Angelita didn't like him much either, since she'd said there was no other family. "Your father comes from the Leewolds?"

"Yes." She ticked the lineage off on her fingers. "Aunt Ida's sister. She went out West and married a guy—from Santa Fe, but his family came from Mexico. Their son in my father."

"So your father is Ida's nephew."

"Yes."

"And there are no other Leewolds left? Or branches of the Leewold family? It's just you and your father?"

Angelita looked at the fingers she'd counted on. "As far as I know."

"And where is your father?"

Her head went down. "He's been in jail in Florida since I was little."

I raised an eyebrow. "Which institution?"

"I don't know. I never see him."

I wrote down Florida to have something to do. "So great Aunt Ida was the Leewold. Was Ida short for something?"

"Idetha. It was a heritage name."

"Heritage name?"

"That's what we called it. It was a Black name. They brought it up with them from slavery."

I made more notes. "Was your family connected to the settlement in Tawawa Springs?"

"Aunt Ida talked about that name. I really don't know what it was."

"I didn't either, until this morning."

Angelita took a moment as if she were sorting through her thoughts. "Why are you interested in my family history?"

"That's a good question. It's probably not going to help me solve whatever is bothering you out here."

"And how did you know that about Tawawa Springs? I mean how did you not know until today?"

"The Google."

Angelita straightened her back. "Do you check out all of your clients like that?"

"Generally."

"And what did you find about me?"

"Not much. It was more of the family history."

"My family?"

"That depends on which one you're thinking of. I read a lot about the Leewolds in Greene County."

"And the Leewolds before that?"

"I know that one of your ancestors bought his way out of slavery and then brought the family up here."

Angelita raised her foot and tamped it back down on the ground. "This very spot." She pointed to the cabin. "And this house. They built it with their own hands."

"Your family lived here a long time."

"And now I'm all that's left."

"Somebody else appears to want something with it, from what you've been telling me."

"You haven't even seen that yet."

"Let's take a closer look now. Have you slept here at all?"

"No. I've been at the B&B for three nights since I got here."

"Good choice. I probably wouldn't have slept here either."

I noticed that the back door had been open when I passed through, but Angelita had unlocked the front door. "Did you leave the back door open?"

"No."

"It was open when we got here."

"I don't have a key. I can only unlock the front. The back has a deadbolt I can turn from the inside."

I bent to look closer. The door showed scrape marks by the bolt. I pointed. "Were these here at any time during the past few days since you've arrived?"

Angelita bent to see. "I don't know. The door was unlocked the first time I was here. I closed it and locked it from inside."

"These marks are fresh. It's a good bet someone had been getting in and didn't like you locking them out."

Angelita recoiled.

"Hang on. This might just be someone taking advantage of an opportunity. Show me what else you've seen."

Angelita walked me through the house for second look. There wasn't much inside, but what was there had been rifled and scattered. An old metal-frame bed drooped in the front bedroom. All that remained were springs and rusted metal. The closet door was open and hanging from one of the hinges. A smattering of old accessories lay about—gloves, scarves, a woman's dress hat.

In the kitchen a few of the cupboard doors were open, revealing wooden shelving in need of paint and some reminders of canning days— dusty jars, bands and lids, a water bath canner.

A few glass jars with food remained tucked into a back corner of a shelf. There were no utensils or cookware. The house had electricity, and an ancient electric stove squatted beside the long counter. A plug remained for a refrigerator, but the space was empty.

There was some scattered debris on the floor where it looked like an animal had gotten inside, maybe a skunk or a possum. Whatever it was had ravaged a sack of bird seed that was left behind.

When we'd quickly navigated the place again, Angelita twisted to take in a view of the kitchen and bit her lip. "They were supposed to clean it all up. The realtor hired a service. They were supposed to get rid of the perishables and whatever wasn't in good shape. They were supposed to leave the personal items. The family things."

"Family things?"

"The guy said they would get rid of the perishables and the—he didn't call it junk. They were supposed to just clean it up. He said that's what they did."

I took out my little notebook. "Let's back up a little. You hired a realtor? Who hired a cleaning service? That came before you got here?"

"It was all…kind of a mistake. It all happened through the lawyer."

Well, that would do it.

"They thought I wanted to sell the house, without ever coming here."

"But you didn't want to do that?"

"No."

Angelita gave me a couple of names. I wrote them in my notebook. "Well they sure cleaned it out, but they didn't clean it up."

I could see the regret on Angelita's face and I wished I hadn't said it. I tried another angle. "It looks like the house has been getting some pretty steady traffic for a place that's supposed to be empty."

She tapped my arm. "Come look at this."

We went to the bedroom that accessed from the kitchen and Angelita lifted a sleeping bag that lay in the corner. Beneath it was a thin sweat jacket that was balled up like a pillow. Angelita pulled the bag back farther to reveal several cans of food arranged against the wall.

There were vegetables and baked beans, some cooked pasta. The label was the store brand for the dollar store in town. I toed the blanket with my shoe and uncovered a can opener.

Angelita motioned me to the bathroom. She opened the cabinet and inside was a shriveled half-bar of soap stuck to the shelf.

I tried the faucet. Water came out. "Does the toilet work?"

Angelita nodded.

It would be a well and septic. The well pump appeared to be working. "Is this how you remember it when you stayed here when you were younger? The house in general?"

"Aunt Ida kept it really clean."

"Besides that?"

"I guess so."

"And you haven't been here since then?"

"Not since I was a teenager. More than fifteen years."

That put Angelita a little older than I'd guessed. Early thirties. "And your aunt was in her nineties and living alone. Did she have any help?"

"I know she had deliveries. There's a senior center or something from the county. They brought food and checked up on her."

"What about doctors' appointments?"

Angelita's face clouded. "I don't know. I guess they did that too. Aunt Ida didn't have a car. I should have—I know I should have called her more often."

I went to the kitchen and lifted the big black phone receiver from the wall. There was no signal. "You called her on this line?"

"Aunt Ida had a cell phone."

"OK. So people came out here. They knew about your aunt. People knew about this place. Your aunt wasn't just a recluse. Is there anything else you want to show me?"

Angelita took me out back to the trail that led to Massies Creek.

After a few minutes walking through trees and sparse undergrowth, the path merged with another better-defined trail that traveled along the water's edge. In another minute we came to a small clearing.

Massies Creek might have been better named a river. Even in late summer it ran steady and sure. Where we stood there was a wide turn in the creek and a low, flat entry to the water. A couple of smooth broad rocks near the bank were large enough for several people to sit or sun on at once.

Angelita pointed to the ashy remains of a recent campfire. Empty tallboy cans of malt liquor sat neatly turned over at the edge of the ring. I didn't need to look closer. "These are recent."

Angelita was looking out at the swimming hole.

"It might be just kids."

"Probably. It's what I did when I used to come here to visit."

Angelita stepped to the water's edge and took off a shoe and dipped her foot into the gravelly creek bed. "It doesn't look much different."

It probably hadn't changed at all. It didn't look much different than a lot of places in the county, or in the state, or anywhere. It was where kids went in the summer when it was hot and they were bored. I scratched the back of my neck. "Nature abhors a vacuum."

"Well, Aristotle thinks so."

My estimation of Angelita went up.

She took her foot out of the creek, tried to swipe the water off, and put her shoe back on.

"I don't think you have much to worry about." I pushed an empty beer can over with a toe. "You can clean this up. Show whoever has been coming here that there's someone watching the area. It might not do any good, but it won't hurt."

We walked back to the house. "More important, you should clear out the blanket and canned goods at the house. Get rid of those. Call a locksmith and have the locks changed. Put a sign on both doors—*No trespassing*. Put another at the road. Add *Private Property*."

Angelita nodded dutifully.

"And all of that probably won't keep everyone away. The place has to look lived in. If you intend to do that?"

She nodded curtly. "I do."

"Then this is a job for the sheriff. Or private security."

"Do you do that?"

"I used to be with the sheriff. You've already tried them and they appear to be doing what they can. I don't do private security."

That wasn't exactly true. I'd done some security work, and I could be tempted to do it again under the right circumstances. But sitting around in the heat doing nothing and waiting for kids who probably wouldn't be scared off by me anyway wasn't the right conditions.

"Would you make an exception?"

"My business cards say Jackson Flint Detective Agency." I put some emphasis on *detective*.

Angelita laughed.

"What?"

"You don't mind being called a detective?"

"That's what the cards say."

"Magnum always corrected people when they called him a detective. He said he was a private investigator."

"Magnum lived in Hawaii. On a TV show." And I was no Magnum. But I was warming to Angelita.

"True. So you won't take the case?"

"I don't think there is a case."

"Well I need something. Some kind of help."

"You could put up some cameras. That and the internet are squeezing people like me out of business anyway."

"And the cameras? What will they do?"

"You might find out who's coming here."

"And I'd give that to…"

"It might at least discourage people. If you put up signs that the place is being surveilled."

She scrunched her face.

"What?"

"Is that a word?"

"What word?"

"Surveilled."

"What else would you call it?"

She knitted her brow like she was filing the word away for later use.

"You want it to look like someone lives here. It's not abandoned anymore."

"You think any of that would help?"

"It might. Cameras would be cheaper than hiring me."

We reached the back door and Angelita let her hand linger on the knob. "I inherited some money."

I knew where this was going.

"With the house. Aunt Ida left me some money."

"You probably don't want to burn it up paying me to sit here watching the place."

"It's more than you might think. Aunt Ida had municipal bonds. When you live as long as she did, they add up."

"Look, I don't really need details about your inheritance."

Angelita looked stung.

"I'm not good at surveilling. I don't like to sit still. And I don't want to play the heavy and try to scare some kids away. And maybe a squatter."

"So you won't help me?"

"It doesn't sound good when you put it that way."

"I don't know what else to try. You're the only detective I could find in Yellow Springs. I guess I could look somewhere else."

I sighed. "All right. I know someone who might be able to help you."

4

J'LEAH DAWKINS WAS A LOT OF THINGS that I wasn't. She was a tech wizard. Put that together with a head hard-wired for math and the specialized training she'd received compliments of the U.S. Marine Corps, and J'Leah was built for the future. If cameras, closed circuit TV, the internet, and phones were squeezing P.I.s out of business, they were opening space for people like J'Leah.

And for surveilling, she could sit for hours with little sleep waiting for something or nothing to happen, then jump up and turn on the afterburners in a heartbeat if something did.

J'Leah was in her late twenties and in shape like she still wore the uniform. Her ebony complexion was the opposite of my pale white skin, and I'd seen her use that to disappear into the shadows and night like an illusion.

And like Brick, she still carried a touch of PTSD. Brick worked with a group that helped veterans transition to civilian life. J'Leah was one of the transitionees, and Brick had connected me with J'Leah earlier in the summer when I worked a missing person case that got complicated.

I slipped up the back way to my office, opened the window to let in some summer air, and texted J'Leah.

Up for some work?

When she didn't reply after a few minutes I grudgingly went back to the work I hadn't finished that morning. I filled out an invoice for serving paper to the guy at the mall. I cleared emails and started a file for Angelita, noting time and mileage. She'd paid me with Venmo, and I checked that the transfer had cleared. I updated my profit-and-loss sheets.

When there was nothing left to distract me I went to the window and looked down at the village. It was a Friday and perfect weather. Weekend visitors were already starting to fill the sidewalks. Ye Olde Trail Tavern was doing a solid lunch on the patio. A couple of women busked on the steps in front of Tom's Market. Accordion and banjo, Americana with a Creole-Dixieland twist. They were making it work.

I was restless and wanted to call Marzi, but my head wasn't all the way wrapped around that yet. A good workout would help clear my thinking. But a workout was better done with Brick, and it was still radio silence from him.

I gave in to the urge to text J'Leah again.

Have some work for you if you want it.

This time she replied right away. *I already have some.*

This isn't a Monty Python sketch.

??

I searched for a link and sent it to her. *From Search for the Holy Grail. I told them we already have one.*

J'Leah sent an emoji that I interpreted as a face pretending to laugh. Then my phone rang. "What have you got?"

"Client needs some help. Requires some briefing."

"Is the client a man or a woman?"

"Yes."

"Not funny, Jackson."

"Does it matter?"

"Not really."

"Woman. About your age. Maybe a little older. Someone is getting into her house in the woods and she needs help running them out."

"I'll take it."

"I haven't told you the details yet."

"You like her?"

"Who."

"The client."

"Her name is Angelita."

"You like her?"

"I do."

"I'll take it."

OK.

"This is where you fill me in."

"I'm wondering what other work you have."

"Does it matter?"

"No."

She took up the bait. "Data software."

"Uh-huh."

"Dumping in numbers and setting up analytics."

"For what?"

"What do you mean for what?"

"What are they trying to do with the numbers?"

"I don't know."

"Then how can you help them?"

"The point is they don't want me to know too much."

Huh. "Doesn't that bother you? You're doing work, but you don't know what it's for, exactly."

J'Leah laughed. "I was in the military. You get used to that."

I leaned out the window. The buskers had switched to Creole. A classic. Chanson de Mardi Gras. They were good. My foot started tapping. "You like it?"

"Like what?"

"The work."

"Better'n sitting around wishing I had money to spend."

"You could work anywhere. Go to Google or Amazon or GoDaddy or one of those kinds of things. They'd love your skills."

"You really don't know me that well, do you?"

I guess I didn't.

"You don't have to say it."

"We only just met…"

"I said you didn't have to say it."

"I'm not."

J'Leah grunted. "Civilians." There was the feel of a grin in her tone. Maybe I was wrong. We didn't really know each other that well yet.

"What's your boss think of you talking with me while you're at work?"

"My boss isn't here. It's not that kind of work."

"You're not in a cubicle?"

She laughed. "Contract work. I'm my own woman."

"Sure you are. But is running numbers for a thing that you don't know what it is as good as working with me?"

"It has its appeal. Numbers don't give me any shit. People do. Numbers are just numbers."

She had a point. People will give you shit just for the joy of shoveling it. I'd seen a lot of that in my line of work. "You didn't really have to answer."

"You didn't have to ask."

True. "You want to do this over the phone?"

"Do what?"

"The briefing."

"I can be free after two. Got a long lunch meeting."

"I thought you were your own woman?"

"You know that thing about numbers not giving me shit?"

"Okay, okay. Can you come out this way? Put the time and mileage on your ticket even if you don't take the work."

"You know I like that little village you live in."

I did know. "I'll set up a time with the client."

"Angelita."

"What?"

"You said her name is Angelita."

"I did."

"So set up a time with Angelita."

Now it was my turn to laugh. "So personal."

"I'm just trying to get used to this civilian stuff."

"Aren't we all."

Then something else tapped on my frontal lobe. "Hey, have you heard from Brick recently?"

"What's recently?"

"Past couple of days. Today."

"No."

I gave her the skinny on what had happened. The kids and the money and the gun. Brick going dark.

"Jesus. Hang on."

"What?"

"Hang on."

I did. J'Leah came back a minute later. "He'll text you." Then she ended the call.

Huh.

I sent a series of texts to set up the meeting time with Angelita and J'Leah. That took about five minutes. Cell phones. The modern detective's toolbox.

I thought that left me some free time. I went back to the window and leaned out over Yellow Springs. Chatter sifted up from the sidewalk. The buskers were doing a Dixieland number. The smell of coffee wafted up.

My phone jangled. *Feeling manly?*

Brick resurfacing. I gave the only right answer. *Always.*

ETA?

20. My gym bag was already in the truck.

I'll go wake up Betty.

I grabbed some water bottles and headed down to the street. I could already feel a grin tugging at my psyche.

Betty was a 1978 Buick Skylark that hadn't run since probably 1979. What was left of Betty peppered the weeds and grasses around Brick's cabin, rusty glints of orange and brown and gray in the sunlight.

When I cleared the trees that shaded the narrow, rutted lane to his cabin, Brick was slouched on Betty's engine block. Nothing remained of Betty's body. Only innards squatted in the clearing that ringed his home.

I parked by a patch of coneflowers and black-eyed Susans that had probably sprouted from seeds blown in on the wind. Tall, spindly prairie dock kissed the front bumper.

Brick stood up and squinted in the sunlight. "Your pain awaits."

I came over and bent to one end of the engine block. "As always."

We carried the engine block slowly once around the cabin. When we set the weight back down again where we'd started, Brick curved his shoulders and stretched his back. "That's once around the block."

He kept the pieces in roughly the shape and alignment of the actual car. Rims on the outside, ragged chassis, engine block up front. A discarded drive shaft looking for its rightful place in the mix.

I raised my end of the block again. "What are you just standing there for?"

He grinned. "I thought you might need a break."

"You see me sitting down?"

"Nope."

We retraced our route backward, side-stepping and grunting. When we dropped the block again Brick immediately reached for the rims and hoisted one in each hand. Sweat glistened on his skin and dotted his t shirt. "You need me to slow down for you?"

I picked up a set of rims. "I'll let you know."

Brick's biceps flexed as he worked the rims up and down. His t-shirt told me *If it's easy it's not worth doing*. Haw. Brick might have been stronger than me, but I wasn't in the habit of letting him know it. I took off with a rim in each hand. "See you on the other side."

I held him off for two loops before Brick closed the gap. Then we moved to the chassis, a series of lifting and carrying maneuvers Brick had devised to get to what muscles remained to be worked.

Then we sat and wiped sweat away and drank water, sitting in the roughed-out frame of what had once been Betty. I think Brick loved that old car more than if it had been running. And no one else I knew was still getting mileage out of a '78 Skylark.

I rolled my shoulders to get blood back into them. "Barn climbs?"

Brick had secured a sequence of two-by-fours and scrap lumber to the outside of the barn to make an elaborate climbing pattern. He shook his head. "Could work the bag."

I lifted an arm to show that it had been worked pretty good.

Brick rolled a shoulder. "Maybe a run."

"Hot out there on the road."

He drank some more water and set his bottle down. "Manly man like you can do it."

A run is when Brick and I would usually talk. Or not. But if there was something to say, the run is where it would usually happen.

Today it didn't. Brick didn't say a word about what he'd done with the two kids from the mall. After a mile or so when our muscles loosened and the pace evened out, I gave him an opening. "So…"

Instead of talking, he took off.

After the run when we were rehydrating I tried again. "What'd J'Leah tell you?"

"About what?"

"To get you to text me?"

Brick got a confused look. "She said you needed some reassurance."

"She what?"

"She said you thought I might've done something I shouldn't have."

I let it sit between us until the moment grew too fat to ignore. "Did you? With those kids?"

"Hard to say."

"Well, try. What happened?"

He ran a sweaty hand over his forehead. "It didn't look good."

"I don't disagree. We should have called it in."

"Maybe. That's what people do. Doesn't always lead to the best solution though."

A fat horsefly buzzed my ear and tried to land on my arm. I flicked it away. Those things hurt. "So you let them go?"

Brick spent some time finding his words. "Sort of."

"Sort of?"

"I don't know…exactly how it's going to play out yet."

OK. I was tired of pressing. If Brick didn't want to tell it, he wouldn't. I got up and stretched. "I have to go get cleaned up."

"Big date tonight?"

"Client. I'm putting J'Leah together with someone who needs help controlling the neighbors."

"She'll be good at that."

"A little finesse goes a long way."

"J'Leah's got a lot more to her than just finesse."

The horsefly came back. I swatted it away again. "I know it. Why I wanted her for the work."

Brick wiped his brow. "So, it's Friday night…"

"I noticed. I'm thinking of asking Marzi over. Her and Cali, pizza and salads on the porch."

"Lucky man."

"Maybe. I haven't asked Marzi yet."

His mouth made an O.

"You want to join us?"

"Nope. Sounds like you haven't got that all worked out yet."

So I headed out. Something caught my eye when I turned. A shadow framed in the jamb of the open front door of the cabin.

The shadow moved out into the sunlight and became a person. I turned to Brick. "Is that the kid from yesterday?"

"It is."

The younger one. The kid who had looked scared. The kid holding the money. "You want to tell me what's going on?"

Brick shook his head. "Not yet."

5

WE MET AT THE LEEWOLD HOUSE. I arrived before the others.

When Angelita pulled up to the chain that blocked the drive I signaled her to wait and walked over to her window. "I think we should leave the vehicles out here at the road."

"OK. Why?"

"Establish a presence. Let people know someone is here."

"You think that will help?"

"I don't think it will hurt. Might at least get the neighbors looking over. Get some eyes on the place to discourage uninvited visitors."

"You don't think it will draw the wrong people?"

I didn't, but I said, "Let's see what J'Leah thinks when she gets here."

"J'Leah?"

I spelled it for her. "I'd never heard the name before either."

"No, I mean…"

I leaned in so Angelita would say whatever it was that had her tongue tied up.

"I expected it would be a guy."

Oh, that. "J'Leah can get the job done. I think you'll like her." I hoped it went the other way too. I didn't want to have a repeat with J'Leah of our conversation that numbers were less trouble to work with than people. I knew she was right.

A moment later a maroon Honda Civic hatchback in need of a wash pulled off the road. J'Leah stepped out and went directly to the window of Angelita's truck and stuck her hand in. "You must be Angelita."

Angelita offered her hand and they shook. "You're the specialist."

J'Leah laughed. "Specialist at what?"

"Jackson said he's not good at surveillance."

"Well, that's true."

"He said you were better at it."

J'Leah laughed again. "Also true."

I moved closer to the two women. "So the question of parking."

They both looked to me.

"Whether leaving the vehicles out at the road might discourage un-wanted visitors."

J'Leah looked up and down the road at the approach angles. "Jackson is right. You want to let them know you're here. This is your place and you're not going to be shy about it."

"I don't know how the swimmers are getting in," Angelita said. "Or if the guy who's been sleeping here is one of them. And I haven't met any of the neighbors yet."

"Doesn't matter," J'Leah said. "You want to park here on the chance that it might help. And it'll be good for your confidence."

I wouldn't have put it that way, but Angelita was nodding vigorously.

J'Leah pulled a pair of light-rimmed sunglasses off her nose and looked at Angelita. "You think it's a man who's been sleeping here?"

"I just meant, in general."

"You said the *guy* who's been sleeping here."

"I don't know if it's a guy. I guess I just assumed."

J'Leah tucked the sunglasses into a shirt pocket and pointed down the drive. "Come on. Let's take a look."

They did. And that left a lot of room for me to stay quiet during the briefing. Angelita walked J'Leah through everything we'd seen and talked about that morning—the house and family history, the sleeping bag and food, the forced entry at the back door.

Then Angelita led J'Leah down the path through the trees to the swimming hole and they looked at the fire ring.

When we got back to the house after the walk to Massies Creek, J'Leah seemed to remember that I was there. "Hey, Jackson."

"Uh-huh."

"Anything else?"

I gave it a little thought. "Angelita did a thorough telling of it. I think the questions now are who's coming to the house, and why, and if we can deter them."

"Deter?"

"Didn't they teach you that word in the military?"

"They did. We called it running the fools off."

"I knew you'd bring tact and grace to this."

J'Leah tapped her forehead. "And brains and beauty." She flexed a bicep in a Rosie the Riveter pose. "And a little more."

I grinned. Angelita looked confused. I spread my hands. "Sorry. It's Friday."

"That's all right," Angelita said. "You two look like you've known each other a long time."

Funny, I guess it did look that way. "Not entirely," I said. "But I think J'Leah will have some good ideas about cameras. And maybe signs or some other things to—" I looked to J'Leah. "How did you say it? Run the fools off?"

"If that's what Angelita wants."

"I'll leave that to you two…"

J'Leah cut her eyes to me. "Are you in a hurry for something?"

"No. I just think you two can handle this…"

The corners of J'Leah's mouth ticked up. "Got a big date tonight?"

"How is it that you're the second person who's asked me that today?"

"What did you tell the first?"

I pinched my fingers a few inches apart. "Little date." I hoped. I still hadn't asked Marzi.

"Think you might get lucky? You want time to go home and freshen up first?"

"That how they teach you to do it in the military?"

"That's one thing they don't have to teach." She put her focus back on Angelita. "Sorry. Friday, like he said. I don't have a date tonight like the fancy detective. So I can stay and help you. Assuming you don't have a date either?"

"No date," Angelita said. "I don't even know anyone here yet."

"Then it looks like you and me, sister."

"I'd put on a pot of coffee. If I had coffee. Or a pot."

J'Leah laughed. "I think I'm going to like you."

Angelita smiled. "I hope so."

I said, "I'm glad you two are getting along so well. Is there anything else?"

Angelita turned to J'Leah. "Is one of the options that you might spend some time out here surveilling?"

"You mean watching the place?"

"Jackson explained to me today that the word is surveilling."

"He would. That could be an option."

I made another attempt at an escape. "If I'm not needed here anymore…"

Angelita raised a hand. "Wait."

J'Leah took out her phone and began lining up shots of the house. She moved away for other angles, and Angelita said, "Do you think there's any chance we can find any of Aunt Ida's things?"

"You mean that were taken from the house?"

"Yeah."

"I doubt it."

"But you're a detective."

"Says so on my business cards."

"Is there anything you can do?"

I could see how much she wanted it. "They'd be long shots."

"Like what?"

I really didn't want to do this. "You'd have to put some money out on it, couple of days plus some modest expenses. And most likely it won't turn up anything."

"What would you do?"

"The service who cleared the house. I'd start with the realty company that hired them, then dig from there. See if I can find who worked that job."

She was quiet, then "Anything else?"

"The neighbors. Sometimes people see things, and I've found that they're often eager to tell."

"Okay."

"And I can coordinate with J'Leah. If you have any return visitors, which I suspect you will, they might be persuaded to…share whatever they might know."

"Uh-huh."

"And the county workers, or the people who came out to bring groceries and give your aunt rides. I could look for them."

"That sounds like a lot you could do."

It did. "But the most likely thing is that the items from your aunt's house are just gone. You won't be able to recover them."

"I understand."

Good. "So J'Leah and I can help you try to discourage uninvited visitors. Make you feel more safe here."

"I want you to do it."

"Uhm?"

"All of it. Those other things. I want you to see if there's any chance you can find some of the things from the house."

"I thought we…"

"You're a detective, and I've hired you. This is what I want you to do. I want to be sure everything is lost. I don't want to wonder if there was any chance to get something back. Anything I could have done. It will be worth it to me to know there isn't anything left to do if you don't turn up anything."

It was a good speech. "You're sure?"

"Yes."

I sighed. "I just want to make sure you understand—"

"I understand."

"OK." I took out my little notebook and wrote it down. Phones and the internet hadn't taken over everything yet. Paper and ink fit into my pocket as easily as a phone.

Then I went to J'Leah, who was checking the windows at the back of the house. "You have a second?"

She grunted as she tried to lift a sash. I took that for a yes and caught her up on what I was going to do for Angelita.

"Sounds like you're going to take her money."

"If you can talk her out of it, go ahead."

She moved to another window and tried to raise that with no luck. "I don't think I could talk Angelita out of anything. She's kind of…"

"Convincing?"

"I was going to say charming, but convincing will do."

"And listen, did Brick tell you anything about the kid?"

"The kid?"

"Yeah."

"Brick?"

"Yeah."

"So Brick and a kid?"

"I'm guessing he didn't tell you."

"No."

"Then I'm sorry I mentioned it. Listen, don't tell him I asked you, okay?"

J'Leah shook her head. "That's not going to be a problem. I don't even know what we're talking about."

I left her trying to open windows.

I stopped at Tom's Market on the way home. It was where you went if you were in Yellow Springs and you were hungry and trying to put a meal together. Fridays at Tom's could get giddy.

The two women who'd been out front in the morning busking on the accordion and banjo had been replaced by a school kid with a music stand and a violin. He was short and held the violin high so that it hid most of his face. That didn't seem to discourage him as he sawed through a simple tune I thought I recognized. Maybe Hot Cross Buns.

Yum, hot cross buns. Whatever those were. I dropped a few dollars into his violin case and followed my hunger inside.

The produce section was clogged with three young women entertaining a fairly serious discussion about vegetables. One of them wore a rainbow shirt and another sported a BLM t-shirt and skinny suspenders. I picked up some portobellos and lingered behind them while I eyed the peppers.

The woman in the rainbow shirt noticed me. "Are we in your way?"

"Not if you'll hand me a pepper."

She stepped aside.

"See, now I'll have to decide. Green, red, or yellow. If you'd just handed one to me, I wouldn't have that problem."

It took her a moment to decide to go with it. "First-world problem."

I smiled. "Ouch."

She looked into my basket. "What are you making?"

I held up the hand basket to show her red onion, the mushrooms, soy sausage. "Pizzas."

"Hmm. What else are you going to put on them?"

"Broccoli? Black olives?"

"Good, good." She reached for a pepper. "You're going to want some color in there." And she dropped a yellow pepper into my basket.

"Thanks."

She lifted two fingers to her forehead and pulled them away in a salute. "Happy to be of culinary service."

It could be like that in Yellow Springs. Maybe it was something in the water. Whatever it was, it kept things interesting.

I picked up items for a salad. A bag of nutritional yeast. Pita bread. Then I headed home for my little date with my daughter and Marzi.

Cali was home and we cut vegetables. Marzi had agreed to come over. It was like the weirdness with her from the night before had never happened. For that I was thankful, and a little leery.

Cali sliced neatly, precisely, with exact motions. Knowing exactly how she liked the onions. Just how a cucumber should be cut.

I chopped with more whimsy and abandon. Why make everything the same size or shape? Lettuce is shredded, tomatoes make chunks.

Put together, Cali's pieces and mine made sense, a good base of regularity, with some surprise tossed in.

We were arranging slices of tomato on the pizza crusts when Marzi came in. She looked over our shoulders. "Where's the sauce?"

Cali maneuvered a tomato slice carefully into position. "Just tomatoes, but watch this." She arranged a thick layer of basil leaves in a careful pattern over the tomatoes. Then she scattered soy nuts over the top and laid on slices of fresh mozzarella.

Marzi nodded appreciatively. "Caprese."

Cali drizzled olive oil over the pizza. "I think maybe a little more like pesto than caprese."

"Kind of like both," Marzi said.

"Capresto," I offered. Neither of them appreciated the neologism.

I pointed to the other items on the cutting board. "Marzi? What else here looks good?"

Cali answered. "Um, Marzi would probably like meat, but there isn't any here."

Marzi looked over the chopping block and I could see she was already mentally pushing the items around on the imaginary plate in her head. Taking off the soy nuts. Pushing the mushrooms to the side. "What have you got?"

"Let's see. Olives, banana peppers, onions, nutritional yeast." I opened the fridge and pulled out a plastic container. "Soy meat." I dug deeper into the fridge and came out with two more containers and looked at them. "Potatoes? And is this pasta?"

Cali rolled her eyes. "Now he's just trying to show off for you. He's not going to put all of that on the pizza."

I opened a container. "I'm not?"

Cali relented. "You might."

Marzi lifted a bottle of shiraz from a bag she'd set on the table. "Can we go halvsies? I'll think I'll stick with just the capresto. You can put whatever you like on your side."

"Don't encourage him," Cali said.

Marzi winked. "I think I already have."

Cali drew two precise lines on the pizza. "Marzi and I should get two-thirds, not half."

"But I'm bigger," I said. "And hungrier."

"You're always hungrier," Cali said. "You put all that stuff on your piece, it'll be twice as thick as ours."

Marzi picked up a blob of mozzarella and tasted it. "I think that's fair."

I did too. And right then life became very, very good again. Nothing else mattered except the three of us in that kitchen. For the moment, it was working.

We slid the pizza into the oven and went out to the porch with the salads and the red wine. Cali took an iced tea.

The weather was mild and there was a light breeze from the southwest.

The food didn't last long. Mrs. Jenkins discovered us during the pizzas and meowed like we'd done something wrong by not inviting her to the party.

Cali pinched off a little piece of crust and set it by her feet. Mrs. Jenkins sniffed it, batted it once and watched it skitter, then took off after the crust in a frenzy of battering and skittering.

When we'd finished eating and Mrs. Jenkins was done playing with the remnants, Cali took the dishes inside. Marzi whispered over to me. "Hey."

I gave her my attention.

"Is it OK that Cali invited me over last night?"

I rolled that through my head twice to make sure I'd heard it right. "I guess so."

"It's new."

"It is."

"And it implies something we haven't talked about."

It did. But I couldn't say exactly what.

Marzi set one arm on the table. "Something that we don't know if it's true yet?"

Right?

"So it really wasn't such a good idea that I accepted an offer from Cali to come over without communicating with you first."

This is where it can get weird dating your former counselor. I dipped one toe in, slowly. "You probably thought it was me? That Cali had talked to me about it first?"

"I didn't really know that."

Okay.

"So it was kind of not OK for me to presume."

I felt my head shake. I hadn't asked it to do that. "I didn't say that."

She patted my hand. "You don't have to."

Marzi left it there. I hoped she knew what all of that meant.

Cali came back out a few minutes later and said, "The dishes are done. Is it OK if I go over to Asia's?"

"Of course."

She lingered.

"You want me to give you a ride?"

"Of course not."

Half the fun of being out in the village on a warm summer night was not having to be in a car. You could drink in the vibe better on foot or a bicycle. Or a skateboard. Golf cart. Pogo stick. Anything.

Cali lingered still.

I raised an eyebrow to her.

"My curfew?"

"It's still summer. School doesn't start for another week."

She hadn't really had a curfew over the summer. Cali was generally a careful and mature teen, or if she wasn't she'd been careful and mature enough to hide from me whatever indulgences she'd been enjoying. As far as I knew she'd been spending her time in the village with friends and coming home at an hour that didn't seem outrageous for a teenager.

"You said this weekend."

Oh. I did. To set a curfew for the school year. "You were supposed to start now so you'd have a week to get adjusted."

She bobbed her head yes.

And when I hadn't given her a curfew, she reminded me about it. Exactly the opposite of what I would have done with my father when I was a teenager. And exactly the opposite of what I expected now from Cali after the awkwardness of last night. If adolescence was confusing to teenagers, it was to their parents too.

I pushed my chair back from the table. "Actually, I've been thinking about this."

Cali waited.

What I'd been thinking was that I didn't know the best answer. That I wanted Kat here with me to help us make that decision together. But it was Marzi at my elbow, not Kat, and Marzi was staying out of it.

"I think when you come home should be flexible. And I think you should decide. If you're in a good place and you feel comfortable, you don't have to come home at any specific time. So long as you're healthy and staying alert for school."

She nodded enthusiastically.

"So it's not an exact time. It's more a healthy decision about where you are, what's happening, and how you're getting up in the morning and doing at school."

Cali didn't move, but her eyes said yes, yes, yes.

"And I'll make suggestions or adjustments if I think I need to, and I expect you'll go along with whatever changes I decide if I have to do that."

She still didn't move.

"OK?"

"Yes, OK."

I waited.

"So tonight?" Cali asked.

"Let's start tonight."

I knew I might regret it. And I knew that was part of raising a child, when that child was ready to start trying to become an adult. I had to trust that we could both weather whatever choices Cali was going to make.

Then Cali walked over and placed a gentle kiss on my forehead and right then I didn't regret a single thing. Just come back to me, safe and sound. Show me I did the right thing letting you go. That some things are hard, but we'll stick together through them.

After Cali left, Marzi arranged the hem of her summer dress over one leg. She pushed a strand of soft brown hair behind one ear and exposed a long, dangling earring. "So?"

"I'm not going to make a curfew for you. Yours is flexible too."

She laughed. "Then what *do* you have in mind?"

"Whatever pleases the lady." I picked up the wine bottle and felt its weight. "There's a little left."

Marzi raised up. "Maybe we can play a game of chance."

"A game of chance?"

"Yes."

"What kind of game would that be?"

"Something that involves an element of wonder."

I couldn't wait to learn more.

Marzi picked up the wine bottle and went inside.

I was picking up the glasses when my phone buzzed. I almost didn't look.

It was a text from J'Leah. *Have you heard her stories?*

I tapped a quick reply. *Whose stories?*

Angelita's. You've got to talk to her. There may be something else going on out at the house.

Can it wait until morning?

Anything can wait if you want it to.

I sighed and texted Angelita. Just an opening volley. *Have you got some time in the morning?*

I waited a minute and didn't get a reply. Maybe Angelita was wiser than me and had set her phone down for the evening. An image of her tossing a frisbee to a dog who chased it like that was the best thing in the world flitted through my head.

I put my phone to priority only and turned it over.

Then I went in to see about my game of chance.

6

I WOKE EARLY with Mrs. Jenkins on my chest. The sun wasn't up, but some quality of the air, and of the cat on top of me, told me that daylight was imminent.

Marzi lay silently beside me. Mrs. Jenkins looked from one of us to the other. *Which of you is going to get up and give me some attention or a treat?*

I held my ground and stayed in the bed. Reached with one hand to scratch Mrs. Jenkins' ear. That settled her enough that she curled under my chin and purred.

The room was warm and getting warmer with the cat on me. I wanted my coffeepot, but the cat was well and truly content. And that's the rule. You can't get up when the cat is on you.

Then Marzi rolled over and Mrs. Jenkins' reverie was interrupted and she thumped to the floor and slumped away. Marzi rubbed sleep from her eyes. "What time is it?"

"Early."

She reached for her phone and checked. "I should get up."

"Me too."

Marzi was very quiet, as she always was when she stayed over and Cali was still asleep in the morning. I made coffee while she got dressed, then we sipped together at the table.

After a moment I set my cup down. "So."

Marzi sipped.

"I know you heard."

"I did."

Cali had come in very late. I'd rolled over to check the time. Marzi pretended she hadn't woken up.

"It was almost two o'clock."

Marzi looked up. "And is that what you were thinking? That's an appropriate time?"

"It's way later than she's ever stayed out before."

"Uh-huh." The counselor in her working, encouraging me to say more. It usually worked.

"I don't think it's a coincidence. It's like she did it on purpose. Right after I told her to make her own decision."

"And are you OK with her coming in then?"

"Of course I'm not. I think she's trying to make a point."

"What point?"

Good question. "She didn't even have a curfew before. What the heck is she doing?"

Marzi sipped. "She's testing you."

"Well, it's working. Why is she testing me now, after things have been so good all summer?"

"There are some dynamics shifting. That could have something to do with it."

"So what do I do now?"

"Exactly like you said. You pay attention. You give her some room and see how she does. If you feel you need to, you make some adjustments."

"After the first night?"

"What do you think?"

"I think that's too soon. It hasn't given her enough room yet. It would be like…"

"Like what?"

"Like the test isn't complete yet."

Marzi leaned back. "So there's your answer."

"For one night. What about the next time? How will I know when the test is done?"

"This might be a multiple-part test. There might be variables. Cali could have been acting last night on the way she felt yesterday, which might not be the same as she'll feel today or tomorrow. Or another day."

"Great. So she's human."

"Aren't we all. I don't think anybody ever said raising a teenager wasn't interesting."

It might be getting a little too interesting. I finished my coffee and stood up and stretched. "How about some breakfast?"

"I should go. I have to change and get cleaned up before work."

"On a Saturday?"

She shrugged. "Everyone can't live the exotic life of a P.I."

"How's this for exotic? I have refrigerator oats."

Her expression asked the question.

"Refrigerator oats? You put them in the fridge the night before and…"

Nothing.

I pulled a bowl from the fridge, dropped walnuts onto the tray in the toaster oven, and set a plate of blackberries on the table. Marzi showed interest.

A few minutes later, she gave her verdict. "Jackson, you eat the weirdest things, but you know how to keep a girl fed."

"It's one thing I can do."

She helped herself to another blackberry. "I can think of another."

So could I. "Look, I don't want us to get ahead of ourselves, but…" I was noticing Marzi's dress. How she had shimmied back into it this morning. How that had been a nice thing, but it nagged at me. "It seems…inconvenient for you to have just the one set of clothes if we're going to…"

Marzi wiped her blackberry fingers on a napkin. "That does seem like it's getting ahead of ourselves. But on the other hand, here we are. I'm wearing last night's dress, so we're not ahead of ourselves. And we are not two teenagers after the prom."

That brought awkward thoughts of my own daughter's first prom, which would probably come this year. Getting ahead of myself. I pulled my thoughts back to Marzi. "It's not quite as convenient for me to stay at your place."

"No. But you should be here with Cali."

"So…?"

She put a hand against the side of my face. "That gives us something to think about. But right now I have to go."

She did, and I cleaned up the table and made a breakfast sandwich of egg and cheese for Cali and left it in the fridge with a note. Then I went out to face a day that I hoped would remind me that the internet, smart phones, and video cameras hadn't yet put the kibosh on the sleuthing business, that I could make my time worth Angelita's money.

But the road ahead was muddled. Angelita had told me some other details. Her Aunt Ida's will was very old and specified the executor as simply her oldest child or living relative. Her father was alive in a jail somewhere in Florida, and the court had deemed him unable to execute and so named Angelita as the executor.

Angelita was living near Santa Fe and learned of her Aunt Ida's death from a clerk at a law firm where the will had been drawn up. Angelita told me that she really didn't know what it meant to be an executor. The clerk suggested that Angelita should contact a local real estate agent and have them prep the property for her since she couldn't come to Ohio right away. The clerk had been happy to recommend her brother-in-law, who had recently gotten his real estate license.

Angelita arranged to have keys to the house sent to the realtor, who had mistakenly assumed that she wanted to sell her aunt's house. By the time Angelita had gotten her head around what an executor is and what was happening with her aunt's house and estate, the realtor had already called the estate cleaning service, believing he had Angelita's implicit okay to do that.

It had been a series of unfortunate and rookie mistakes. Angelita called off the realtor, got some funds released from her aunt's estate, and drove from New Mexico to Ohio. It took her three days in the truck. That sounded like a Jimmy Buffett song, but when Angelita got here she found an empty house instead of a party on the beach.

For starters, I skipped the lawyer and started with the realtor. I had nothing against lawyers, but I tended to err on the side of Shakespeare when it came to members of the bar.

The realtor was working out of half of an old storefront a shade outside of the downtown district in Xenia. The other side of the building was empty and had an ancient sign for a vacuum repair business. I peeked in the window. It was dusty and looked like it hadn't been swept for a long time. The irony.

The realtor looked maybe forty, trying to pass like he was still in his twenties. He had dark, short-cropped hair, sunglasses with reflective lenses hanging from the neck of a button-down shirt, and a sports coat that was a size too small for him.

I went with it. First impressions don't always tell you the whole story. I extended a hand across his desk. "Fred Markson?"

He extended his own hand. "Freddy."

We shook once and I sat down. "Jackson Flint."

"I know." I'd called. He was expecting me.

"I'm here about the Leewold property."

"Right." I had the feeling that Freddy was sizing me up like we were on point across from each other at the line of scrimmage in a high school football game. I resisted the urge to flex a bicep.

When the game of quiet had gone on a little too long, I leaned back in my chair. "Angelita Rojas Flores hired you?"

"Her estate executor did, yes."

"Idetha Leewold's estate executor."

Freddy's eyebrows went up. "I guess that's right."

"And that executor is Miss Rojas Flores."

He nodded like he didn't want to agree to it. "Said she was out of state or something."

"She was. She's here in Ohio now."

"I guess she is."

I gave Freddy a long look. "And Miss Rojas Flores talked to you yesterday."

"Yeah."

"About me."

"About a Mister Jackson Flint."

"Which is me."

"So you say."

I reached for my wallet and took out my P.I. and driver's licenses and laid them on his desk.

Freddy squinted at the documents for a moment and then waved them off. "I can see it's you."

I tucked the licenses back into my wallet and returned my attention to Freddy. "So?"

Freddy ran long, thin fingers through his flyboy hair. "This is unusual."

I shifted in my chair. "Makes it interesting."

He pulled his hand off his head. "I don't like it."

I tented my fingers, leaned forward, and planted my elbows on his desk. "What's not to like about it? All you have to do is provide me with a name and contact for the estate removal service you hired for the Leewold property. It's something you should have done for Miss Rojas Flores when she talked with you on the phone. I shouldn't have to come here and get that from you."

"Hey, she never asked me." Freddy's hand was out, palm up, as if he was trying to wipe away that suggestion.

I tented and re-tented my fingers. "Freddy." I pulled an index finger out to point at him. "There is a simple solution here."

He squirmed back into his chair and his hands fidgeted with the back of his desk. "I don't want to get caught up in no scam here."

Suspiciouser and suspiciouser. Maybe my time today and Angelita's money would be worth something after all. Or maybe Freddy was just a good 'ol boy who didn't know how to show proper hospitality. I pointed to the phone on his desk. "Why don't you call Miss Rojas Flores? Your client. Ask if it's her wish that you share this information with me?"

Freddy looked at his phone. "How do I know it's gonna be her that answers?"

"Freddy." I hadn't thought any of this would lead anywhere. But this was weird. "What are you worried about?"

"I just don't want to get anybody in trouble."

"Why would there be any trouble? This is a lot of effort just to find out where a respectable cleaning service may have taken some of poor old Aunt Ida's things. What trouble can there be in that?"

Freddy's jaw worked back and forth. Unless he was grinding coffee beans in there, that was a bad sign.

"It was a respectable service you hired, wasn't it, Freddy?"

His fingers went to the edge of his desk.

I pointed to his phone again. "Call Miss Rojas Flores if it will make you feel better."

Freddy picked up the phone and tapped on the screen. After a few rings I heard Angelita answer. Freddy looked at me as he spoke. "Miss Flores, I have a guy named Jackson Flint sitting here in my office."

I didn't correct him to use both of Angelita's surnames. She would likely also overlook the Gringo slight.

I bent forward. "Ask her what I told you."

He did, and listened. Then Freddy's face soured. "Do I have to tell him?"

He listened some more and ended the call.

"What did Miss Rojas Flores say?"

Instead of answering, he opened a drawer on his desk and took out a pad of paper and began to write. "It's J Guy Estate Removal Service. I'm giving you the guy's name and number."

"Give me the address too."

"He doesn't usually…"

"What?"

"He comes to you."

I extracted my phone from my pocket. "I can look him up."

"Wait—" Freddy held a hand up, the pen drooping between his fingers, then wrote again. He tore the sheet from the pad, folded it twice, and dropped it onto his desk. "Look, just keep an open mind, OK?"

I reached for the paper, unfolded it and glanced at what was on it, and slipped it into my pocket. "I don't know why that was so hard."

Freddy stood up like he didn't know where he was going but couldn't wait to get there. "There's no trouble. You're just not going to like it."

I cut my eyes up. My question was in them.

"He's a friend of mine. From way back. He can use a little help, you know, so I pushed some business his way."

I kept the question in my eyes.

Freddy shoved his hands into his pockets. "It's just that he's not a—his business is a little unconventional. I don't want him to have any trouble."

I would have offered my hand, but Freddy's were in his pockets. I gave him a friendly finger point instead. "If there's no trouble, Freddy, then there's no trouble."

I drove one block down, parked at the curb, and looked up Freddy's friend. Google told me J Guy was John Guy, aka the Junk Guy. He had a Facebook page that hadn't been updated for more than a year. There were a couple of photos of pickup trucks loaded with boxes and furniture and old appliances, one with a truck hitched to a trailer filled with downed branches. A single posting said *John Guy Hauling and Removal. We haul anything so you don't have to. Let the junk guys do the work.* There was a phone number that matched the one on the note Freddy had given me.

I called.

"Guy hauling and removal."

"Hey, guy." I couldn't resist.

"Can I help you?"

"You've been recommended to me."

"By a satisfied customer?" He sounded hopeful.

"I suppose so. Freddy Markson."

"Oh, Freddy. You have a house you want cleaned out?"

"Something like that."

"If it's not too far I can come out and do an estimate. Probably get to that today if you're in a hurry."

"I'd like to come to you."

There was a pause. "That's not the way we usually do it. If I come out and see it I can give you a better estimate. Or if you send pictures I can give you a ballpark number."

"I can come to you. I'm in the area."

A quiet hum travelled through the connection. "What area?"

"Near you. I can stop by."

"You have my address?"

I read the street number to him.

If a shrug had a sound, I'm sure I would have heard it. "Like I said, it's not what I usually do. But if that's what you want."

"I'll be there in twenty minutes."

The rabbit hole was getting deeper. Why was this harder than it seemed it should be? Just bad luck, or maybe something peculiar really was going on?

The drive to Guy's took me through downtown Xenia, past the Greene County Courthouse with the big stone clock tower. If I was lucky I'd drive past on the hour and get to hear the bells chime. But I didn't seem to be having that kind of day.

Even silent, I was grateful that the tower was still there. It was one of the few things left standing after an F5 tornado ravaged the town in the spring of 1974.

The storm was part of a super outbreak of tornadoes, the second-largest recorded and the most violent, with thirty F4 or F5 tornadoes wreaking havoc from Alabama up to Indiana and Ohio. Xenia had a multiple-vortex touchdown, with winds running to three hundred miles per hour. The clouds from which the twister descended rose to sixty thousand feet in the sky.

Back then no one had a cell phone or the internet or data streaming to alert them that danger was coming. Thirty-two people were killed.

Entire neighborhoods were wiped away. Aerial photos showed lightened areas that looked like someone had sprinkled sawdust over matchsticks. That was a path of dust and rubble tossed from the remains of homes.

The twister dropped a school bus onto the stage at the high school where moments before students had been practicing for a play. The winds turned over train cars and toppled headstones. The swath was half a mile wide. Half the city was gone or heavily hit.

The tornado left town and travelled to Wilberforce and Central State Universities to do damage there before breaking up in the wilds of Greene County. Those wilds were where the Leewold cabin stood, and the tornado had spared it. I wondered what else the family had endured in the years it had held on to that property.

I'd grown up hearing stories that the Shawnee had called this area the land of the devil wind. As if to prove the point, in 2000 a smaller tornado travelled a nearly parallel path to the 1974 storm, but with much less damage. Except to the single man who was killed at the county fairgrounds when a tree fell on the truck he was sitting in.

As I passed through downtown I glanced at the clear blue sky and the rising spire of the clock tower. Still there.

I turned off the state route at Oldtown, a dot on the road that seemed appropriately named. Oldtown had once been called Old Chillicothe. Before that it had been a Shawnee village. It was the place where Daniel Boone had been held captive.

A historical marker down the road kept alive the myth that Tecumseh had been born there. I knew that the Shawnee moved their villages when natural events or white settlers pushed them out, but they often kept the village name and moved that with them. So the *Chalahgawtha* division of the Shawnee had several Chillicothes in different locations. And Oldtown hadn't been settled yet when Tecumseh was born.

But a historical marker is a historical marker, so who was I to speak?

Not far beyond that another sign marked the spot where Simon Kenton had run his gauntlet. I hadn't been given a reason to doubt that story.

I let that history slip behind me and drove the backroads out past where the old Leewold homestead crouched by the waters of Massies Creek, to my rendezvous with a junk hauler who might offer the slim hope that some of Angelita's own history could be recovered.

John Guy was at a rural address with a house set back from the road. A truck parked in the drive looked like a dirtier version of one from the Facebook photos. Maples and a few hardwoods dotted the acreage. The neighbors' places were visible but out of earshot and shrouded by clumps of honeysuckle and overgrown privet.

The house itself was small, a brick ranch with a detached garage. When I pulled the truck up, a side door on the garage opened and a man in a buttoned green work shirt, khaki pants, and boots stepped out. He waved me over. "In here."

I followed him into the garage where it was cool and lit but not bright. A large box fan in a corner provided good circulation.

The man held out his hand and we shook. "John Guy. Sorry about the location. We're relocating the office and I'm working temporarily out of here."

The half of the garage nearest the small door had a large metal desk staged between two low filing cabinets. Beyond that, cardboard moving boxes were stacked carefully to make a partition. Beyond that were garage things—a lawn mower, yard tools, plastic crates, shelves with household items, and more boxes.

John Guy waved me to a metal chair in front of the desk and went around to take a seat behind it.

I settled in. "It's probably nice to be able to work close to home."

He winced. "That's actually my ex-wife's house."

I winced with him.

"It used to be mine—ours. She's got it now. She's letting me work out of here for a little while."

Ouch.

John Guy shrugged. "What can you do? Life goes on, right?" Then he turned up his smile. "You're here about a property?"

"Yes." I pushed a slip of paper across the desk to him. On it was Angelita Rojas Flores' name, the address of the Leewold property, and Freddy's name and phone number. "You cleaned out this property a few weeks ago. I'd like to know who worked that job so the property owner might determine if there are some items that were inadvertently removed and might be recovered."

John Guy looked at me, looked at the slip of paper, and looked back at me for a long time. "We don't usually give that information out."

"I understand that. But my client paid for your services, and that should give her some consideration here."

John Guy leaned his chin into a hand. "Now who are you, exactly?"

We went through it. I showed him my P.I. license and connected the dots between Angelita, me, Freddy, and now Guy Hauling and Removal.

John Guy nodded. "OK, yeah. Freddy hired me. We go way back."

"He said that."

John Guy moved some papers around on his desk but left the conversation where it was.

"And Freddy was hired by and working on behalf of Miss Angelita Rojas Flores, who paid for the services. And Miss Rojas Flores would like to know if there is any chance to recover some items that may have been removed."

John Guy rubbed a few days' beard growth. "Any particular reason why?"

"She is hoping to locate some personal family items that may have been removed by your crew."

"Look, they can't be held responsible. If she wasn't on site and there were no instructions to keep specific items…" He held up his hands in surrender. Not my fault. Nothing anybody can do about it.

"If you'd just look up who worked that job."

He reached for a drawer in a filing cabinet. "I have the order here somewhere. I don't think it said to keep anything. We were cleaning out to prepare for a sale."

"There won't be any problems with your crew's work. My client just wants to find out if there is any chance to recover some personal items."

John Guy dug into the drawer. "What kind of items?"

Good question. I didn't know. And I didn't like the way that made me feel. "If your guys are willing to talk with me, or with her, that would be a place to start. Miss Rojas Flores will understand if the items are gone. She just wants to know for sure."

"Well it's unfortunate, but chances are that all the stuff is permanently gone. We donate some to the local thrift stores. But a lot of it gets hauled to the dump."

"And does anything ever get kept?"

"I'm not following you."

"Items slated for removal. Does your crew ever keep anything?"

"It's possible. But there's nothing wrong with that. The client signs a waiver, and whatever is hauled away can be disposed of however the crew sees fit. It's like if you leave something at the curb for your garbage pick-up and someone takes that. There's nothing wrong with it."

"So it sometimes happens."

"Look, it's one of the perks of the job. Some of these guys are working two jobs. This is a little extra money for them. They've got kids, mortgages." He flicked his head in the direction of the house. "Ex-wives."

"There won't be any trouble. My client would pay a reasonable fee for any items that might be recovered. There's no finger-pointing here. Just a woman who didn't quite understand what was happening and now she's trying to find any family items that she may have a connection to."

"Uh-huh. Who signed the waiver?"

"Miss Rojas Flores was in New Mexico. If you can locate the contract, we should be able to clear things up."

He nodded. "We may have gotten a verbal consent. That may have come from Freddy." He switched to another file drawer, rummaged in there for a bit, then turned to the boxes behind him.

"If you could just tell me who worked the job."

"I don't remember exactly. And I'm not going to give you everyone's name. We have eighteen guys working here."

"Eighteen?"

"OK, some of them are part-time. Very part-time. But yeah, eighteen." Proud of it. Why not?

"So you'll have to keep looking for the contract?"

John Guy twisted his neck and rolled it over a shoulder to work on a kink. "I don't have that kind of time. We've got work. I'm sorry about your Miss Flores, but we didn't do anything wrong. There's probably nothing left to find anyway."

I let out a long, defeated breath. This is what I'd expected. Getting Angelita's hopes up on the slim chance of returns. But she'd wanted me to push it to make sure. Since I was here and it was going nowhere, I went for the cliché. I reached for my wallet. "Is Benjamin Franklin meaningful to you?"

John Guy looked surprised. "I don't really know who's on the bills."

"Then how about a Ulysses S. Grant?"

He laughed. "Is he on the thousand?"

I laid two bills on the desk. "Meet my favorite historical figures." I pushed Franklin forward an inch. "A hundred for you if you can find the names and phone numbers of the guys who worked the job." I inched Grant up. "And fifty—how many guys worked the job?"

John Guy's eyes watched the bills move across his desk. "Two or three."

"Fifty for any of the guys who might be able to locate anything removed from the house. Even if that means just the name of a thrift store where they dropped something."

He didn't literally lick his lips, but if John Guy had been a schnauzer, his tongue would have been hanging out. "If it's worth a hundred, it's worth two."

I pulled the bills back. "No. It's worth a hundred."

His eyes followed the bills. "You're probably expensing this."

I picked up the bills and returned them to my wallet. "Is this information that you feel bound to protect? Some company rule, or some higher authority you feel bound to?"

"No. It's just—the guys who work here."

"What about them?"

"I don't want to bother them."

I tucked the bills back into my wallet. "OK."

John Guy came forward in his seat. "Come to think of it, I don't believe any of the guys would mind if I just asked them about that job."

Interesting how quickly a little money could swing a moral compass. "I don't want to be a bother."

The rub didn't get past him. "It'll take me some time to look for that contract. If I can even find it. Time is money."

"It'd be a nice little windfall for you."

"A wind...?"

I explained what a windfall was.

"Ok, then yeah. It'd be that."

I put the hundred back on the desk. "This is to keep you company while you look. If you can find the names, I'll add the fifty. That seems pretty lucrative for looking through some files."

He looked uncertain.

"Lucrative means—"

John Guy waved me off. "I know what lucrative means." He wasn't insulted. Not at all. His left hand came down to cover the bill and at the same time he extended his right. "Nice talking to you."

I exited into the sunlight and rising heat and climbed into the truck. The whole thing was a rabbit hole of confusion. A clerk at a law firm recommends her brother-in-law, a newly minted real estate agent without an agency to work for, who misinterprets Angelita's intentions. Freddy gives the job to a buddy who's working out of his ex-wife's garage, and I'm explaining what a windfall is to him and trying to track down guys who probably won't remember where they dropped what they hauled out of the Leewold house. And Angelita isn't even sure what she's looking for.

And all of this would probably lead to nothing but a bigger bill for Angelita. Some days you feel like you're in a Raymond Chandler novel, and some days it's a comedy of errors.

7

ANGELITA WANTED AN UPDATE. And I wanted to hear her stories.

We agreed to meet at my office. She wanted to come up the hill to the village and step into the Saturday summer vibe. It was hard to argue with that. The sun was canting over the rooftops across Xenia Avenue and dancing the fandango on my windowsill. I leaned out.

We were more than a month away from the autumnal equinox, so there was still more daylight than darkness. The humidity was low and the air was warm and comfortable. Hardly like August in Ohio at all.

The village hummed with its weird dance of chill spiked with the anticipation of a weekend summer night. I felt the draw and I wanted to get out in it.

My phone beeped to remind me of just that. Cali and Marzi planning a Saturday night picnic for the three of us. They were walking to town to look for food. I messaged them to wave up at my window when they got there.

My phone buzzed again. Angelita, on an actual phone call. "I'm here in the alley."

"Good. Come on up."

"I can't find the door you said to look for."

"Where are you exactly?"

"There are a bunch of murals."

"Then you're close."

"But there are murals painted on all of the buildings."

"Are you near some Black Lives Matter things?"

"I think. And some clouds and trees and stars and mountains and psychedelic stuff and some more faces—and is that a weird cat face down in the corner?"

It was. "Do you see a door?"

"There are a bunch of doors."

I told her which one to go in.

"I didn't even see that one there. It kind of disappears."

"That's the one."

A minute later Angelita called again. "Um, so I'm on the stairs…?"

"Go left."

She stayed on the call. "This doesn't look like it goes anywhere."

I heard her down the hall. "Keep going."

I opened my office door as far as it would go, which was awkward. The door was hung backwards so it swung out, scraped against the far wall, and blocked the hallway. To get in, you had to step past the door then reach back and open it. To get out you had to go the wrong way, close the door behind you, then turn the other way to exit.

I stuck my hand out from behind the end of the door and wiggled my fingers.

"Got it." Angelita ended the call and I retreated into my office so she could do the dance around the door to get in. Swing your partner, do-si-do.

She stepped inside and looked left, then right. "It's very small."

"Thanks. I hadn't noticed."

"And that's a weird way to get in."

"If the door opened in, it would take up more space in here." I gestured to the room. One folding seat set up for sitting, two more closed and leaned against the wall. The filing cabinet with the coffee maker on top. My desk, and the window behind me.

Angelita's eyes went to the window.

I turned with her. "Best feature of the place."

She smiled and sat. Tucked the hem of a floral sundress under her knees.

That reminded me again that I'd been meaning to buy a cushion for that chair, or better yet, a better chair. "Sorry about the seating arrangements."

"It's fine."

"So, updates. My day. I'll go first?"

"Yes."

I told her about my talks with Freddy the realtor and John Guy the junk guy.

Angelita's first question surprised me. "You found them both on a Saturday?"

I shrugged. "There's no weekends anymore. I don't think either of them had anything better to do."

Angelita's face darkened.

"Did I say something wrong?"

"No."

OK. "And you never talked to John Guy, right?"

"John Guy? No."

"And you found Freddy because the clerk at the law firm—" I read the names to her from my notes. "The clerk gave you Freddy's number because Freddy is her brother-in-law?"

"That's right."

"So Freddy hired the estate cleaning on his own?"

"Uh-huh."

"And he did that because he thought you wanted him to do that and sell the house."

A tinge of color rose in her olive-brown complexion. "I didn't really know...what..."

"I understand." We'd been through this before. But checking the stories after you've talked to the players was Detective School 101.

"They said I was the executor, and I..."

"I know."

"It was so far away. Now that I'm here I feel like—I remember how much I liked it here. In Yellow Springs. When I would come to stay with Aunt Ida in the summers." Her eyes went to the window again. Sounds from the streets broke through. Cars. The buzz of skateboard wheels on pavement. Snippets of voices and laughter. The faint sounds of a drum circle in the making.

I supposed the village hadn't changed much since Angelita was here when she was young. But Angelita had changed. Returning as an adult to a small town where you had family roots could stimulate a bit of existential reflection.

I hadn't asked Angelita about Santa Fe, what she'd driven away from to come to Ohio and step into her family's ancestral roots. I wondered again, but I stuck to business now. "Can you give me an update on J'Leah? What's happening there?"

"You mean the cameras?"

"And we talked about some other things."

"We're going to do the cameras. J'Leah is really good. I'll be able to look at them from my phone."

"Uh-huh. Good."

"There's a motion sensor, so they come on when something's there."

I imagined bright-eyed deer in the dark. Raccoons and possum. Squirrels and skunk. Maybe a mink. Redtail hawk and crows.

"And a video doorbell. That's already set up."

J'Leah was fast. I wrote some notes in my little book. I'd transfer them to the laptop later. "Where are the cameras going to go? How many?"

"J'Leah is still figuring that out. One at the road. It has a battery that will need to be charged, but it's portable and I can move it later if I want."

I wrote that down. One at the road. Two if by sea. The British are coming. I scratched out the last. Punchy. The weekend was here.

"One in front of the house and one in back."

"OK."

"That's all. J'Leah is making suggestions. I'm letting her do what she thinks is best."

"And will J'Leah be able to tap into the feeds too? On her phone, or some other way?"

"We haven't decided that yet. She's against it long-term. She wants me to have my privacy. But we might set something up for her to have access for a little while. Until we see what happens."

I tented my fingers. "Did J'Leah tell you this might not turn up anything that leads directly to who has been entering your house? That all of this might go away on its own, without the expense of the cameras and equipment and her time? That once it's clear that the house is inhabited it won't be as much of a target?"

Angelita nodded curtly.

Of course J'Leah had told her that. But there was something here that felt to me a little like overkill.

Angelita smoothed the fabric of her dress around her legs again. "I think it's a good idea anyway. It makes me feel safer."

Well, that's what the client pays for. "So you'll be moving out of the Airbnb? And into your aunt's house?"

"Yeah." She grinned. "I'll miss that dog. And his frisbee."

And the dog would miss her. But I brought us back to business. "If John Guy finds the paperwork and the names of the guys who worked the job at your house, that will probably happen soon. I could ask to talk to all of his crew, but there are a lot and I don't know if that will get us anywhere."

Angelita gestured that she was following.

"And even if the guys come forward, there's only a slim chance this will end up getting any of your family things back."

"I realize that."

"And if we're very lucky we might find a thrift store somewhere in the area where you could go to look around for…I don't know if there's even something specific you know to look for, so I can't predict."

She looked like she expected more, so I plodded on.

"Tomorrow might be a good day to try to talk to the neighbors. It's Sunday, so people might be home. If you still want me to try that. It'd be another day's expense."

"Yes."

"For the folks from the county and the senior center who were coming out to help your aunt, I suggest we wait on that and see how everything else goes. You have a lot going on here for what are probably going to be slim returns."

I still thought this whole thing might just go away on its own. The family items wouldn't turn up, and the squatters would move on. A little time, and all of Angelita's worries might just melt away.

She didn't seem to be thinking the same way. Angelita's shoulders slumped.

I regretted my commentary. If this was what she wanted and it made her feel better, who was I to judge? I took us to the last thing. "J'Leah says you have some stories you should tell me."

That got her interest. "I don't think I ever really believed all of those."

But she believed them enough to tell something to J'Leah. I waited.

"She was asking about my family."

I leaned back in my chair—relaxed, open, safe. Tell me more. "Your family?"

"My father always told stories. Always."

I very discreetly opened my notebook and took out my pen.

"It was like that was who my father was—the guy in the stories. Or who he wanted to be. Like he was never completely there with you. He was trying to make this other guy in the stories be more real than he was."

Angelita slowed, like there wasn't much to tell. I gave her a little push. "Are there some stories that you think might be relevant here? Anything that sticks out?"

"The stories about a family treasure. He was always talking about this big, valuable thing that he had hidden away and it was going to change everything, make everybody's life easy. Easy street, he always said. He was going to put the family on easy street."

"These are stories from when you were young?"

She blinked. "I've never really known my father when I was an adult. He went to jail when I was in grade school."

I jotted notes. "And your mother?"

Angelita's eyes dropped. "She was sick a lot. She died when I was in college. I lived on campus after that until I graduated."

I paused my note-taking. "I'm sorry."

"Thank you. I remember Aunt Ida telling me it was a big scandal when daddy married my momma. He was black—or mixed, you know, or biracial or multiracial, or whatever it is you want to call it so I don't risk offending you." She flicked a sideways glance at me.

"I don't have a lot here to be offended about. I'm more likely to do the offending. How about we just call him human?"

A tiny lift came and went at the corners of her mouth. "Daddy was what a lot of people descended from slavery were. But he was different from my momma. She was Native American, or indigenous, or whatever...?"

"I don't know the best terminology, but I think I get the idea."

Now Angelita let a whole smile out. "My mother always liked to do that. Test people. She said the answer was Navajo."

"So your mother was Navajo."

"She was, but that was also diluted. You know, by the whites again."

I did know.

Angelita said, "What does your family call itself?"

Good question. "Well, my grand-daddy used to say we were too damn much kraut. I don't think he meant pickled cabbage."

The more you try to side-step racial insensitivity, the harder it becomes not to just step into it.

"You do kind of look a little like pickled cabbage."

Okay, we were doing this. I held up a beefy white forearm and pretended to sniff it. I found myself to be mildly amusing.

The moment passed, and I attempted to steer us back from the weeds again. "So your mother. That's your connection to Santa Fe?"

"Good guess."

"The Navajo reservation out there."

"Navajo Nation. My daddy went out to New Mexico to see where his family came from, and he found my mother to bring home with him."

I picked up my pen again. "Tell me more about the family treasure stories."

"They kept changing. Daddy had a story about a poker game. He and another guy were delivering money for the mob. Like couriers. They used the money to buy into a high-stakes poker game and won half a million dollars, on top of the money they had to deliver."

I raised an eyebrow. Had I seen this in a movie once?

"I know, right? And then the other guy disappeared, and daddy had to find him to get the money. He said when he did we were going to be on easy street."

I motioned for her to keep going.

"Another story was that he'd been smuggling drugs into the U.S. from Cuba—he really did work on a fishing boat in the Florida Keys, so this one has...something. He was supposed to have skimmed some of the—product? And sold it and stashed the money away."

Angelita took a breath. I waited.

"There's one more that kind of fits. My father said he knew a guy who stole some diamonds from a jewelry store. The guy got shot during the robbery. He was friends with my father and gave him the diamonds, but the guy died and daddy hid the diamonds until things cooled off so he could figure out how to sell them."

I jotted it all down. Then I turned and looked out the window, imagined myself out in the beautiful Saturday Yellow Springs day, and turned back to Angelita. It was a lot to take in. "Do you know why your father is in jail?"

"No. I know it was something bad. They wouldn't tell me. Mom was going to tell me before she died. She said she would, but then she died while I was away. I do know that he got into more trouble while he was in prison. They added time to his sentence."

"Do you know what that was for?"

"No."

"OK. Do you have any idea if your father was capable of doing any of the kinds of things in these stories? Was he connected like that? Could any of the stories be true?"

Angelita shook her head. "I have no idea. I was a kid. They were just stories."

"You didn't believe them?"

"I guess I did when I was really young. They don't make as much sense now."

They didn't. But you never knew. There may have been enough of a kernel of truth in at least one of them to amount to something.

Then Angelita added one more thing. "My father said he was going to bring the treasure here. To the old family house. He was going to keep it safe there until the time was right."

"Right for what?"

She shrugged.

"Do you ever remember him being at your aunt's house?"

"Not while I was there."

"And your Aunt Ida never mentioned that your father had been to her house?"

"No."

"But he probably was."

"He probably was."

I pushed the notebook aside and set the pen down. "Is that why you want to try to recover things that the estate cleaners took from the house? Because you think there's something valuable that might have been in there?"

"It's silly, I know. My father was such a mess. But still…part of me wants to believe. I think I really don't believe, but I want some sort of closure."

I measured my words before I let them out. "Can you ask your father?"

"I've thought of that, more than once. I don't know where he is."

"Is he still in prison?"

"I think so."

"We can probably find him." I made some more notes. Then I set the pen down again. "Look, I don't know if any of this gets us anywhere. If you still want me to I'll continue to follow up on the guys from the cleaning crew, and I'll go try and talk to the neighbors. See if there's anything left to keep tugging at. But this may be just about played out, or it will be soon. I think J'Leah is going to get you squared away with the squatter, or squatters, and whoever else might be coming around the house. Then you may have to let the rest of it go."

Angelita did the smoothing of the dress again. But the dress was already completely smooth against her legs. "I want you to keep on."

I knew she'd say that.

"Plus, I don't really have any physical connection to my Aunt Ida, or to the family before her that came up here out of slavery and made the new life that I came from. I'd like something, if I can find it."

"You have the house."

"I do. I meant something personal. Something handed down."

"That's fair enough." I pushed my chair back. It thumped against the wall beneath the window. I looked out the window just as Cali and Marzi were coming out of Tom's Market. I lifted the screen and leaned out and waved.

It took a second, but Cali looked up and saw me and waved back. She pointed to a fabric bag she was carrying and shouted. "You won't believe what we found."

I pointed down and called back. "I can be down in a minute if you can wait."

Cali gave me a thumbs-up. The real thing. Not the emoji.

Angelita was standing. "I'll let you go."

"Thanks."

But then she lingered. I closed the office window. "What else?"

"Nothing."

But she still lingered. I figured there was something else she wanted to tell me. I sat down.

Angelita made it to the backward-hung door, stopped. "What is there to do here on a Saturday night?"

I spread my hands toward the view of the village below.

"I don't really know anyone."

Oh. "Just go down and see what happens. I'll bet you'll find someone to talk to."

She swung the backward door closed to slide behind it into the hall. "See ya, Jackson."

8

THE PICNIC DINNER WAS A PLOUGHMAN'S LUNCH. An hour earlier Cali had never heard of a ploughman's lunch, but now that Marzi had explained it to her she was excited like a penguin waiting in line to jump into the water.

"Dad, it's just like bread, cheese, onions, and pickles, right? But then you can add whatever else you want."

We were on the front porch, under the steady swish of the overhead fan. Cali reached into the shopping bag she'd carried home and pulled out a loaf of bread. "Baguette from the Emporium." Then she set three chunks of cheese onto the cutting board. "From Tom's Market."

I looked over the cheeses. "Green, orange, and white."

Marzi made a face. "Gorgonzola, smoked gouda, sharp cheddar."

"Well, that sounds more appealing. And less like the Irish national flag. No Wensleydale?"

Cali's eyes slid from me to Marzi and back.

I winked.

Marzi got it. "Whoa, Wensleydale. That's serious stuff. Wensleydale broke up Wallace and Wendolene."

Cali groaned at Marzi. "It really pains me that you get that. You two deserve each other."

Marzi gestured a tiny bow. "Indubitably."

Cali ignored us and unloaded more items from the bag. Radishes, baby carrots, a red onion, cherry tomatoes. A little tin of sardines and one of smoked trout.

I picked up one of the tins. "Fancy."

Cali waved at Marzi. "Courtesy of." She took out a big bunch of purple grapes and considered them. "Let me go in and wash these." She picked up the radishes. "These too."

While she was gone, Marzi and I set out plates and the cutting board and I sliced half of the baguette.

Cali came back with the grapes and had also snagged soft boiled eggs and hummus from the fridge.

I picked off a grape and looked at all of the food. "That's some ploughman's lunch."

I twisted another grape from the bunch. "Here's the problem though. I don't think the language has caught up yet."

They both looked at me.

"Well, the two of you are women."

Marzi rotated in her seat. "Let's start right there. The language hasn't even caught up with the word women yet."

That got Cali's attention.

Marzi wiggled a finger between herself and Cali. "Why is it that woman sounds like a diminutive form of the word man?"

"But it's not supposed to be. Historically those were different words, and it just sounds like the word woman comes from man."

"Historically, schmistorically. Like Eve from Adam's rib."

"Ah, so history is dead. Would you rather have it the other way around?"

Marzi said, "Men defined based on women?"

"What would the men be called in that case? Wom*un*?"

Cali hung her head. "Are you trying to be funny?"

"Is it working?"

"No."

"Then no."

Cali positioned a block of cheese on the cutting board. "So what are we going to call the picnic dinner then? If we can't call it a ploughman's lunch?"

"I leave that to your generation," I said. "I think they've already got a good start on redefining gender roles."

Cali cut the first slice of cheese with a precise motion that delivered a perfect yellow wedge. "Your generation is leaving a lot to my generation."

"I've noticed that. My generation has screwed up a lot of things. Yours will have to do better."

Cali let loose an enormous sigh. "I don't even know where to start with that."

"How about global warming? And whatever else you have in that bag?"

She reached in and took out three brownies from Current Cuisine. "How about we start with this: We're calling it a ploughman's lunch. It might be his lunch, but I'm eating it. Woman eating the plough-*man*'s lunch. How's that for gender role reversal?"

Marzi didn't try to hide a grin. "Wom*en* eating the ploughman's lunch."

I reached for a pickle. "Is this going to go on all night?"

Marzi said, "I'm afraid so, Mr. Ploughman. And you've got yourself to blame. You started it."

I crunched the gerkin. "As long as I get to eat the pickles I don't care what we call it."

Cali sliced more cheeses. Neat, even, precise slices that were all the same size and shape. She spread the pieces in an equally precise fan across the cutting board.

Marzi and I less elegantly laid out the rest of the fixings.

I picked up a piece of cheese from the center of a fan. "I appreciate your artistic impressions here, but the cheese tastes the same whether it's sliced all the same or randomly hacked up into a pile."

Cali cut another slice of cheese and replaced the missing piece from the array. "Eat from the edges, please. This is a classy operation."

"I'm just a poor ploughman."

Then Mrs. Jenkins rustled out of the wildflowers and stretched. She hopped onto the one empty chair at the table. I knew the cat had never heard of a ploughman's lunch before either, but she seemed to know exactly what it was and what to do with it.

After the picnic dinner Cali got a text from her friend Asia. Some of her friends were going over there to bake cookies and do what teenagers find to do. She looked up at me from her phone. "Um."

"Yes?"

"I hate to be a Yoko."

"How do you even know that reference?"

She held up her phone. "My generation knows everything."

"That's what I'm afraid of. But I'm glad you've found the Beatles in your world of everything."

Cali gave me a blank look. "The who?"

I almost fell for it. "Funny. Now go. Make cookies with your friends. Post pictures for all the world to see."

Her fingers worked across the screen of her phone. "Of course we will. And I'm taking the chocolate chips."

"The chocolate chips?"

"In the back of the pantry?"

Pantry?

"That thing in the kitchen with all the food stored in it? The chocolate chips have been hidden in the back for an emergency."

"Oh. I didn't know we had chocolate chips."

"We don't. There's like half a bag. I'm taking them to Asia's so I won't eat them."

"You're not going to eat the cookies?"

"Of course I am."

Oh. "Is half a bag enough? Why do we only have half a bag?"

"Because they're the emergency back-up chocolate."

"And there have been emergencies?"

"Jeez, dad. Have you been following any of this?"

"I thought I was."

Cali went inside to get some things to take to Asia's, and Marzi helped me clean up. It didn't take long. Stick the remains of the ploughman's lunch into the fridge and rinse off a few dishes. Sneak a few more bites of brownie while Marzi wasn't looking. Catch her trying to do the same thing with the brownies when I wasn't looking.

Cali came out with her backpack on her shoulders and the bag of chocolate chips in her hand. She tossed some chips into her mouth.

I said, "You'd better take those to Asia's so you don't eat them."

She didn't laugh.

Then there was that moment I knew would be coming and I didn't know how it would go. And we had to do it in front of Marzi again.

When Cali stepped toward the edge of the porch I said casually, "How late do you think you might be?"

She stopped. "Is that important?"

"Yes."

"I thought you were letting me decide."

"I am."

"Then why are you asking? If it's my choice?"

"That's part of it. Communication. We talk. There's flexibility, but not a vacuum."

Cali's eyes went to Marzi.

Marzi smiled back but said nothing. She rose from her chair. "I think I'll go in and use the facilities."

Cali tossed her head and said, "Before midnight, probably."

So much for trying to get on a schedule for school.

"OK. And I'm not going to remind you that you'll have to start getting up early next week."

Cali spread her arms. "You just *did* remind me."

"But I didn't want to. Now go. Make cookies. Save me from the chocolate."

"You wouldn't eat the chocolate. You didn't even know it was here."

"Marzi might. You'd better go before she comes back."

Cali did.

Marzi stepped back out onto the porch a moment later. I sighed. "How'd I do?"

"It's too soon to tell. And that's a better question for you to answer than for me."

Marzi was right, of course. Once the counselor, always the counselor. "At least that's settled for now. What shall we do with the rest of our evening?"

We settled on a summer evening bike ride. It was one of the things I loved most about our little village.

We pedaled north and the ride almost got short-circuited when we reached the Yellow Springs Brewery. Having avoided that temptation, we rode past the edge of the village to Ellis Pond, where we took the bike path spur up to the Little Miami Scenic Trail. The corn was high and the undergrowth along the creekbed was thick and full and made a tunnel around us as we climbed the spur.

We pedaled north. A few minutes later when we reached the Jackson Road crossing Marzi circled her bike in the path. "We could keep going."

I circled behind her. "That's the plan."

"Up toward Springfield."

"That's what's to the north."

"Or…" She pointed her bike toward the lights to the east. "But we shouldn't."

I angled toward Jackson Road. "Just this once."

She was already ahead of me.

The bright lights were Young's Dairy. The big red barn. The miniature golf and the driving range. The water features. The cows and goats.

The ice cream.

Young's was crowded. We got in line for ice cream. Marzi scanned the list of flavors. "We should share something."

"Of course." I only wanted one bite anyway.

"Maybe cow patty?"

I scrunched my face. "I'm not eating cow patty."

"Wooly Wonka?"

"You're kidding?"

She grinned. "Actually, I was thinking of butter pecan with two spoons."

"You've earned it. You can eat with both hands."

She turned her back. "For that, I just might."

We took the ice cream outside and I got at least two bites before Marzi took over and showed me that butter pecan really was her favorite.

Then we rode back down to the bike path and cruised to the village, behind the Brewery, past the skate park and the train station building that was the visitor center. We circled back to the heart of the village for a back-alley tour at dusk.

The alleys of Yellow Springs are an overlooked peek into the arteries of the village. An intimate and slightly voyeuristic indulgence, with overgrown right-of-ways, outbuildings and patios, gardens, and an army of skunks looking for the local compost piles to raid.

Marzi had planned to spend the night at her place, but we were closer to mine and stopped there to refill our water bottles. Once we'd stacked the bicycles against the side of the house and sat down on the porch, inertia was taking over.

I put a hand on Marzi's arm. "Sleepover?"

"Jackson, I really want to be in my own bed tonight."

"All right."

"I'm sweaty and I want to shower. It's getting late, and I'm tired."

"It's OK."

"Maybe another time."

"Sure."

It was fine. We were trying things on for a fit. This was part of the fit.

I went in and finished cleaning up the dishes and took a book to bed.

9

IN THE MORNING I was drinking coffee and waiting for a more respectable hour on a Sunday to knock on the neighbors' doors out by the old Leewold place.

Some time between not late enough and getting there my phone burbled. Text from Brick.

The boy needs to run.

It was an odd way to put it.

I texted back. *Devil's backbone?*

Be there in 15. I'm gonna bring Quando.

Huh? Brick got a dog?

I was waiting when Brick's dirty green jeep lumbered into the dirt pull-off at the bottom of the steep and twisted road locals called the devil's backbone.

Next to us the old Grinnell Mill hunkered by the banks of the Little Miami River where it had weathered time and floods for more than two hundred years. Now it was a B&B. At our bumpers was the old mill race that still dug its course to the water wheel. On the front steps of the mill an overnight guest lounged with coffee.

Threading its way up through the trees was the hill climb.

Brick's door opened and he stepped out into the dappled sunlight. He stretched his arms back, and the tree of life tattoo that covered his scars spread up over his shoulder.

Then the Jeep's passenger door opened and a kid stepped out. It was the kid who had held the stack of bills in the mall parking lot. The kid I'd seen at Brick's.

The kid stepped out and yawned. He had ear buds in and was looking at his shoes.

Brick and the kid shared something of a mocha tinge to their complexion, but that's where the resemblance ended. Brick was hardened muscle and sharp angles, and the kid was all aloofness and slouch.

Brick centered his eyes on the hill as we approached the base. "You're not gonna ask?"

"I figure one of you will tell me if you want to."

Brick angled a thumb toward the kid. "Quando."

I looked back. So not a dog.

Quando caught up to us and pulled the buds from his ears and tucked them into his waistband. "I know you were talking about me."

I said, "We were. Your name. Quando. I've never heard that before."

He rolled his shoulders in what might have been a shrug if he'd given it more effort.

"Where's it come from?"

Brick and the kid looked at each other. When the kid didn't say anything, Brick did. "It's his banger name."

The kid's nose came up. "I told you that ain't what it is. And people don't say that anymore."

I said, "I thought that other guy called you Deek?"

Quando frowned.

"When you were holding all that money."

"That ain't nothing. That's just talking shit."

"So your name's not Deek?"

Brick made a slicing motion under his chin. So Deek was maybe something bad?

Quando said, "I ain't no Deek."

OK. "So where's Quando come from?"

The kid stuck his chin out. The fear I'd seen on him at the mall was gone now. "My daddy give me that name."

"Ah. What's it for? Mean anything?"

His eyes narrowed. Too many questions.

"I'm just asking if you know where he got the name. It doesn't mean anything. It's just interesting." I turned away to show I didn't care too much about it.

That did it. "I don't know where he got it."

"So? Your father never told you?"

"I never knew my daddy."

Hmm. "But you know it was your father who gave you your name?"

"I guess so. My momma tol' me."

I stretched my neck. Shook out my legs. Glanced to Quando. "You like it?"

"Like what?"

"Your name?"

"Quando?"

"Yeah, that one."

"I don't know. It's just my name. Why you askin'?"

"Trying to show a little interest. It's a unique name. I like it."

The kid waved a hand like he was trying to swipe the idea away.

"Unless you've got another, what do you want me to call you?"

"It's whatever."

I looked up the hill. "Then it's Quando. Let's see if you can do this."

He took off up the devil's backbone.

Brick and I started a steady climb. He matched his movements to mine. "Glad you two are getting along."

"You think?"

Brick didn't have to answer.

We caught Quando at the second curve. Brick and I were picking up the pace, beginning to stretch our legs out. Quando was still moving up the hill, but he was grinding down.

The road straightened a little for the last hard climb. Quando fell behind us, bent over at the guardrail, breathing hard.

I upped the pace another notch, legs and lungs working hard against the climb.

Brick kicked up beside me.

I lifted my legs higher. "Today is not the day."

Brick stuck beside me. "Every day is the day."

It was never a competition, but it was always a competition. And this was one thing I could consistently beat Brick at.

When I reached the mailbox that marked the top of the steepest part of the slope, I was one step in front of Brick. He threw his hands down, turned and started walking back down the hill. "That's one."

I came up beside him. "Of many."

Quando was about three-fourths of the way up when we met him. His feet were pounding like he was running, but he was moving at something slower than walking speed. He gave up and walked down with us.

Quando was sweating hard. He put his eyes to Brick. "You're just trying to make me look bad."

Brick shook his head once. "Not what's happening here."

"Then why'd you run past me?"

"Came here to run, I'm running. That's about me. Not about you."

"But I can't—"

"This one thing," Brick said. "It's one thing I can do that you can't yet. Doesn't mean anything unless you want it to."

We descended a little more.

Quando said, "What am I supposed to want it to mean?"

"That's up to you."

Some more steps down.

"So I don't have to do this?"

"You never had to. Your choice."

Closer to the bottom. I knew that if Quando could have beaten us to the top he would have wallowed in it. Brick knew.

We reached the bottom of the hill. Brick lined up for another climb. "Jackson and I are going to run. That doesn't mean we're trying to make you look bad. You can run against yourself or you can sit it out. There's no shame in either. You choose."

Quando swatted at sweat on the back on his neck. "You're just going to do one more?"

Brick laughed. "Not a chance."

This time Brick was the first to the top. By a step.

We ran another. And another. And more.

Quando grunted it all out. He never got his speed above a crawl, but he never stopped. And he made sure we saw that as we ran past him again and again.

After seven climbs I'd made it to the top first four times. After eight it was a dead heat.

The day was heating up. We were hot and sweaty and tired. I had doors to knock on. I gulped deep breaths to re-oxygenate. "I guess that's it. I've got to go."

"Not a chance."

"It's not a competition."

"It's not," Brick said. "But today is the day."

It wasn't the day for Brick to beat me. I dug deep and beat him by three steps.

I bent and wheezed. "I've got more where that came from."

"You don't look like it."

I raised up. "Another?"

"I'll let you have this one. You look like you could use some rest."

Uh-huh.

We picked up Quando about halfway down. He trudged beside Brick like a dog that had been left out in the sun. "You guys are crazy."

Brick lifted a hand toward the kid and for a moment I thought he would lay it on Quando's shoulder. But he didn't. Brick said, "Next time will be easier. You're running against yourself. It's not a competition."

"It looked like a competition."

At the bottom we drank water. Quando sat in the Jeep with the windows down and his ear buds in. Brick and I stood in the shade by the mill race.

I waited a long time for Brick to answer the question I hadn't asked. Then I said, "So what's going on with the kid?"

Brick crossed his arms. "He's still with me."

"I see that." I drank water, tried to keep the conversation going. "What about his parents?"

"Ain't no father."

"Mother?"

"He wasn't living with her."

Brick's look said don't ask. So Quando was on the streets, then. Somewhere.

I said, "Somebody's probably looking for him."

"Not his parents."

"I don't doubt that, but…"

It hung between us for a long time. Then Brick said, "Someone is probably looking for him. Not his parents. He can't go back there."

I shrugged. OK.

Brick wasn't ready to let it drop. "Say it. What you're thinking."

"Not much. It just—doesn't seem like something you'd do. Taking him in."

He stared out into the ruins of the old mill race. "It's surprising me too."

And that was it. The conversation ended. I finished my water and tossed the bottle into the cab of the truck. "You have any idea what comes next?"

"None."

"What's the kid want to do?"

Brick looked to the Jeep. "I don't know."

"What do you want to do?"

"I don't know that either."

Some cool air drifted up from the direction of the river. We both leaned into it. "Is there anything I can do?"

"Not yet. I don't know."

"Well, if the time comes…"

It hung there.

"You can't just…"

Brick turned toward the kid. "I can't do nothing." Then he joined Quando in the Jeep and backed out onto the road.

I hadn't even asked about the stack of money. Or the other kid. Or what Brick had done when he caught up with them.

Maybe I'd ask him later. Or maybe I never would.

I went home and got cleaned up. The most interesting part of my day was probably over. What were the chances on a sunny summer Sunday that I would find Angelita's neighbors at home, that they would allow me onto their property and answer the door, and then be willing to talk to a stranger about what would likely feel like spying? I knew that some people just liked gossiping, and that could be a P.I.'s salvation, but even if all of that fell into place, what were the chances that I might learn anything useful?

You'd think the life of a P.I. would be exciting, but a lot of it was sitting at a laptop or drudgery like I had to do today. Some days that was what paid the bills.

At least it was rural enough that there weren't many neighbors. Maybe I could put this to rest for Angelita in a hurry.

The houses on that stretch of county road were set far apart and back from the berm, often hidden from view by trees and winding lanes. At the more secluded entries I drove slowly and honked my horn a few times. It could be a mistake to surprise someone.

I had marked fourteen homes along a little under half a mile that ran to either side of the Leewold property. At five of those I found no one home. At three residences the owners politely but firmly closed the door to me. At six I got long looks at the explanation I gave to why I was there, but no one who could tell me anything useful about the Leewold place. I did get one offer of a cold glass of sweet tea, which I respectfully declined. Sweet tea was best left to the South.

After I'd run through the fourteen residences I pulled off the road in front of the chain that blocked the entrance to the Leewold home. I could walk up the drive and see if Angelita was home. Give her a report then instead of having to do it later. But I'd gotten nowhere, so there was nothing to report.

I found myself interested in whether the camera that should be pointed where I sat had been tripped by its motion sensor, and if that would alert Angelita to check her phone and see me sitting there in the truck.

What happened instead was that I caught movement through the trees behind Angelita's nearest neighbor's house. It was one of the addresses where I had found no one home. But out back now was what looked like someone jumping through the trees.

I looked closer. Another figure leaped through the trees, followed by the faint sound of a crash.

I took out my phone and used the camera to zoom in on the view. It was enough to tell me that the crash hadn't been a crash, it had been a splash. And the leaps hadn't been from the trees, they had been from a wooden deck beside an above-ground pool.

I left the truck where it was and walked over to the front door. The doorbell rang from somewhere deep inside the house.

After a moment, a woman who looked like she was probably in her thirties came to the door with a dish towel draped over her shoulder. She was thin and fit and showed sun like she'd spent some time outside. The garden in the side yard might have been the culprit.

The woman craned her neck forward. "Hello?"

I launched into a repeat of the explanation I'd already given to the other homeowners.

The woman stopped me a little ways in. "This is about Ida?"

"It is. And her grand-niece who has inherited the place."

She tipped her head. "Would you care for a glass of iced tea while we talk?"

"Sweet tea?"

Her eyes crinkled mischievously. "We don't have sweet tea here. That's for Southerners."

"Then I would be much obliged."

She slipped the towel from her shoulder. "I'll just be a minute."

I waited at the door and she came back in much less than a minute and handed me a tall tumbler of ice and tea. She kept another glass for herself and motioned us to a set of outdoor chairs in deep shade at the corner of the house. We sat and I went into the explanation of why I was there again.

The woman was attentive and when I was finished and asked her if she'd seen anything unusual or noteworthy, or if they had any security cameras that might have recorded something, she set her tea on the table between us. "We've lived here since the kids were little. Mark was four and Sheila was still toddling when we bought the place. My husband cleared out the honeysuckle, built the garage, and tilled up the ground for the gardens. We spend every summer out in the yard. Working on the place or swimming in that pool. And we barely knew Ida."

I nodded like it meant something important.

"What I'm saying is that she was very reclusive. Not anti-social, just private."

"Uh-huh."

"But Ida was as sweet a little old lady as you'd ever want to meet. Which I did maybe twice a year."

I nodded again. "Of course."

"I worried about her living alone out here. There were some people who would come by now and then and, I don't know, I guess they helped her out."

"Right. What about more recently?"

"You mean after she passed?"

"Yes. If you noticed anything, it could be useful."

"There were some folks who came and, I don't know, I guess cleaned the place out some."

"J Guy Estate Removal Service."

She squinted again. "So you know already."

"Yes, ma'am. That's the part I'm here about. They weren't supposed to remove everything. It seems like an honest mistake. I don't think anyone is going to get into trouble over what happened."

She waved a hand. "If there's trouble, there's trouble. I'm not afraid of stepping into anything. But I don't think we can tell you anything. There were trucks there one day, maybe two. We heard them over at the house, and then they were gone."

"So you didn't talk to them? Anyone who came to the house after Ida passed?"

"Neither I nor Duke did. The kids were probably here swimming."

I reached into my pocket for my little notebook.

"Duke is my husband. David."

I wrote that down. It probably wasn't important, but it would show that I took her seriously.

She held a hand out. "Stephanie Dunders."

We shook. So her husband was Duke Dunders. That name was worth noting, just for the fun of it. I did. Then I asked Stephanie if any of them had met Angelita yet.

"Angelita?"

"Ida's grand-niece."

"You said that. No, we haven't seen her."

"Well if you do, I think she wouldn't mind meeting the neighbors. I don't think she really knows anyone out here."

"Out here?"

"Ohio. Angelita came out from New Mexico when her aunt passed."

Stephanie Dunders sipped tea. "Is the niece a Leewold? I know that family's been here for a long time."

"Not by name, but Angelita comes from the Leewold family. She's Ida's grand-niece. It's her father's line. Her last name is Rojas Flores."

"You mean like red flower? Lord, some culture has come to us out here to these sticks."

I laughed. You never knew what you were going to get when you came down one of these twisting drives in the woods.

Stephanie rose. "Let's go ask the kids if they know anything that could help you."

I stood too. "Good idea."

But it was unexpectedly quiet when we rounded the back of the house. The pool was empty. Wet footprints marked the deck, and towels hung from the railing.

Stephanie called out and went into the house to search for her children, but she came back shaking her head. "They do that. Probably walked over to the Petermans'. You can try another time if you think it would be worth your while."

"I might do that. But I thank you for your time, regardless."

"It was nothing."

It wasn't nothing. It was a terrific glass of tea, at the very least. I drained the last of the melting ice from my tumbler and set it on the back step.

10

MONDAY MORNING STARTED QUIETLY. Cali was torn between sleeping late while she could before school started the next week and getting up early to adjust to the schedule. I wasn't surprised that sleeping in was winning.

I was getting a late start on work and not feeling guilty about it. I'd put in the weekend working and could afford a slowdown in billable hours. I made coffee and waited a long time for Cali to get up. When she didn't, I made her a breakfast sandwich with veggie sausage and peppers and left that in the fridge.

Mrs. Jenkins looked into the truck cab when I opened the door. She liked getting inside closed spaces, but she seemed to recognize that nothing good ever happened when she got inside a vehicle. She flipped her tail and headed into the weeds.

I spent an unhurried morning in my office, typing notes, updating expense reports, copying and filing receipts. It wasn't a lot of work. I never understood how fictional guys like Sam Spade had enough business to have both a partner and a secretary. But then who wouldn't want to share an office space with Effie Perrine?

My phone rang and I took a call from a guy desperate to have me take pictures of his wife with another guy so he could beef up his divorce case. I quickly and politely declined. That kind of work made a person feel dirty, and for the worst kind of work it had a high likelihood of trouble. People hated snitches, especially snitches who caught them cheating. It was a recipe for revenge, or for someone taking a crack at you while you're trying to get the goods on them.

I had a lengthy and lucrative security and personnel review for a local company scheduled for the fall, and there had been steady work serving papers. I could afford to wait for something more digestible to come along.

I finished the office work and considered the loose ends to clear up with Angelita. John Guy would probably want to get the extra fifty, and his guys would probably go for the cash for a quick talk, but I didn't expect it to lead to anything.

I could go back and try to talk to the Dunders kids next door to the Leewold house, but ditto.

Angelita should put up signs at the road and house announcing the video camera, but that was something J'Leah could do.

I could introduce Angelita to Stephanie Dunders and maybe she'd make a friend, but I didn't like to play match-maker.

That left Angelita's father's stories, which I thought were just that. She may be disappointed to have lost some family items in the confusion of her inheritance, but I didn't believe there was a family treasure to be found, or any lost items that could be recovered.

Angelita's obvious options were to settle into her Aunt Ida's house or sell it and go back to Santa Fe. But unless there was more trouble with the squatters, this thing with Angelita was probably just about over for me.

The more I thought about the loose ends the less I wanted to do them. Talk to the neighbors. Track down the Dunders kids. Look for the county and senior center workers who had come to Ida's. All of that might make Angelita feel better, but none of it was work I cared to do. This is why Sam Spade had a partner and a secretary. And why I was no Sam Spade.

I called John Guy.

"J Guy Estate Removal Service."

"John, Jackson Flint. We talked a couple of days ago about the Leewold estate?"

"Yeah."

"I was trying to find out if there is any chance some of the items removed might be recovered."

"I remember."

I waited and gave him a chance to do some of the work in the conversation. He didn't take it. "You were looking up the guys who worked the job."

"Yeah."

His vocabulary wasn't getting any larger. I'd have to walk him through it. "You remember our arrangement? Have you found anything?"

There was an awkward pause. Guy closed it with an awkward response. "You gave me a president. Lincoln."

"Lincoln is on the five. I gave you a hundred."

"Yeah."

"John, have you found the names of the guys who worked the job?"

He grunted. "I'm not giving the fifty back."

I ignored the downgrade in currency. "You don't have to. Did you not find the names?"

"I can't tell you."

"You can't tell me if you found out who it was that worked the job?"

"I can't tell you their names."

Huh. A couple of days ago he tried to up the ante to two hundred for that information. "Because you don't know?"

"They don't want me to tell you."

"The guys don't?"

"Right."

"Any reason why?"

The sound of air came through the connection, like Guy was breathing too heavily or had his nose too close to the phone. "Look, some of these guys, they don't want any trouble."

"There's no trouble. Miss Rojas Flores is just hoping there's some chance that some of the items may have been dropped off in a place where she can go look for them."

"That's unlikely."

Now I breathed too heavily through the phone. "I know."

"And I don't know Miss Rosie Floors."

I didn't think he was trying to make fun of her name. I thought he couldn't pronounce it. "My client is still willing to offer a financial incentive if there is some information to follow, regardless of whether it leads to recovery of any items or not."

"You've seen my office, right?"

"In the garage?"

"Yeah. So you know a hundred dollars ain't gonna save me."

I tried not to let it, but a laugh slipped out.

John Guy didn't seem offended. "Look, there's nothing to find. Everything is gone. I can't have my guys upset. I need them to work for me."

"OK, John."

He tapped off the connection. It wasn't the hard close to this loose end that I'd wanted. Sam Spade would have had someone to put on it and make sure the book was closed, but I would have to let this one go. One down.

I reluctantly went out to tug on another of the loose ends. I retraced my way to the five addresses near the Leewold home where I hadn't found anyone the day before. At two of those, someone came to the door. But all I got for it was a couple of long looks and quick send-offs.

On a whim I tried the Dunders next door to Angelita, but no one was there. On another whim, I left the truck at the road and walked around the chain in front of the Leewold place and down the shaded drive.

Angelita's truck was parked out front, and J'Leah's Honda was next to that. The front door was open and I called out. "Hello the house."

Angelita and J'Leah were outside and came around from the back of the house. J'Leah said, "Did you just say hello the house?"

"I did."

"My gramma used to say that. I never knew what she meant."

"It's just what you say so you don't surprise people."

"You could just say hey."

"I could."

"And then you wouldn't sound like a gramma."

I shrugged.

J'Leah looked down the winding drive behind me. "Or you could have driven down instead of walking and we would have heard your car."

"It's a truck."

"Whatever. We would have heard you."

Angelita stood quietly a few feet behind J'Leah. I felt like I'd stepped into the middle of something. I turned to J'Leah. "I thought you had a job you had to be at?"

"Welcome to the gig economy. It's flexible."

I turned to Angelita. "Since I'm here, do you have a few minutes for an update?"

"Sure. I'm flexible."

She was having fun. Gig economy. Flexible. My news wasn't so fun. "I don't think you're going to get back any of the things that were removed from the house. I'm sorry."

"I guess that's what I expected."

"I haven't talked to absolutely everybody, but I think we've reached the point of diminishing returns here."

She took a moment. "I guess I'll have to be able to live with that."

"If you want to think about it and let me know if there's anything else you want to do, you can take your time with that."

"I will."

"There's still the sleeping bag, and who it belonged to. And whoever else might have been coming around. I think J'Leah is helping you with that?"

"She is."

"You might consider putting up some signs. Let people know there are cameras so they'll be more of a deterrent."

J'Leah stepped in. "I'm on that."

"I figured." I looked at the two women. Something was off. "Am I interrupting something?"

Neither of them had a complexion that would let them blush much, but color looked like it was trying to rise on both of the women's faces.

They looked at each other.

Angelita said, "We were going to go swimming."

Oh. Okay.

"Down at the creek, like I did when I stayed with Aunt Ida when I was younger."

"I remember you told me."

They were still sharing the looks.

"Well this doesn't look like my party and I didn't bring my swim suit, so I guess I'll leave you two to it."

J'Leah flipped a towel over her shoulder. It didn't look like she'd brought her suit either.

Oh. It seemed like maybe Angelita was finding someone to do a little bonding with.

I got out of there and left them to it.

That afternoon and evening were quiet. I picked some tomatoes and zucchini from the yard and cooked them with black beans for dinner. Cali spent a lot of time texting on her phone. Marzi had worked late and wanted to stay home and go to bed early. I sat on the front porch with Mrs. Jenkins and a Don Winslow novel and read about California sun and surfing. The exciting life of a P.I.

The surprise came at two in the morning.

I knocked the phone onto the floor when it rang and fumbled to pick it up. Angelita. I swiped.

"Jackson?"

"Yeah."

"You have to come help me."

"What? Where are you? What happened?"

"I'm at my aunt's house. I shot someone."

11

A COUNTY SHERIFF'S CAR sat at the road, floodlights glaring through the foliage. My headlights swept a motorcycle that had been pushed into the trees beyond the county car. Out of habit I stopped at the berm and took some photos of the bike with my phone.

The chain at the drive was pulled back. I hesitated. The Smith & Wesson M&P40 was clipped on my belt. I thought about it longer than I wanted to.

Then I unclipped the weapon and pushed it into the glove box. I drove up slowly with the headlights on and both windows rolled all the way down. Hello the crime scene. Nobody shoot at me.

The house and yard were lit up by headlights from more county cars and an ambulance squeezed into the clearing of trees.

A siren whooped once when I arrived in the clearing. I took the truck out of gear, set the parking brake, and brought both hands to the top of the wheel. Then I dimmed to the running lights and waited while a flashlight held head-high battered my eyes as it approached the driver's window.

When the light was a few feet away, the angle canted to my eyes and a voice came from behind it. "Sir, leave one hand on the wheel and with the other turn the vehicle off."

I did, then returned the hand to the wheel. I knew from the time I'd spent working for this same sheriff's office that this was exactly the kind of situation that would put a deputy on edge.

"I have a private investigator's license. My client called me. Angelita Rojas Flores."

The light flicked around inside the cab.

"I want to tell you that there is a loaded pistol in the glove box. It's registered to me, and I have a concealed carry permit."

The deputy stepped closer. "Jackson Flint?"

"Yes." The light flicked around the cab some more and over the glove box. "May I show you my ID?"

"Yes, sir. We're aware of the call Miss Rojas Flores has placed to you."

I reached for my wallet and gave him everything. The deputy kept the light and his eyes on both me and the identification as he scanned it. Textbook.

Then he handed back the items and clicked his flashlight off. "We served together. For about a year when I first started."

I looked at the deputy.

He said, "Bronigan."

"I remember." It had been a while. "How've you been?"

He tucked the flashlight into a pocket on his duty belt. "Actually, you remember Molly? Worked for dispatch? We're married now and she had our first a couple of months ago. Little Henry."

"Congratulations."

He shifted his steps. "Yeah. She's actually been pretty much on edge since Henry was born. Thinks something is going to happen to me. It gives me the spooks. I'm sorry about the treatment."

"Don't be. It was by the book."

We both knew even that was sometimes not enough.

Bronigan pointed across the clearing. "Park it over there. Leave the weapon in the glove box and lock the vehicle. We'll see if we can get you a few minutes with her."

I did what the deputy said and nosed the truck into the black cherry and elm branches.

I stepped out into a glowing dome from the lights, tempered by muted squawks from the deputies' and EMTs' radios. Then as if to drive home Bronigan's wife's fears, an EMT exited the rear of the ambulance, secured the doors, and got into the driver's seat. The big overhead lights came on and the ambulance rumbled away.

Angelita stood in front of the house close to another deputy.

I walked up slowly and held my hands up. "Hello the house."

Angelita brightened and stepped close to me. If I had raised my arm for her, I think she would have tucked under it.

The deputy's eyes followed everything.

I said, "Are you OK?"

"I'm all right."

"What happened?"

The deputy answered in Angelita's place. "She wasn't harmed. We're trying to determine the details now."

I flicked my head once to where the ambulance had been.

The deputy understood. "It's serious, but he's alive."

I turned away from the deputy. "Angelita?"

She swallowed once. "I shot him."

"Tell me."

"He was coming at me."

"Who was?"

"I don't know."

"What was he doing?"

"Yelling. He said he was coming for me."

"Coming for you?"

A nod.

"Why would he say that?"

"I don't know."

I glanced to the house and hoped J'Leah had gotten those cameras in.

"And that's when you shot him?"

She pointed into the circle of lights. "Right there."

"How many times did you shoot?"

Angelita's eyes widened. "I don't know."

The deputy stepped back in. "More than once. Who are you again?"

I pointed to Bronigan, who was examining something on the ground in the lights from a cruiser. I went through it again and showed the deputy my P.I. license.

He squinted briefly at the ID and pushed it back. "So not her lawyer?"

"No." It was nearly two-thirty in the morning. I couldn't imagine a lawyer on site at this hour. The deputy probably couldn't either, but he'd made his point.

The deputy pressed me again. "You were working on something for Miss Rojas Flores?"

"Squatters. Trying to keep them out of here. The place had been empty for a while and some undesirables had moved in."

The deputy flipped through some hand-written notes but didn't share what he'd written there.

"Your office should have records of a call from Miss Rojas Flores to report that someone had entered her property without permission. They sent someone out and put her on the drive-by sheet."

The deputy's eyes came up. "I'm aware of that. We're going to have to ask Miss Rojas Flores some more questions. You'll have to wrap this up."

I remembered how it was. You try to control everything on the scene as much as possible.

I tossed out a question. "Who called it in?"

The deputy angled a thumb over his shoulder. "Multiple. First call came from the neighbors—over there."

His thumb went to the Dunders, where a light sifted through the trees. "Did Miss Rojas Flores call?"

"She did."

"And after you arrived you let her make the call to me?"

He checked his notes. "That call may have been placed before the responding officer arrived on the scene."

"And that was Bronigan?"

The man's eyes narrowed. "You know Deputy Bronigan?"

"We worked together. For this office." Giving it back to him. A little push.

The deputy didn't look like he believed it. He glanced to Bronigan. "I'll check on that."

I clocked some mental notes. Whatever the details were, there hadn't been much time between the shots and the calls to the sheriff's office and to me. It had all happened fairly quickly.

The deputy listened to something on his radio, then clicked the transmitter. "Standby." He looked at Angelita but spoke to me. "She's going to need a lawyer."

Then he took two steps back and listened to his radio again but kept his eyes on us.

The deputy was right. Angelita was going to need a lawyer. I knew a good one, who had helped a family come back together twenty years after the teen daughter ran away and disappeared. Maybe Shakespeare didn't know everything about the often beleaguered legal profession. You didn't want to put all of them up against the wall just yet.

I put my attention back on Angelita. "Are you really all right?"

"I think so."

"Where did you get the gun?"

Her face twisted a little. "I brought it with me when I came here."

"Why didn't you tell me you had a gun?"

"I didn't think I needed to."

"It was pertinent. You were worried about being out here alone. A gun changes things."

She didn't disagree. It had certainly changed things in this case.

"What was it?"

Angelita understood the question. "A thirty-eight."

Good at close quarters, but not for much more. She'd probably just been in range. "You're comfortable with a handgun?"

"Lots of people where I come from know how to use a gun."

She didn't have to convince me. My limited knowledge of New Mexico geography gave me the Navajo Nation and Zuni Reservations, Los Alamos, and lots of empty spaces. It fit.

Angelita pointed into the melee. "They took it."

Of course they did. "Is it licensed?"

"It is."

"In New Mexico? Does that transpose to Ohio?"

She gave me a blank look. That's why she was going to need a lawyer.

"I know a guy. Samuel Thomas. He's a lawyer. I can call him in the morning if you want a recommendation."

Angelita wrapped her forearms together. It was a warm night. The gesture would be more for comfort than for warmth. "I think he's in bad shape."

"They guy you shot?"

"Yeah."

"Tell me."

"I was…" She gestured to the house. "Sleeping. I bought a sleeping bag and pillow. And I brought some coffee and things. I just wanted to—J'Leah said I'd have to get used to being out here alone if that's what I wanted to do."

"J'Leah suggested you sleep out here tonight?"

"No. I think she meant…eventually."

"But you didn't want to wait."

"With the cameras and everything. I thought it was OK."

Obviously it wasn't. "The camera woke you? The app on your phone gave you an alert?"

"No. I heard the noise."

"Where's your phone now?"

She pointed to Bronigan.

"The deputy asked you for it?"

"Yes. He said he'd give it back."

OK. "So you heard a noise…"

She nodded. "They were noisy."

"They?"

"I think there was another guy."

"Did you see a second person?"

"No, but they were noisy. I think I heard two."

"Did you tell the deputy that?"

"Uh-huh."

"And what happened when you heard the noise?"

"They were walking up."

"Up the drive?"

"I turned the light on. But I couldn't see anyone. They were out in the dark."

"Then what?"

"The guy was shouting. *I'm coming for what's mine.*"

I waited. "That's it? Just *I'm coming for what's mine?*"

"That's all I remember for sure."

"The deputy said you told him it was something like *they were coming for you.*"

"I can't remember exactly. I was scared. I told him to stop. I said I had a gun. He kept coming. I think he was drunk."

"What about the other guy?"

"I don't know if he was drunk too."

"No, I mean where was he? What was he doing?"

"I didn't see another guy."

"But you heard him?"

She looked out past the vehicles and the curtain of lights. "Farther back. He didn't come up to the house."

"But the guy you shot did. He came toward the house?"

"I told him to stop. I told him I was going to shoot."

"He was still coming at you?"

"When I shot him?"

"Yes."

"Right there." She pointed again. It added up.

"And he stopped then?"

"He stopped when I shot him."

"After the first shot?"

Angelita flinched. "I didn't realize I'd shot him more than once."

That was for the lawyer. I changed course. "What do you think he meant, *I'm coming for what's mine?*"

Angelita jabbed her palms into her eye sockets. "I don't know."

But we both knew her father's stories were sitting there between us.

I ticked through some mental images, trying to picture the scene. "What about the motorcycle?"

"Motorcycle?"

"There's a motorcycle out at the road, pushed into the trees."

"I don't know."

"Did you hear motorcycles? One or more than one?"

"Maybe. The shot was so loud. And I heard the guy running away."

"The other guy?"

"The other guy."

"After you fired the gun?"

Angelita nodded.

"So you're sure now that there were two?"

She looked into the dark again, as if remembering. "I'm sure."

"But you didn't hear him leave on a motorcycle?"

"I don't know. Maybe. I heard something."

And then the deputy came back from talking into his radio and held a hand out to Angelita. "Ma'am, we're going to want you to come to the office in Xenia for more information. And we're going to have you checked out, make sure you're OK, there's nothing we might have missed." He turned his attention to me. "Sir, you can contact your client later."

"If you can just—"

"Later." He signaled to one of the cars, then guided Angelita to it. Angelita bent and got in.

I went over to Bronigan. He shook his head before I even got close. "You're going to have to go. That's all we can give you right now."

It was more than they usually gave. I tipped my fingers in thanks. "Give my best to Molly."

Bronigan pulled a tight smile at the edges of his mouth and turned away to the house.

I backed the truck out slowly from under the trees. Something didn't add up yet. Either Angelita hadn't told me the whole story, or there was a missing piece I hadn't found for her yet.

Or both.

12

I WOKE WITH THE SUN HIGH and Mrs. Jenkins perched on my chest. She had that curious feline look on her face, probably trying to decide whether I was going to get up and do something that interested her, like going to her food bowl or scratching her ear, or whether I was dead and she should start eating me.

I moved to show her I wasn't dead. She followed me to her food bowl where I dumped what was left there back into the cat food bag, shook things around, and scooped out another half-bowl's worth of food and set that on the floor.

Mrs. Jenkins purred like I'd given her the keys to the golden city. She dug one bite of food from the bowl, jerked her head side-to-side rapidly to kill it, then ate the one piece and was done.

With the threat of the cat's imminent demise from starvation averted, I found my way to the coffeepot to try to avert my imminent demise from lack of caffeine.

By the time I had a cup of hot joe in my hand, I'd seen the news from last night breaking everywhere. Video clips of reporters standing in front of the Leewold house pointing with conviction down the shady drive, explaining the seriousness of what had happened.

Angelita's picture was popping up everywhere. If I'd been more interested in social media, I probably could have spent the rest of my phone's battery touching and swiping to follow the stories and comments.

I didn't like it, both for the intrusion into Angelita's life and into the investigation I was plotting out in my head. But I knew the news was fickle, like a starving cat with a bowl full of food. Unless there was another kick of excitement, this story would become yesterday's lover like the morning after a frat party.

I soft-shoed to Cali's bedroom door. It was partway open. I knocked and peeked in. She wasn't there.

I pulled out my phone to text her, but before I was finished tapping out a message I'd reached the fridge and found a breakfast sandwich with a note stuck on top.

Dad ~

So I made you a breakfast sandwich, because you've made me like a thousand. I can't remember the last time I was up before you. (So ha!) I'm with Asia and Jenny (and probably Nadia) shopping for clothes.

Shopping for clothes probably meant online. I'd always believed that was quicker than going to a store and trying things on, until I saw my teenaged daughter spend a whole day looking at clothes on her phone. It wasn't just the clothes. It was looking up various people wearing those clothes doing different things, and there was something called wardrobe planning apps that I understood the attraction of, but there wasn't enough bandwidth in my head to allow patience to look at one.

And then when the clothes arrived, Cali would pretend it was nothing. That she'd bought them on a lark, just for fun, without any real thought to how much she might like them. I knew better.

I'd grown up without sisters, and when I was a kid and we shopped for school clothes it was with mom. She whipped us into the car, took us to JCPenney, picked out what we would try on, and had us back home before her coffee got cold. I hadn't even realized that new clothes for school was a vital and necessary function for high school girls until Marzi explained it to me.

So I told Cali she could use the credit card I'd given her for emergencies only, gave her a budget, and told her to have fun. With that kind of green light she might not surface again until Monday morning when classes started.

I peeked under the top of the breakfast sandwich. Veggie sausage, red pepper, and an egg. It was on a homemade biscuit. Cali was showing off a little. I could get used to this.

I poured more coffee. My phone buzzed. Text from J'Leah. *Talk?*

I dialed. J'Leah answered.

I said, "So I assume you've heard?"

"I have."

"I should see how Angelita is doing."

"She's at home. Sleeping."

"Home? The Leewold house? How do you know that?"

J'Leah said, "I picked her up from the station this morning. She called me to come get her."

"The county guys didn't take her back home?"

"It was a woman doing the interview with Angelita. They would have taken her home. But Angelita called me."

"I could have done that."

"Angelita thought maybe you'd want to sleep in."

Well, she was right. "I was going to give her Samuel Thomas' number. She's probably going to want a lawyer."

"I already gave her ST's number. She's called him."

ST? I didn't even know J'Leah had stayed in touch with Samuel Thomas after we'd cleared the case with the missing girl. And Samuel Thomas had never seemed to me like anyone but a two-name guy. Now he was ST?

Jeez, Jackson. You sleep late one day and the world passes you by.

I sipped more coffee. Maybe caffeine would make me more relevant.

J'Leah had a better idea. "We need to catch up."

"We do."

"How about lunch at that funky pizza place by you?"

"Lunch?"

"Lunch."

"It's not lunch time."

"It will be by the time I get there. The day's almost half over for us working people."

I checked the time. I was way off my game. "Ha Ha."

"That's the best you've got?"

"No. The place is called Ha Ha."

"The pizza place?"

"Yeah. Ha Ha Pizza. Is this conversation getting silly?"

"It is. How about I just meet you there?"

"Why don't we just talk now?"

"There's more to it. And you're not tech savvy enough to do it on your phone. Plus, I wouldn't get to come out there and eat pizza."

"And they have the best salad bar in town."

J'Leah exhaled. "It's just like you to want the grazing option."

"Ha ha."

"Don't start that again. Noon. Be there. Keep the sun at your back." She ended the call.

I put the breakfast sandwich back into the fridge. We'll meet again, my eggy friend.

What was I thinking? I ate it.

Then I did a couple of chores around the house and bicycled to town. J'Leah was sitting in the front window of the pizza place, looking out on the main drag into Yellow Springs. I went in and slipped into the bench across from her.

J'Leah was studying the menu. "Why do they call it Ha Ha?"

"No idea."

"You think it has something to do with the sixties?"

"Probably. The sixties lasted into the seventies around here."

J'Leah looked around at the bright yellow walls and the local art for sale hanging on them. "At least."

In the eighties a print of Picasso's Guernica hung on the wall just above the pizza oven doors. Years of heat, smoke, and grease had morphed the print into something even more distorted and psychedelic than Pablo's original work. The print was probably more cheese and tomato than paper and ink when it had come down.

Now the defining image for the place was the picture on the pizza box of a smiling guy looking over a pie and holding something that suggested the pizza dough wasn't the only thing he'd hand-rolled. Yeah, this town held on to character.

A guy came to the table and asked me if I'd like a menu.

I waved it off. "Lunch special. Mushroom and black olives."

J'Leah groaned. "They have meat here."

"Feel free."

She sighed and looked up at the guy waiting our table. "Broccoli and onion."

I laughed.

J'Leah shook her head. "When in Rome."

We filled our bowls from the salad bar that had the usuals plus things like tofu, beans, and Aegean dressing. J'Leah stuck to just the usuals. I looked over her greenery choices. "Hmm. Not very adventurous. Save some."

"Save some?"

"For your pizza."

"To eat with my slice?"

"To put on top of it."

She made a face but didn't disagree.

The pizza came and I stacked peppers, beans, and olives I'd saved from my salad on top. J'Leah's salad bowl was empty. We ate.

When the pizza was gone, we got down to business. I started. "How's Angelita doing?"

J'Leah reached for the bag on the bench beside her. "Not good. She's freaked out about shooting the guy. And about the police."

"You have any idea how the guy is doing?"

She pulled a thin laptop from the bag. "Just what I've seen on the news."

"Me too. It doesn't look good."

"Medically induced coma."

I touched my temple. "Swelling in his head. It's to try to protect him."

J'Leah frowned. "Guy I served with got put under after he tumbled on a bumpy chopper ride. Didn't have his helmet secured."

"This guy wasn't wearing a helmet when Angelita shot him."

J'Leah winced. It wasn't the right thing to say. I tried something else. "Angelita shouldn't feel so bad about what happened."

"I think she's confused. She didn't want to shoot the guy. But, you know. He was coming at her."

"When did they let her out?"

"I picked her up about five o'clock this morning."

I drummed a finger on the table. "You have any ideas about what's going on?"

"There's something missing here. Something we don't know yet."

"Or those stories her father told…?"

"But why would this happen just now? What's the connection? If there was something valuable at the house, why did nobody come for it until now? And why didn't Angelita know about it?"

"Those are all good questions. I have another one for you. Did you know Angelita had a gun?"

"No. I wouldn't have pegged her for that."

"Me either. She said it's common where she comes from."

"Texas?"

"New Mexico."

"Close enough."

"Don't you think that's a bit of a stereotype?"

"I do."

"Well as long as you're OK with it." I pointed to her laptop. "I'm hoping you have something there that will help."

"That's why I came out here."

"That and the pizza."

J'Leah opened the laptop and sorted through some windows.

"Angelita said the app on her phone that would alert her when the camera came on didn't wake her up."

"She's still learning it. And that's not quite the way it's set up. If she had the app alert her every time some critter set it off, she wouldn't get any sleep."

"So it's mostly for while she's away?"

"Or during the day while she's home. Kind of like a video doorbell. Let her know someone is coming before they get there."

"So at night…?"

"It can be set to record when it senses motion, but not wake you up. That's what happened last night."

"Can you get to that. Whatever it recorded?"

"It records to the cloud."

"And you can get to it?"

J'Leah scooted over on her bench and motioned for me to come around and sit next to her. "Already did."

I came over, and J'Leah touched the laptop screen. "I pulled some stills and video clips. The one I'm going to show you is the most useful."

"Where is the camera?"

"Under the eave near the corner of the house. It's got a wide angle and gets the front door and a slice of space out front."

She started a video clip. The picture was black-and-white and very dim, and there was no sound. "The camera starts recording a little before this, but here is where we start to see something."

The front door of the house opens. The outside light does not come on.

"The camera has a low-light sensor, but with the trees and no moon up, the frame is a little dark."

Angelita steps from the house. The camera catches her in profile, looking over her right shoulder. She is in front of the screen door.

Angelita stands for a moment, looking away from the house. Her shoulders move and it looks like she might be saying something. Then her arm comes up, and it's clear from the movement on the side of her face that Angelita is speaking.

Angelita stops speaking. Both of her arms are raised. The gun isn't visible, but from what happened it's clear that she is holding it.

Angelita is speaking again, and then there's a flash of light from the blast of the weapon. Angelita stands her ground and shoots again.

J'Leah paused the video, backed it up several seconds, and held the image there. She pinched her fingers and widened them to zoom in on a blurred image that was clearly human. "That's him."

"The guy Angelita shot?"

"Has to be."

I looked closer. Some detail came through, but I wouldn't be able to pick the guy out if I was standing in line next to him at the dollar store. "Angelita said there were two guys. Are you sure this is the one she shot?"

J'Leah advanced forward a few ticks. She started the video and the guy fell and stayed down. "That's him."

"OK, so who is he?"

Instead of answering, J'Leah played more of the video.

A bit of time passes where Angelita stands behind the screen door looking out from the house. She goes inside for a moment, then comes back to the same spot in front of the door again, still in profile, her eyes on the clearing and trees beyond the house. She holds a phone in one hand and places a call.

I touched J'Leah's computer screen and stopped the video, backed it up again to where the guy was falling. "How much time passed from when she shot him to when we see Angelita make the call?"

"I thought of that. It was a minute or two."

I turned it over in my head. "Does that seem to you like the right amount of time?"

"If you were scared, you wouldn't want to run out there."

"I wouldn't want to wait to call for help either."

J'Leah moved the time index on the video a couple of times. "She could have made another call inside. Before this one."

"OK."

"And anyway, the whole thing is just a couple of minutes, so the video fits with what Angelita has said. That's good."

"It is."

We both looked at the screen. "So what does this tell us?"

"It says you should find out who this guy Angelita shot is and why he was at that house in the middle of the night. What he wanted and what he thought was his to take."

I already knew that. "So why did we need to meet to look at the video? What's here that you couldn't have sent me?"

J'Leah picked up the last bit of her pizza crust and waved it around.

"We've already covered your need to eat. But I do have a question. I didn't see a camera at the road when I was there yesterday. Is there one?"

J'Leah spun the laptop. "It's there, but it's not completely set up yet. Still working on it. It's really just snapping stills on a motion sensor."

She swiped and tapped, and some images came up. "We had to pull it back from the road or it would load up with snaps every time a car went past." She pulled up a shot that captured the chain that blocked the end of the drive.

"So it's aimed away from the road?"

"It is. And it gets images like this." She tapped and there was something on the screen.

"Is that an arm?"

"Yes. Watch." She moved through a couple of shots. The camera caught a side and rear view of a motorcycle advancing into the woods next to the chain gate. "The images are one second apart. We see someone push a motorcycle into the trees, and we see his arm—assuming it's a he—and we get a look at the bike but we never see the person pushing it. But Angelita said you already knew about the bike."

I pulled my phone from my pocket. "I did." I called up the photos I'd taken of the motorcycle last night and showed them to J'Leah.

She took my phone and looked closer. "Yours are better."

"Uh-huh. The police are going to want the recordings from Angelita's."

"ST is working with her on that."

I looked at her. "Does Samuel Thomas know you call him that?"

"He does. He says you have a thing about lawyers. You want to keep it formal."

"They trained us for that when I worked for the sheriff."

J'Leah sighed. "I don't doubt that. Are you going to give them these photos from your phone?"

"No. They don't know about these. And they'll have their own shots. And they'll have the bike. They won't need my pictures."

She put her nose closer to the phone. "What's that?"

"What?"

J'Leah zoomed in on a photo. "On the bike."

I looked. "Club patch?"

"Looks like it. Could be interesting."

I shrugged. Bikers and clubs hadn't been a big part of what I saw when I was with the sheriff's office. Mostly it was domestics, accidents, traffic control, a little public disturbance. I knew there were bikers with club patches in the area, but I didn't remember most of them causing a whole lot more trouble than anyone else. Every once in a while we'd break up something noisy with bikers, but most of them went on their way when we showed up instead of going to jail.

I squinted at the image. "Mean anything to you?"

"Uh-uh."

I flicked through the pictures, looking for the best view of the image painted on the gas tank.

J'Leah said, "Lot of vets ride. Some of them are in clubs. Not all bikers are trouble."

"Sure. But this guy pushed his bike into the weeds in the middle of the night and got shot in front of Angelita's house."

"Well, there's that. Why don't you send me those photos?"

I did. Then I set my phone down. "Got any ideas how I can find another one of these bikes with the patch on it?"

"Why don't you start with the guy she shot?"

"He's unconscious."

"Right. My bad. I meant if he wakes up."

"I was hoping I wouldn't have to wait that long."

"Sorry. Lack of meat addles my brain."

"You could have had the pepperoni and sausage."

"I don't want to walk around Yellow Springs smelling like meat."

I failed to hold back a laugh. "The only thing interested in you would be the buzzards."

"Buzzards?"

"Turkey vultures? Fly around looking for fresh roadkill to eat?"

"I know what a buzzard is."

"So if you smelled like meat…"

"I'm not following you."

I waved her off. "You're not the first. You have any ideas?"

"You mean that are useful?"

"That would be a good start."

"I can look around."

"What does that mean?"

"Set up a searchbot. Look for chatter online."

"Chatter? What chatter?"

"Image search. If I can sharpen up your photos I might be able to get the name of the motorcycle club."

"What would you do with that?"

"We're back to searchbot."

"You think that would get anything?"

"Might. It's worth a try."

"Then do it."

I took a pen and the little notebook from my pocket to write some notes, and for a moment it felt silly. There was the internet, data connections and the cloud, note apps for my phone, and digital voice recorders. And J'Leah with all of her tech experience and searchbots.

But my pen and paper hadn't become completely obsolete yet, and neither had I.

13

DARK STAR BOOKS was smack in the middle of the village, right where a bookstore should be. I walked there and stepped from the bright sidewalk sun into the cool shadow of the interior.

Dark Star exuded originality like a unicorn wearing a tuxedo. It was an alternative throw-back to a time when a bookstore could feel like someone's living room, with easy chairs and stacks of comics and rows of books and a sleepy black cat. The books here had been loved once, twice, many times, and were ready to be loved again.

I sauntered back to the mysteries and squatted down in front of the shelves. The cat trundled over and swept beside my knee. I scratched his neck. "Hello, Mr. Eko."

A local guy did radio interviews with authors. He got everyone—superstars, presidents, newbies, breakouts. You name them, he'd interviewed them on the Book Nook.

That guy had turned me onto Don Winslow, and I was looking for Winslow's book with a character who had the same name as Nelson Algren's golden-armed man. As a sleuth myself, I felt it my duty to stay abreast of how the fictional guys did their work.

I had three paperbacks in my hand when a woman emerged from the stacks and looked my way. "Find what you wanted?"

"And then some."

"Yeah, you never know what you'll find on our shelves."

What I was finding now was Mr. Eko curled into the shelf in front of me. They claimed the cat could read. Darned if it didn't look like he was.

I paid up and passed back out of the bookstore world into the sunlight and the street. The rattle of a motorcycle cruising past reminded me that my life wasn't like the sleuths in the books. I had a guy on a motorcycle to find, and he wasn't going to just ride by on the street. Finding him wasn't going to be fancy work like in the novels.

I went up to my office and wrote down the threads I could try to chase.

Look for Angelita's father in prison somewhere in Florida. She hadn't given me his first name. I knew Angelita's father's father had Mexican heritage, and that should be where the surnames came from. And I knew a little about Mexican surnames. Google led me to more explanations. I learned how to pronounce *apellido*.

There were more variables if one of the parents was outside of the Mexican culture. If both of Angelita's parents were Mexican, her father's first *apellido* might be Rojas, but I wouldn't know his other surname. But Angelita's mother might have just taken her husband's full last name. That would make her father a Rojas Flores.

I should just ask her. Sleuthing 101: go to the source. I texted Angelita. *What is your father's full name?*

When a reply didn't come right away, I plowed on. I found the Florida Department of Correction Offender Information Search online database. I entered Rojas. There were several. I tried Flores. There were even more. I tried Rojas Flores. There were none.

I called Angelita. It went to message. I didn't leave one.

I sent another text. *Call me when you can. I have a couple of questions.*

I turned back to my laptop and searched for motorcycle clubs in Ohio. There was a lot to look through. I skimmed.

Most of what I found was people posting pictures on websites and Facebook and other places. Photos with bikes, rallies, cookouts, scenic views. Benign. There were social clubs, veterans' clubs, Christian groups, men's clubs, all-gender groups.

Looking at selfies of people on bikes and eating barbeque got old in a hurry, and it was getting me nowhere. Nothing looked like the image of the club patch from the bike left at Angelita's house, and there was too much to look through to expect to get anywhere without a great deal of dumb luck, which I didn't feel was coming my way.

I could call the county sheriff's office and ask for Deputy Bronigan. Maybe he would be inclined to extend his goodwill even further to tell me if there was anything I could use to find the second biker. Or if the rider Angelita had shot had come to, or who he was.

I hadn't kept a lot of friends from my time with the sheriff's office. This wasn't the first time that I wished I had. I filed Bronigan as a long shot and decided to come back to him after I tackled the next item.

I moved my photos of the motorcycle from my phone to my laptop, searched through them for the best picture of the club patch, and used my snipping tool to cut the image from the photo. Then I tried a Google image search. That got nothing even close to what I was looking for.

I pushed back from my desk and looked out the window. It was a big, beautiful world out there, and I was stuck inside doing my least favorite part of my job.

And Angelita's retainer was running out. I checked my messages. Nothing from her.

My options had dwindled. I could wait for Angelita to reply. Wait for J'Leah in hopes she would find something with her special-ops bot search. Or try Deputy Bronigan.

To ease my decision I went down to the Emporium for an iced coffee. When in doubt, caffeinate.

I filled my cup with cold brew and a splash of cream, then added chunks of crystal ice from the cooler and was careful not to leave the scoop in the ice chest, just as the sign said.

The coffee helped my mood, but it didn't improve my prospects. I sat on a bench on Xenia Avenue and watched the walkers, the bicycles, and people wandering into and out of the local shops.

Some music drifted over from across the street. A young guy in dark trousers, suspenders, and a fluffy white shirt was finger-picking old-time music on a banjo. Pretty good.

My phone doodled.

The guy with the banjo picked up the pace and busted into a version of Foggy Mountain Breakdown that would have made Earl Scruggs shout yee-haw.

My phone doodled again.

The banjo player's fingers flew.

Doodle. My phone. Work. Someone replying to my messages.

I looked at the screen, then swiped.

"Brick."

"Jackson."

I said, "I didn't know your phone could make calls. I thought you could only do texts."

"Har har." Then, "What are you listening to?"

"The village vibe." I held the phone out toward the banjo player.

When I put the phone back to my ear, Brick said, "I heard what happened."

"I'm guessing you mean that my client shot someone at her home last night."

"Good guess. It's all over the news."

"And J'Leah probably told you too?"

"That's how I knew to look at the news."

"Uh-huh."

Brick said, "So things just got a lot more serious."

"They did."

"And how's that going?"

"Well, right now I'm drinking a really good iced coffee."

"And?"

"That's all."

"So it's not going well."

Foggy Mountain Breakdown ended and the music faded. Brick said, "Guy's taking a break?"

"Probably letting his fingers cool down."

Brick steered the ship back to why he called. "How's your client doing?"

"I don't know. She hasn't returned my messages today."

"Huh."

"Late night for her last night."

"And for the guy she shot. How's he doing?"

"Didn't J'Leah tell you? Medically induced coma."

"She did say that. He's still in it?"

"Far as I know. I don't have a desk at the sheriff's anymore."

Brick said, "You need a break?"

"In more ways than one." I tapped the bottom of my cup to dislodge the last of an ice cube stuck there.

"Want to tell me about it?"

"It's kind of a long story."

"If you're not too busy with the coffee and everything, why don't you come over here and tell it?"

"Why not? You'd be saving me from Bronigan."

"I don't know what that means."

"Neither do I. I'm on my way."

Forty-five minutes later I'd gotten my bicycle from in front of Ha Ha Pizza, ridden home, found Cali still out, and driven to Brick's.

The first thing I noticed when I pulled up to his cabin in the woods was Quando out in the yard. He sat in the shade in a kitchen chair, leaning back with his feet propped on the rusted engine block of the old Buick Skylark. Looking at his phone.

I gave him a two-finger salute and said, "Quando."

He looked back at me with eyes I couldn't interpret and said, "Flint."

I laughed.

He glared.

"People usually call me Jackson."

"I called you Flint."

I looked around for Brick. "So I'm asking you to call me Jackson."

"Then why'd you call me Quando?"

I did a hand shrug. "That's what you said."

His eyes went back to his phone.

"What do you want me to call you?"

"I don't know."

So it was still weird with him about the name. I tried another way in and pointed to the skeleton of the Buick arranged around him in the yard. "You've been getting to know Betty?"

Quando shook his head. "White people have weird names for everything."

The kid's skin wasn't dark. He definitely had color, but I didn't know where to draw the lines between who was black and who was brown and who was white or in between. But I did know one thing. "Brick named Betty. He's not what you'd call white."

Quando showed me he didn't like that by not saying anything.

Then Brick came out of the barn, wiping has hands on a dirty rag. He wore work pants and a t-shirt with the sleeves cut off. His biceps bulged as the rag turned in his hands.

His t-shirt was military green with big block letters across the front. *It ain't nothin' you need to know.*

Brick tucked the rag into his back pocket. "What are you two talking about?"

Quando kept his nose down.

I said, "Names."

"What names?"

I shrugged. "Mostly Quando's."

Quando said, "Black people's names."

Brick laughed. "Really?"

Instead of answering, Quando said, "You know that ain't my real name."

I pointed to myself. "You mean me? You said your father named you."

"Quando ain't my birth name."

"OK."

Brick wiped his forehead with the back of an arm.

Quando watched us. "You're not going to ask?"

Brick didn't answer.

I said, "I guess you'll tell us if you want."

I didn't figure he would. But the kid surprised me. He said something that sounded like *Deejan.*

I said, "I didn't quite get that? Did you say Dijon or DeShawn?"

He looked confused. "Those sound the same to me."

"Spell it."

He frowned. Then he spelled. "D-i-j-o-n."

I stifled a grin. Brick put a hand to his chin.

The kid said, "Go ahead and say it. I've heard it all before."

OK. "Like the town in France?"

Quando or Dijon's face said wrong answer. "The what? I don't know no town in France. Dijon mustard. As in Dijon must turd. Hey, must turd. That's what you were thinking."

Brick said, "I wasn't thinking that. Were you?"

"I was thinking of the French city."

"The one that the mustard's named for?"

"That one."

Brick said, "So his name is French?"

"Sounds like it."

Quando or Dijon's nose stayed in his phone.

I said, "Now that makes me think of a veggie dog. With Dijon mustard."

The kid's nose came up. "Real men don't eat veggie dogs."

He was named after a condiment, so I gave him a break. "I'll work on that."

Brick said, "You two are like a couple of kids on the playground."

I didn't disagree.

The kid said, "Can we just go back to Quando now?"

We both agreed.

Quando said, "Whatever will get you guys to stop making fun of me."

Brick stepped closer to Quando. "That's one way of looking at it."

Quando's gaze came up to Brick. "What's another?"

"We're trying to *include* you."

"By making fun of me."

"What do I get out of making fun of you? What does Jackson get? Why would we want to make fun of you?"

Something dropped from Quando's face. "Why would anybody?"

"I'm not talking about anybody. Other people make fun of you for their own reasons. Why would me or Jackson make fun of you?"

Quando stared. "I don't know."

"Then maybe we aren't."

Quando glared, then went back to his phone.

Brick said, "You know my real first name?"

"It's Brick."

"No."

Quando worked hard to show that he was only interested in his phone.

Brick said, "You ever want to know, ask me."

When Quando didn't, Brick tipped his head toward the barn. I knew what that meant. Some progress on his pet project.

When we were in the shade of the barn I said, "What's up with the kid?"

"Same. He needs some time."

"He seems a lot more…"

"Confident?"

"That's a word for it."

"He's a little angry."

Sure. "At what?"

"I don't think he knows. Maybe a little of everything."

"You learn anything else about him?"

"Like what?"

"I don't know. How old is he?"

"Fifteen."

"What about family?"

"Mom's a user. That's why he ran away."

Ran away and ended up with some compadres who landed him in a mall parking lot carrying twenty thousand dollars in used bills. Then he ran into me. And then Brick.

I said, "Rough."

Brick crossed under the wooden barn beams that arced above, past the horse stalls that had been converted into a woodshop and storage, around the weight bench and heavy bag, and to the Shelby.

Brick had been putting back together a 1966 Shelby GT-350 for more than a year now. How he'd gotten the thing was a mystery—not to Brick, but to me. Brick explained simply that is was a favor from someone he'd done a tricky job for. Another time he said it had been compensation. Whatever it was Brick had done to get the car, it must have been significant, because an original Hertz GT-350 in good restored condition would be worth more than I could figure.

This one wasn't restored, and it wasn't in good condition, and I'd never seen it running. But it was still impressive.

We leaned in under the hood. I whistled. "You've been busy."

"Came into a little money I could spend on her."

"Her?"

"'Course."

I ran a hand over some chrome. "She's going to need a name."

"She is."

"Got anything in mind?"

"Thinking on it."

"Maybe Quando or Dijon, if you think it won't upset the kid."

Brick didn't laugh. "What did I tell you about trying to be funny."

I flashed him my dimples. "It didn't take."

He rubbed a spot on the back of the rear-view mirror with a clean rag. "I was thinking maybe Hertz."

"Hurts? Like a hurts donut?"

Brick groaned. "That was a stupid joke when I was a kid."

"Still is."

"Now it's a donut shop."

"Seriously?"

"Whole bunch of stores. Weird donuts. Fruity Pebbles and stuff on them."

"Fruity Pebbles?"

"You know, the cereal."

I thought about it. Cereal? "So like Pebbles and Bamm-Bamm?"

"The Flintstones thing?"

"Yeah."

"How'd we get to talking about the Flintstones?"

I shrugged. "I don't know. I think you brought it up."

"We were talking about donuts."

We looked at each other.

I snapped my fingers. "Oh. I think Bamm-Bamm becomes a mechanic when he grows up. In the cartoons. Maybe you could name the car Bam Bam."

Brick moved the rag over the black paint and gold stripes on the side panel of the car. "Not gonna name her Bam Bam. That's not even a woman's name."

"Maybe Bon Bon?"

"Stop now." He opened the passenger door. "Why don't you tell me about your client?"

I did. Brick listened without saying anything, working a clean rag over the interior of the car.

When I'd told it all, Brick pocketed the rag and said, "You sure she's telling you everything?"

I'd considered whether Angelita had disclosed everything. I didn't like the way it made me feel. I told Brick that.

"You think she'd let me meet her?"

"What would that do?"

"Tell if she was on the straight up."

"You could tell that from meeting her?"

"Maybe. I have a knack."

True. Brick did have a knack for that. And Angelita hadn't returned my calls or texts. She'd had a rough night, but it was late in the day now and she should have had enough time to sleep it off. I checked my phone. No messages or missed calls.

Brick held up a key in his hand. "I've got a knack for something else too."

He motioned for me to get into the driver's seat and tossed me the key. I fired up the Shelby.

Beautiful. The sound of 1966 filled the barn. Beach Boys, the Temptations, and Nancy Sinatra swam in my head. Wilson Pickett.

I gave it a little gas. The car roared. Excellent.

Brick had a big smile. "She's come to life."

"Roadworthy?"

He leveled a hand and wiggled it. "Maybe."

We admired the car a little more and then I turned the engine off. I took my phone from my pocket and checked for messages again. "I'll call her."

Angelita answered. "I saw your messages."

"Well, you had a tough night. Are you up for talking?"

"I think that's a good idea."

"I could come over. Bring a friend. He might be helpful."

"Uhm."

"You can think about it. He and I have done some work together before. He's good at thinking things through."

"Uhm."

"You want to think about it?"

"No. Bring him. Bring anybody. It's lonely out here."

Brick twisted in the passenger seat and looked behind him. "How long have you been there?"

In the mirror I saw Quando standing at the rear fender. I asked Angelita to hang on for a second.

Brick turned fully toward Quando. "You've been listening in?"

"I didn't mean to."

It wasn't convincing.

Brick said, "You hear anything?"

"I heard some things."

"What?"

Quando came a step forward. "I heard her say to bring anybody."

"She wasn't even on speaker."

"You said you were including me. If you want to include me you'll let me come with you."

Smart kid. He'd turned that back around on us in a space of less than twenty minutes.

Brick looked at me with the question.

I took my hand off the mic. "Angelita? There are two others here. Is it OK if they both come?"

I listened, then ended the call. I called back to Quando. "You're in."

14

BRICK AND I CLIMBED OUT OF THE SHELBY. Quando had already disappeared.

Brick stripped off his dirty shirt and pulled a clean black t-shirt from a cupboard bolted to the barn wall. His work pants had somehow escaped the grease stains.

When we reached Brick's Jeep he looked surprised and peered into the back. Quando was already in there, scrunched behind the seat so not much of him was visible.

Brick opened the driver's door. "What are you doing?"

Quando said, "I wanted to make sure you'd take me along."

"We said we would."

"I know. I just…"

Brick gave the kid a long look, then tilted a thumb toward the passenger seat. "Ride up front. We're going to follow Jackson."

Quando scrambled out from the back of the Jeep and came around to the passenger door.

Brick dangled the key from a finger. "You want to drive?"

"Can I?"

"Do you have your learner's permit?"

Quando shook his head. "Not old enough yet."

"Then no."

It sounded a lot like the same kind of conversations I'd been having with Cali. She wanted to drive, but she didn't want to take the exam to get her permit. So it seemed perfectly normal to hear that play out again between Brick and Quando. But nothing here was really normal. Quando and Brick were mostly strangers. Less than a week ago Quando had been carrying a stack of money for a guy who went out of his way to show me he was carrying a gun.

But put Quando in a different situation and he looked like a different kid. Interesting how quickly the view changed when you looked through a different lens.

I left them and got in the truck. Brick already had the old green Jeep queued up behind me.

We drove to Angelita's on back roads, past farm fields in full green and trees shading the waterways. Low bridges at stream crossings. An old Lowell George trucker song about back roads slipped into my head and I willingly let it play.

When we reached the old Leewold cabin, Angelita was outside to greet us before we'd reached her door.

She looked fresh and alert in a lightweight summer dress with flowers against a dark background. The hem of her dress swished at her knees, and Angelita's black hair was drawn back into a wooden stick barrette with a long pin. She'd spruced up for us.

Quando stared. Brick noticed and pressed an elbow into the kid's ribs. I pretended I didn't see it and addressed Angelita. "Did you get some sleep?"

"I did. Long night."

I gestured. "This is Brick. Quando."

Angelita drank in Brick. With the tight black t-shirt that showed the definition in his chest and shoulders, and heavy work pants and boots, he resembled a military operative.

Which, I realized, he had been.

"Brick has helped me sometimes on cases. He served in the Marines and has special training."

Angelita's eyes drifted from Brick to Quando. His long, baggy shorts and oversized t-shirt made him look much the opposite of Brick. Quando put his eyes at his sneakered feet.

Angelita said to Quando, "When?"

We all four looked at each other.

Angelita's eyes stayed with Quando. He said, "Ma'am?"

I didn't even know Quando could get that word to come out.

"No, my name is Angelita." She enunciated invitingly. "Your name is like the song? When?"

Quando shuffled his feet. "I don't know. My daddy named me."

Angelita said, "I think it's a great name. Maybe your father knew the song." She gestured toward the house. "Come on. I'll play it for you."

Quando looked to Brick. Brick flicked his eyes after Angelita and the three of us followed her into the house.

The windows were open and the house was cool and full of sunlight. A small settee framed one wall of the front room, and two simple wooden chairs with cushions faced the settee from the other side. I imagined the Leewolds who had built this place, recently escaped from slavery in Kentucky. Whatever it looked like then, this cabin must have felt like heaven.

Angelita saw me looking around. "I had a few things delivered. Before last night."

She crossed to a shoulder-high shelf made from brackets and a single board that had probably hung on the wall from the time before Aunt Ida. Angelita reached to a speaker on the shelf and turned it on. Then she swiped her phone. "The reception here isn't great, but…"

The room filled with the sounds of Latin bossa nova, and a voice I thought I recognized but couldn't place started singing. A few words into the lyrics, the singer repeated Quando's name several times.

It was weird.

Angelita stopped the music. "Engelbert Humperdink."

Quando looked at Angelita like she was speaking a foreign language. I guess she was.

Angelita said, "My grandmother used to listen to this song. It's one of the few things I remember about her." She swiped her phone again. "You'll probably like this version better."

The same song played, but this time with a female voice. Angelita placed her phone on the shelf, then she lightly pinched her hands to the hem of her dress. Her shoulders started to move just a little with the syncopated beat.

I had expected Angelita to still be distraught from last night. Or at least upset. But she seemed to have shaken it off.

Brick and I watched as Angelita held a hand out to Quando.

Quando kept his hands in his pockets.

Angelita waved him closer. "Come on. It's your name."

Quando shook his head. "My daddy didn't know this song."

She let the hem of her dress fall from her fingers and raised her arms over her head and twirled. When she'd completed the turn she waved Quando over again.

One hand came from Quando's pocket, then the other, but Quando didn't move toward Angelita.

The song changed to a male voice that was rap, or something like it. That caught Quando's ear and he did a couple of small moves with his hands. I wasn't much of a dancer, but I could have done that much.

The female voice returned, and Angelita reached for the phone and stopped the music. "Anyway, you get the idea. That was Fergie."

Now she was speaking a language foreign to me. The Duchess of York?

Quando said, "So my name means *when?*"

"Well, if you're Italian. Or if you just know what it means in Italian."

Now he did. And suddenly the kid had a look on his face like Quando was the coolest name ever. And in that moment it was.

I appreciated the exchange, but I still wondered at how quickly Angelita had put last night behind her. As if the guys on the motorcycles showing up had answered all of the questions.

But those guys hadn't answered any questions. They'd upped the ante on new ones.

Brick was standing a few steps back from everyone else watching quietly, like he does. Angelita noticed him.

Brick responded by tipping his head. "Miss Rojas Flores." His *r*s rolled perfectly.

"Mr. Brick."

Her voice carried a question. I didn't know what the question was, but Brick seemed to. He said, "Nickname."

Angelita's eye crinkled. "It suits you."

I realized then that there was a charm to Angelita I had seen growing. First she'd drawn in J'Leah. Then Quando, and now Brick. I wondered if I was next. Or if I'd been the first.

Angelita said, "Would you boys like something to drink? I have water. Or water."

I said, "In that case, water would be nice."

We all went to the kitchen, which Angelita had cleaned up. The spilled seed and remnants of a critter invasion were gone. The floor was clean. A soap dish and a bottle of vinegar rested beside a stack of clean towels on the counter.

The old electric stove had been pushed away from the wall and unplugged. In the empty spot where a refrigerator should have been Angelita had installed a small table with a mini fridge on top. She reached into the fridge and took out a pitcher of water and poured into three plastic cups and handed them out. "I'm sorry this is all I have to offer."

Brick drank deeply. "This is fine, ma'am."

Angelita shook her head. "Not ma'am."

"Sorry. Angelita."

She refilled his cup, then refilled the pitcher and placed it back into the fridge. "So we should probably talk about why you're here?"

It was aimed at Brick. Quando stood back and looked into his cup.

Brick said, "We should."

Angelita took Brick around and showed him what she'd shown J'Leah and me. Quando followed. They went to the bedroom where the sleeping bag had been, to the back door that had been jimmied, then outside to look at the cameras that J'Leah had installed.

I left them to follow some line-of-sight trails from the door where Angelita would have stood when the intruder came.

Yellow police tape was tied to a stake by the door and stretched to a tree across the clearing in front of the house. I stepped around the tape and walked the sight lines but avoided the spot where the intruder had fallen. That was marked by more stakes and a dark and clumped spot of vegetation.

I walked from where the man had fallen to the tree line. The undergrowth in the thicket around the house was dense and there were no obvious breaks in the foliage. It seemed the unwelcome visitors had arrived by simply walking down the drive.

I walked that and reached the road in a little less than two minutes. I'd gone slowly, maybe two or three miles an hour, so a little math put the distance at a hundred-and-fifty to two hundred yards. Easy walking even in the dark. And very quick for anyone who might be running.

The motorcycle that had been pushed into the trees the night before was gone. I assumed the county had impounded it. The ground was scraped in the space left behind and there were wide tracks from what would have been a large vehicle like a truck.

In front of that space a single, thinner tire track curved back to the road. As if there had been a second intruder, just as Angelita believed, and he had pushed his bike out of the woods and ridden away, leaving his fallen partner behind. Which he likely did.

That's the man I wanted to get to. Him, or the biker laying in the hospital bed, if he would wake from the coma.

I walked the berm in both directions but didn't see anything more except a country road lined by trees and thick growth. There were swimmers in the pool behind the Dunders' house again. I heard their whoops and splashes, the last revelries of carefree summer before school started again. I wished for a moment that I was with them.

There was nothing really of note, so I walked back down the lane. Brick was squatting in front of the house, examining the same lines-of-sight that I'd been following.

Angelita and Quando sat on an ancient wooden bench under a shade tree. Their plastic water cups rested beside them. I could see that they were talking.

I veered to Brick and squatted next to him, both of us looking into the woods. "Did you have enough time?"

Brick's eyes stayed on the trees. "For what?"

"For your special skill to do its work."

"It's not an exact science."

No kidding.

"But I think I believe her."

I waited for more, but Brick just kept looking at the trees. I got tired of waiting. "Based on what?"

He plucked a blade a broadleaf and twisted it between his fingers. "She's covering."

"Covering what?"

"Angelita is shaken up. She's trying not to show it."

"Because she doesn't want us to know?"

"No. She's trying to distract herself."

Oh. So with the song and the dancing.

"She's pretty upset that she shot someone. And that they came here looking for her."

I glanced over my shoulder at Angelita and Quando. "They came for something. We just don't know what it is yet."

"Angelita knows things aren't clear. But she's scared."

"Has she told you about her father's stories?"

"No."

"Did I?"

"Not much."

I filled him in on what I could remember, then I took my little notebook from my pocket and added a few more details.

Brick stood up and stretched. I did too. He flicked the crumpled broadleaf away. "Sounds like her father was full of shit."

"Agreed. But then why did these two guys come here?"

"Might have been coming for someone else."

I'd thought of that. It made sense, and it made the case even muddier.

Brick held one arm out toward the stained and smashed weeds where the body had been, and he lifted the other toward the house, drawing a line between the two. "It looks like what she said." He dropped his arms. "How much do you know about Angelita?"

"As much as any client."

"So not a lot."

I ran a hand over my jaw, thinking. I didn't know a lot about Angelita. "Her retainer is about to run out. I'll have to talk to her about continuing."

"She'll want you to."

"That seems a good sign. Why hire me in the first place, if she was hiding something?"

"Sounds reasonable. You're the detective."

"So what does your spider sense tell you?"

"Spider sense is conflicted."

"But you'd keep going? Working for her?"

He looked to Angelita sitting with Quando on the bench, the two of them still talking quietly. "I would."

Spider sense was better than nothing.

We walked to Angelita and Quando. Quando said, "She's been telling me her family story."

Angelita shifted on the bench. "Some of it."

"They came up from Kentucky. They ran away from slavery."

Brick raised an eyebrow to me, to Quando, to Angelita. Angelita said, "A lot of families did that."

Quando looked at the house. "But not many of them still have the family house to tell it in."

True. There seemed a lot more to say, but none of it was my story. Then Quando said, "I don't even know where my family came from."

I had no clue to Quando's history, but he and Angelita and Brick shared a common thread that was a much more complex tapestry than the white-on-white my family had sewn.

My phone blipped.

Angelita stood up. "I wonder if I should show Brick the swimming hole?"

"Good idea." I took out my phone. "I'll catch up. I want to check this."

The three of them sauntered away around the corner of the house. I read a text from J'Leah. *I've got some places for you to start looking. Call me.*

I walked the news back to the others at the swimming hole. Angelita settled the retainer right then, just as Brick had said she would.

When I suggested we cut the visit short so I could get the details from J'Leah, Angelita shook her head. "Call her now. I want to hear this."

She was right. It was her case. I held my phone up and out. It got a good signal there on the bank of Massies Creek in the middle of rural Greene County.

J'Leah answered on the second ring. "You've got something?"

"Roger. Three biker bars. Real cowboy stuff."

"Hang on a second." I sat on a log at the fire ring. "I'm putting you on speaker."

The others had already moved over. Brick stood behind me and Angelita sat beside. Quando squatted across the fire pit from us.

I laid the phone on my palm. "What did you do?"

J'Leah laughed. "That's too technical for you, Jackson."

"Humor me."

"You can take the woman out of special ops, but you can't take special ops out of the woman."

"You just made that up."

"Yeah."

"So what did you do?"

There was a pause. "You sound funny. Where are you?"

"We're outside."

"Who's there?"

I told her.

"Quando?"

"It means *when*."

"I know what it means. Who is he?"

Quando and I looked at each other. I said, "I'll let Brick tell you later."

"He will. You want everyone to hear this?"

No, but it looked like that's what we were going to do. "Let's see how it goes."

"All right. We got hits right away. That's a little unusual—but not, you know, unheard of. I plugged the photo into an image search and linked that to…it's something like a spider bot. I set a query to ask for data-crossing of items if there was a convergence of more than three parameters in any two—"

"OK, that's enough. You're right. It's more than I need to know."

"You want me to just tell you what I found?"

"I do."

"That club patch on the bike pops up consistently at three places within a roughly twenty-mile range."

"At biker bars."

"You got it."

"So you think our guy has been at one of them."

"I think some bikers with that patch have been at all of them. One of those places looks more likely than the others."

"Based on what?"

"You want me to explain it again?"

"No. I'll just trust you."

It seemed a long shot. Everything in this case had seemed a long shot, yet here we were still moving toward something. Or something was moving toward us. More specifically, something was moving toward Angelita, and I wanted to find it before it found her.

"And Jackson?"

"Yeah?"

"The best bet has biker night on Tuesdays."

It clicked. "Today is Tuesday."

"Very good."

I looked up at Brick. He nodded once.

"Brick can go with me."

"Good. Here's the thing. These are biker bars."

"Uh-huh."

"And if you're not a biker…"

"What? They don't let you in?"

"Something like that."

"Well I'm not interested in trying to find a broken-down old Harley and a ratty leather jacket to go there and try to cozy up to the locals."

"Then you're going to have to find some other way to cozy up to them."

"We could do the usual."

"What? Just sit and watch?"

"It works in the mystery novels."

"You're not in a mystery novel. And you're not good at sitting and waiting."

She was right. "Have you got a better idea? What do you think our chances of finding this guy are?"

"Zero, if you don't go."

Brick spoke over my shoulder. "You think a 1966 Shelby GT-350 would get their attention?"

The connection went quiet. "A what?"

Brick repeated it.

"What's that?"

Brick was tapping something on his phone to send to her, so I answered. "It's a fancy old sports car."

"Fancy?"

"Well, that's not quite the right word for it. It's more—"

Brick put a hand to my shoulder to shush me. Then he said into the phone, "Check your messages."

"Roger that."

We waited. Massies Creek burbled. A squirrel nattered in a tree. Another squirrel nattered back.

J'Leah came back on. "So it's an old car. Like Jackson said."

Brick raised his voice. "Google it."

J'Leah's voice came in snippets. "Shelby...350..."

Brick said, "GT-350. Nineteen sixty-six."

"Got it." The squirrels nattered some more. "OK, that might do it. But how is a picture of the car going to get their attention?"

Brick said, "I'm not going to show a picture. I'm going to drive up in one."

J'Leah mumbled. Googling again. "I doubt it. Do you know how much these things cost? And how hard they are to find?"

Brick's grin could have cracked the ice on the St. Marys River in January. "Got one out in the barn."

"That thing up on blocks?"

"Ain't on blocks no more."

"I thought it didn't run."

"It'll run well enough. Looking cool will do the rest."

"Does that mean you looking cool, or the car?"

"Both."

J'Leah didn't laugh. "How the hell did you get one of those?"

That was something I wanted to know.

Brick said, "Somebody owed me a big favor."

Quando wiggled in his squat. "What'd you do?"

"Part of the favor is to keep that a secret."

Angelita had her own phone out and had been tapping and swiping. She brushed a strand of hair behind one ear. "Maybe you'll take me for a ride in it some time?"

Brick winked. "Sure thing."

I jumped in before Angelita's charm could take over again. "I think we're getting off track here."

J'Leah cleared her throat loudly. "Still here, folks."

I took the phone off speaker and raised it to my ear. "You catch all that?"

"Unfortunately."

"So tonight?"

"That's your best bet. I'll send you details."

I ended the call. We walked back to the house. When we got there Angelita stopped. "You're all going to leave?"

We were. I had a rule. Don't get too close to clients, and never let the work follow you home. If Angelita didn't want to be at the cabin alone at night, she could try to get back into the Airbnb. Or find another place in town. Or maybe J'Leah would come out and stay with her.

The secluded house and woods were quiet and peaceful and still in the daylight, but the yellow police tape was a bright reminder of what just happened. Maybe I could break the rule, just this once. What would be the risks to Cali if I offered to take in Angelita for one night?

Angelita saved me from deciding that. "OK, go. This is what I hired you to do."

She turned and walked to the house.

Then Brick and Quando got into the dirty Jeep, and I slid into the truck, and we went our separate ways to get ready.

15

GETTING READY for me meant going home to Cali, cooking dinner, and checking in with Marzi.

Cooking was the easy part. Marzi came over after work and she and Cali sat on the porch while I made fried potatoes, poached eggs, and a salad. I filled it in with hummus, carrots, olives, pickles, and cucumber slices. I put it all on a big tray with drinks and carried that out onto the porch.

Cali and Marzi both stopped talking when I swung through the door. "So, talking about me again?"

Cali smirked. "We can do that when you're here."

Touché.

I set the tray on the table. Cali inspected. "Dad, is everything you make some sort of ploughman's lunch?"

"A couple of days ago you didn't know what that was, then you thought it was the coolest thing ever."

She rolled her eyes.

Marzi lifted a carrot from the tray and winked. "I approve of the ploughman's work."

The energy shifted from Cali's side of the table toward me and Marzi. Cali shifted forward on her seat. "Dad? Did you know that Marzi has never been married?"

Marzi's eyebrow went up, and the hand with the carrot went down.

I sighed. "I knew that. And so now I'm not going to ask what you two were talking about while I was making dinner."

Cali's eyes glinted. "Haven't you talked about it?"

"We did. Briefly. But only that Marzi hasn't been married. Nothing else." Marzi looked away.

I said, "Look, this is something that maybe we can talk about another time, OK?"

Cali said, "You can't not think about it."

"We can. That's not a conversation for now. Let's enjoy our dinner."

Cali blinked. Blinked again and looked at Marzi. Then the teenager in her emerged and she reached for her phone and set it at her elbow and dived in. The great escape.

I waved a hand over the food. "Shall we?"

We did. Cali softened a little but stayed mostly more interested in her phone than in me or Marzi. That wasn't exactly something new.

The women cleaned up while I changed clothes to go meet Brick. That was the hard part. Cali and Marzi yammered away in the kitchen, cozy again as ducks in a pond, while I climbed into the truck and backed away.

Getting ready for Brick had meant getting the Shelby ready. He'd taken it for a test drive, checked the brakes, and checked the gauges on the instrument panel. The car was back in the barn with a charger clipped to the battery. Brick wore a tight black t-shirt that said simply *The Few*. Quando was nowhere in sight.

It was an old analog battery charger. The needle hung around two amps. So the battery was still drawing current.

Brick saw me looking. "Ain't nothing to worry about."

"Do I look worried?"

He pronounced our chances at eighty or ninety percent.

"Eighty or ninety percent chance of what?"

"Of not-Betty doing just fine."

"Not Betty?"

"The car is sure as hell not going to be named Bam-Bam."

"Not-Betty is worse."

"Can't be called Betty. Betty is out in the yard in pieces."

"Can't be called not-Betty."

Brick twisted the clamp on the charger against the battery post. "Shelby is too obvious."

"What's Bamm-Bamm's last name? I think it's Barney and Betty Rubble? So their kid would also be—"

"Car's not going to be called Rubble."

"Of course not. How about Wilma?"

"Should be something manly. Like Horse, or Musclestang."

"You said it's a she. Wilma."

"Stop saying that."

"I think it's going to stick."

"Ain't gonna stick." He unhooked the charger and carried it to the workbench. "Ready as she's going to be. Get in."

I crawled feet-first through the passenger window, movie star style.

Brick laughed and in an elaborate show he cracked his neck, cracked his knuckles, flexed an impressive bicep, then reached gently to the door and opened it. "How that works," he said, and slid in through the door.

"But not as cool."

"Not cool if you get stuck in the window."

I said, "It's going to be one of those kinds of nights?"

"We're in a sixty-six Shelby. What do you think?"

"Night of my life."

"Probably so."

We tooled out of the barn. Brick saw me look back and said, "Quando's in the house."

I hadn't asked, but that was what had been on my mind.

"Somebody has got to trust that kid sometime, or he'll never know if he's trustworthy."

That sounded right. But like a bit of a gamble. Leaving the kid home alone.

Brick wheeled the musclestang onto the paved road. "I know what you're thinking."

"You usually do."

"Let's just call it the price of doing business."

Brick drove the narrow roads with a finely tuned economy of motion that was instinct and practice. A subtle turn of the wheel, a subdued flick of the shifter. Like the car, he was coiled muscle waiting to happen.

We saved our best chance for finding a connection to the club patch for last. That place was the farthest away, so it was an easy choice to cruise through J'Leah's two other prospects before hitting Tuesday Bike Night at Dorado's.

There wasn't much of a plan. The locals won't talk to you unless you're a local. Or maybe if you had a cool car. That was about it.

We came at the Rip Rap Roadhouse from the north, Brick cruising the Shelby down Rip Rap Road along the river.

It was dark and the wind blowing through the windows carried the damp smell of the Great Miami River. I'd briefed Brick on what J'Leah had sent. Google maps described the roadhouse as a lively biker bar with outside live bands. Another site labeled it a *raucous* biker bar. I guess it depended on who you went with.

I read more as Brick turned into the lot. "Guy who owns it is a vet. Says it's a family place but they get a thousand motorcycles on bike night. That's tomorrow."

"A thousand is a lot to look through."

"It is."

There was a good crowd for a regular weeknight. Rows of bikes mixed in the parking lot with the cars. Diners and drinkers sat at outdoor tables behind the old barn. Brick circled and slowed in front of them. Revved the engine and made like James Dean.

A few people looked over briefly.

Brick frowned. "Ol' Wilma's not feeling the love."

"We'll have to come back on classic car night."

"They have that?"

"Looks like it. Sometimes."

"So what do we do tonight?"

"We could walk the grounds, look for the club patch. If it turns up on any of the bikes, see if we can trace one to the owner."

Brick looked over the diners who had turned back to their meals. "Let's call that plan B."

The next place was smaller, tucked along the edge of a plat of homes that nestled a bend in the river. A row of Harleys was lined up in front of the building. Two guys sat on a wooden picnic table smoking cigarettes and they were up and pointing at the Shelby before we were off the road and into the lot.

"That's more like it," Brick said.

The guys came over and took selfies with the car, Brick standing by and doting like a father whose daughter was dressed up for her first prom.

I went inside and bought two beers. When I came out and handed one of the bottles to Brick, there were half a dozen guys fawning over the car.

Brick had the hood up and they were taking pictures. I stepped away and walked through the bikes looking for the club patch.

After a second loop through the cluster of bikes, I gave up. The guys were trying to get Brick to start the Shelby and peel out. I flashed him a quick thumbs-down on finding the patch.

Then a guy with short hair and a long beard came out of the bar and stepped directly in front of my face. "You can't have drinks outside of the marked area."

Huh. Nobody except me and Brick had carried our beers outside.

The guy pointed behind me. Apparently the picnic tables were the marked area.

I shrugged, plucked the beer from Brick's hand, and set both of our bottles onto the nearest table. Then I pointed to Brick and to the car, and we got in.

He squealed the tires as we rolled out.

We cruised through the dark toward the last place and I reached for the radio. It squawked on with a splash of AM sound. I twisted the dial. "How do I get FM?"

Brick laughed. "She's built for speed, not for comfort." He punched the gas and the car jerked forward. I forgot about the radio.

It was clear from the moment we arrived that Dorado's was a different kind of animal from the other places. It hunched back from the road in an industrial-residential mix of a neighborhood. Work trucks sat on the street next to gated gravel lots surrounding concrete-and-metal buildings. Jumbled in with them were small houses stuck onto small lawns, with more work trucks parked in front.

The street was dimly lit and the front doors of the houses were shut, and probably locked. Brick coasted to the side of the street across from Dorado's and said, "What do you think?"

I looked around. "Pittsburgh Stealers."

"The football team?"

"No. S-t-e-a-l-e-r-s. Kendalls. Country song."

Brick's blank look deepened.

I sang a few of the opening lines in my best profundo, then added, "Make a good soundtrack for this neighborhood. Very blue collar."

"Jackson, you are very weird sometimes."

"Hasn't killed me yet."

"Well, don't let the neighbors hear you, or it might."

I would take my chances. The only neighbors out to hear anything were at Dorado's. There were a lot of bikes lined up out front and an American flag hanging in the window that threw off a country bent. If you believed what you read in mystery novels, it was the kind of place that should have David Allan Coe's *You Never Even Called Me by My Name* playing on an old jukebox.

But the front door opened as a shadowy back-lit figure filled the frame and instead the chorus of *Up Against the Wall, Redneck Mother* drifted over to us. To the casual listener the two songs might have seemed much the same. But I had a feeling that what we were dealing with here were connoisseurs who could suss out the subtle differences in meaning.

The figure in the doorway moved to the side of the building and peed against the wall. As if taking the song literally.

Brick tapped his fingers on the wheel. "I'm not sure this is the kind of place you want to leave a Shelby parked at the curb."

"That's what I was thinking."

"Then why don't you go in first? Leave me here with the car."

I couldn't think of a reason, so I angled away to the far edge of the parking lot and walked back past the row of bikes before I went in. None of them showed the club patch we were looking for, but around the corner of the building a couple of tight clusters of bikes sat on the broken pavement.

I avoided the wetted wall and identified four bikes with the patch painted onto the gas tanks. Score another win for J'Leah and her searchbot.

Under the shimmer of the mercury vapor light above the door I signaled Brick the affirmative, and I went in.

It was bigger than it looked from the outside. The bar ran the length of the back wall opposite the door. To the right were four bar-sized pool tables arranged in the center of a large room with booths along the sides. I guessed that the room might have once been part of an industrial building.

There were twenty or thirty people inside, most of them men, most entering or exiting middle age. All of the skin was light and most of the clothes were dark, jeans and black t-shirts with eagles. Leather jackets, even in the summer heat.

It was clear to me just how thin our plan really was when a guy entered from behind me and announced to no one or everyone, "There's a guy out there sitting in a Shelby."

"Nah."

A game of nine-ball went to pause.

"What Shelby?"

"Looks like a sixty-six."

Another voice cut through. "You wouldn't know a Shelby if it was your old lady's snatch."

"I might know it if it was your old lady's."

So that's how it was going to be. At least the Shelby had gotten the natives' attention.

Then the love fest started. A couple of them went out to see. I leaned on the bar and asked for a bottle of Pabst. The sound of the Shelby cranked up outside.

When the first guys didn't come back in, a few more went out to check on the situation. Then a few more went out.

I let several minutes pass before I rolled out to join them. No one stopped me from carrying my beer outside.

Brick had the Shelby in the lot out front with the hood up. Biker guys made a ring around it, looking at the car from every angle. Brick stood with them. Someone had given him a beer.

For a burly looking leathered bunch, they were nimble with their phones, pointing and clicking and swiping and probably sharing and posting. I could see what J'Leah meant when she'd said these people's, and most people's lives, were permeable when they had their phones out. I wondered if her searchbots would pick up something that was happening right now.

Brick got in the car and started her up again while a couple of guys shot video. Then he came out and handed me his beer and went to point out something under the hood.

One of the guys who'd seen Brick give his beer to me stepped closer. "You come with that guy?"

I nodded.

He tipped his beer bottle toward the Shelby. "Is it fast?"

"You wouldn't believe it."

Then they were trying to get Brick to come inside and have another beer with them. He looked around the parking lot and up and down the street.

A good old boy in jeans stained with grease clamped his hand onto Brick's shoulder. "It's OK, my friend. Ain't nobody gonna touch nothing in this parking lot." Reading Brick's mind. And thinking what he'd do if he found a Shelby unattended.

But best buddies now. Love your car, love you.

We went in. They wanted to play nine-ball. Just for laughs, not for the Shelby. Ha-ha.

I knew it wouldn't be just for laughs, and I slipped Brick some bills before he could ask me. He kept his hand out and I dug deeper and added some more bills.

Then I settled in at the bar with some others who weren't shooting pool or watching others play or outside gawking at the car.

It was obvious that Brick and I didn't fit in. I had shaved and was overdressed in dark work pants and an old Schoenling Beer t-shirt that had been my father's. Brick fit a little better in black jeans and a black t-shirt, but where the others relied on bulk and sagginess to show their size Brick was rock and veins. He didn't have a beer belly or leather. He was also the only one with any kind of color to him unless you counted cigarette-stained fingertips.

A Reds game was showing on a TV mounted behind the bar, and I gave that some of my attention while I watched and listened to what was going on around me.

Some time passed. Brick won a game of nine-ball, then another. Then he moved to another table and played someone else. I lost track of his scorecard.

I couldn't find the club patch anywhere on the jackets, shirts, or tattoos visible from where I was sitting. I let Brick scan the other room where he was shooting pool, but he hadn't given me a sign that he'd found anything except another game of nine-ball.

I listened and waited. The bartender pointed at my beer asking if I wanted another. I waved one over even though I was still nursing my first.

One of the few women in the bar sat at a table to my right and had looked over a few times. I got the bartender's attention and told him to send a drink over to her, whatever she liked.

Without asking what her pleasure was he poured a whiskey sour from a mix, added an array of candied cherries and a lot of ice, and carried it over to her table.

I watched the game, and a minute later the woman came over and perched on the stool next to me. She looked like a modern version of the pinup girls on the old biker calendar tacked behind the bar. Sleeveless black t-shirt that was too tight, cut-off jean shorts frizzed at the ends. Clumsy black boots that my momma used to call special purpose boots. When I got a little older, my daddy winked and said that meant knock-me-down-and-fuck-me boots. It made me feel grownup, in a weird way.

The woman pointed to my shirt. "I never heard of that."

I looked down at the front. "Gimme that good ol' SB Schoenling Beer."

She tilted her head.

"Was a Cincinnati Brewery. My father's favorite."

The woman lifted her plastic cup. "I'll drink to that."

We clinked bottle to cup and I sipped my Pabst.

"Your friend has a fancy car."

"He does."

"Think he'd take me for a ride in it?"

I slid my eyes to the other room. "Looks like he's busy right now." I ignored the snub. Brick over me because he had the car.

The woman turned on her stool and watched as Brick bent to line up a shot. The cut of muscle on his arm and shoulder sharpened as he drew the cue back.

She took another swallow from her cup and said, "He looks like a movie star."

"I don't think he'd mind you saying that."

"Where'd he get the car?"

I shrugged. "Nobody knows."

Her eyes went over me, back to Brick. "Doesn't seem like the kind of place you'd come to with a car like that."

I tipped my beer bottle. "I was looking for a place to stop and use the can." Not exactly a compliment for what was likely her regular dive, but there it was.

She watched Brick some more. "Your friend plays a good game of nine-ball."

"He does. He's good at a lot of things."

Then something got her attention. She turned toward me so her back was facing the other room. Then a guy who had a good frame and some muscle but was carrying too much weight came up behind her, leaned in, and set his hands on the bar. "Where'd you get the drink?"

The woman pointed at me.

The guy leaned around her to jaw at me. "And who are you?"

I shrugged. Just a guy.

"I said, who are you?"

I pushed my stool back from the bar. "Jackson Flint."

"What're you doing buying Merry Christmas a drink?"

Merry Christmas? Was there a joke here I was missing? "Just a little friendly conversation. Doesn't mean anything."

"I'll decide if it means something. Miranda likes her friendly conversations." He made air quotes, but I didn't know which word he was indicating. Maybe that her name was really Miranda, not Merry Christmas. Maybe that they weren't really conversations. Maybe he was just demonstrating that he knew what air quotes were. It hurt my head to think about, so I gave up.

I held my hands up. You win. No offense.

The guy put the stink eye on me. "You with the guy driving the Shelby?"
I nodded. Yessiree.

He softened a little. "Damn nice car."

"It is."

"How d'you get something like that?"

I put my hands up again. "Beats me." Just the friend along for a ride. I took a pull from my beer. "They wouldn't really play for the car, would they?"

The guy snorted. "Hell, no. What would they put up against it? Their house?"

I laughed. Playing along. "Well I was thinking of the bikes. Some of them look like custom jobs. You probably wouldn't want to give one up, would you?"

The stink eye creeped back. "What d'you mean?"

"Oh, just the paint jobs and such. Some of them have eagles and flames and things. Personalized."

His eyes crinkled. "Some of them's got them all dolled up. They're tighter than a bunch of prison buddies' assholes."

Jeez. I didn't want that image in my head.

The guy tossed a thumb over his shoulder. "Ol' Charlie spends more on his paint job than his bike. The thing could fall apart under him but he'd have his tank newly painted and polished."

Miranda inserted herself into the conversation by lifting her drink. "Bike is just a bike without some bling."

The guy laughed and I was just starting to feel a plan coming together, like George Peppard on a good day. Then the shouting started.

Brick was folding money into his pocket with one hand, pool cue in the other. A guy much too close to Brick's face yelled, "You can't do that." A weird tattoo bobbed on his neck, something that looked like a pretzel but was probably a lumpy heart.

Brick set the cue carefully onto the table, inviting the other guy to do the same. "We can play another. Give you a chance to win it back."

The guy waved his arms, a pool cue bobbing in one. "You ain't gonna steal any more money from me."

Brick stayed still, his feet apart and his hands open.

I slipped off my stool. My next move could go either way. Go over and stand behind your buddy and you're either helping chill the situation or stepping up the ante. I hoped it would chill and we might still have a chance at finding a connection to Angelita's late-night visitor. I was just getting friendly with Merry Christmas and her burly buddy.

It didn't go that way. Before I reached Brick a pool cue came flying at my neck.

Attached to the other end of the cue was a guy swinging the cue. I flipped my head down and stepped under the arc and came up with my right elbow into his jaw. It dumped him backward onto a pool table.

Then black shirts and dirty leather went into motion. Brick popped two straight jabs into the guy nearest him, kicked backward into another, and vaulted up onto the pool table.

I took a fist into the back of my neck. The swing was slow and the punch glanced off without any damage. But it took my attention from the big hand that came in and connected with my left temple. I swallowed the stars and tucked my elbows in and threw my hands up. Another blow came at my head but I was protected enough and got off an underhand jab that felt like it hit a soft spot.

Then there was a hard foot in my back that jerked me into the corner of a table and jammed my thigh but missed my more important regions.

Another sucker punch came in under my arms and rattled my jaw. I covered and tried to keep myself from going down to the floor, and a hand grabbed me under the armpit and yanked up hard.

It was Brick pulling me up onto the table he was standing on. His shirt was ripped and there was a wicked mark across the back of one upper arm.

A loud crack froze the room. The guy from behind the bar had slammed a baseball bat down into one of the tables.

Someone grabbed for Brick's leg, and the guy with the bat dropped it and lifted a shotgun from the bar. "Stop!"

Somebody from the floor said, "There's no way he didn't steal that car."

The words were as ugly as he'd intended.

A thin guy who looked maybe forty pushed through to the pool table and looked at the tear in Brick's shirt that slashed through the words *The Few*, and said, "He's a Marine."

Someone shouted, "Was."

The guy raised a finger to his baseball cap. It had a veteran's emblem. "Once a Marine, always a Marine. Leave him alone."

"He stole my money."

"He fought for your country."

A very brief quiet moment passed. Then someone hissed, "Pussy" and knocked the vet's ball cap off.

The cap fell onto the pool table in front of Brick. He bent and picked up the hat and carefully handed it back to the veteran.

The biker who'd knocked the hat off hit the veteran with an open-handed slap that rang on his cheek. Before the slap was complete Brick's leg came out and knocked the slapper to the floor.

Black leather went into motion again and the room was alive and another ungodly loud crack rang out and stopped the room again. The guy from the bar had the bat again and he'd broken a table with it, and now he swung the shotgun up again and held the room with both barrels. "You two. Out. Now!"

He nosed the barrels of the shotgun to indicate he wanted to make room for us to go. Brick and I jumped from the pool table and ran.

We'd almost made the door when a beer bottle clunked against the side of my head.

Then we were outside and in the car and Brick had Wilma fired up and there was the engine roaring and tires peeling and we were moving *fast*.

I expected a parade of Harleys to chase us, but the neighborhood was dark and quiet and Brick executed a series of quick lefts and rights and then turned to cross a rusty one-lane metal bridge that dropped us close to an on-ramp for the highway.

Brick zoomed up the slope and merged into the highway traffic.

He burned the left lane up for few miles then slowed to speed and drifted into the center lane. Then Brick glanced over. "How's your head?"

"Hard as ever."

He pointed to the glove box. "Towel in there. Try not to bleed on the car."

"Thanks for the concern."

He looked again. "For real. You OK?"

I wiped my head behind my ear and looked at a red smear on the towel. "Could have been worse."

There was another cut on the other side of my head that hadn't bled much. My thoughts were clear and sharp and nothing hurt too much.

I looked in the rear-view mirror and found a cut on the side of my jaw. That completed the inventory.

I surveyed Brick. The mark on the back of his arm was the size of a grapefruit and already starting to darken in color. I pointed. "You get much besides that?"

"Nah. They couldn't reach me."

"That's good."

"The important thing is there's not a scratch on Wilma."

"Thanks again for the concern." I leaned into the cool night air rushing in the window and didn't mention that he'd called the car Wilma. "How the hell do you cheat at nine-ball?"

"He said I missed the combo."

"Did you?"

"Hell, no."

16

WE STOPPED at an all-night gas and convenience place. It was an odd setup, a little place tucked under the curve of the off-ramp on a dark stretch of highway. The little store behind the pumps was weathered and old and looked like it might have once been part of a barn.

The entry dipped down from the road then flattened at the pumps. Brick parked on the slope beside the building, with the nose of the Shelby dipping toward the big Home City Ice chest. He looked at my chin. "Better get the big bag."

"Har-har."

"You should stay here. Don't want to scare the poor kid working the register."

He left the key so I could listen to AM radio while he was gone. I didn't.

Brick came back a few minutes later with a towel, a couple bottles of water, and a paper cup with ice from the drink machine. He handed me the towel and a water bottle and I stood outside the car and stooped to the side view mirror to clean up the smudges of blood on my face and over my ear.

Brick wrapped the ice in the towel and I pressed that to flesh. "Not so bad," he said. "Doesn't look like we'll need the big bag."

"Marzi and Cali will hardly even notice."

He laughed. "I meant I don't look that bad."

"Good one."

I leaned against the fender and looked up at the night sky and held the ice against my head for a few minutes. Then I adjusted the ice pack and patted the car. "Ol' Wilma did all right."

"Stop calling her that."

"You said it."

"Might've slipped out once. It's not gonna stick."

"Already has."

"Well, damn."

I held the cold pack some more and we watched lights from cars going by up on the highway and then I shook the ice out of the towel and squeezed it.

We got in the car and Brick turned the key and Wilma didn't start.

Brick turned the key again. Nothing. Again. Nothing.

He tried a couple more times.

"Are you going to keep doing that, or do you want to get out and take a look under the hood?"

He turned the key to nothing again, then opened his door. "Look under the hood."

We did the headlight trick. Turn on the lights, turn the key, see if the headlights dim. They didn't. That suggested no juice was getting to the starter.

We twisted and checked the connections to the battery terminals and the starter solenoid. Brick reached down into the engine compartment and gently tugged on the starter ground wire. Everything felt tight.

Just to make sure we hadn't twisted something just enough to get a better connection, Brick tried the key again. And again and again. Nothing.

I put my ear to the solenoid and motioned for him to try again. There was a single click when he turned the key. I waved him out. "Solenoid."

Brick reached for the connections.

"We did that already. They're tight. It looks like the solenoid is bad."

"Why would the solenoid be bad?"

I looked at the pitted metal surface. "How old is it?"

He didn't have to answer.

"You have jumper cables?"

"In the Jeep."

"That's not going to help."

He pulled the hood down. "Feeling manly?"

"Manly enough."

"You're going to have to push her."

But the car was at a downward slope, up against the ice chest. I couldn't even keep from losing ground when Brick took the Shelby out of gear and released the parking brake.

I came to the driver's window and leaned in. "You look like a strapping young man. You want to give it a try?"

Brick looked me over. He was built like a, well, a brick, but we were about the same size. He shook his head. "Not even worth a try." It was the best compliment he'd ever given me.

I said, "You have a couple of screwdrivers?"

"Sure. At home in the tool chest."

"Better go back inside and look for jumpers. Or screwdrivers. Or anything that's got enough metal to jump the solenoid."

Brick knew what I meant. He went back into the store.

He came out a few minutes later carrying a couple of little bags of peanuts.

"I don't think that's going to do it."

He tossed a bag to me. "Nothing in there but junk food and beer. And the guy is getting nervous. Wondering why we're still here."

"Just a couple of guys hanging out on a slow Tuesday night, looking cool."

"Because nothing is cooler than two guys at a gas station in the middle of nowhere at one in the morning, one of them a little busted up, and a fancy sports car that won't start."

"When you put it that way…" I tossed the peanuts into the Shelby. Too salty. "I guess we'll have to call for help."

Brick reached in and picked up the peanuts I'd discarded. "You first."

"What?"

"You call someone first."

"It's one in the morning."

"Exactly."

"I don't really want to ask Marzi. And Cali doesn't have her license."

"Uh-huh."

"And I don't think anyone else will answer their phone or a text this late."

"You remember when landlines rang all the time? No sleep mode? If it rang in the middle of the night, you knew it was trouble and you picked up."

"Tell me about it, old man."

"I just did."

"Sounds like an old wives' tale. I guess we'll have to call a tow truck."

"Not a chance. They're not touching this car."

"Triple A?"

He didn't even answer.

"Quando?"

"You know he doesn't have his license."

"I know he's not old enough, but I'll bet he's driven."

"He has, but that boy can't risk it."

"I wasn't honestly suggesting he should drive out here."

"If he got pulled over they'd put him away."

I held my hands up. Stop. "I wasn't really suggesting."

But Brick had turned serious. "He's got no momma."

I let him talk.

"Woman is in jail. Left her son to foster care, but that was no good and he ran off."

I nodded. Listening.

"You saw what that group he was running with was doing to him. Put him out front. Carrying a stack of money across the parking lot. I mean, what the hell was that? Did they want him to get caught? Did they even want their money?"

Uh-huh.

"And that dumbass he was with? He actually came after you instead of tucking the money under his shirt and just getting out of there?"

"Like he had something to prove."

"He had something to prove. That he's stupid."

We were getting to it. Took a broken-down Shelby in the middle of nowhere for Brick to spill.

I tossed something out. "You see anyone else. Besides those two?"

"You mean who they were delivering to."

"Yeah. Like that."

"I saw them."

I waited.

"Bad news. Big SUV."

"Uh-huh." Which meant what happened? What did you do?

"I didn't let them take him."

"Quando."

A tight nod.

"They got their money?"

Another very tight nod. "And the other guy. Showing off for them with that stack of bills."

"Yeah." A long pause. "What'd you do?"

"I just opened the door and he got in."

"Quando?"

"Yeah."

"That's it?"

"That's it." Brick let out a very long sigh. "Sort of. The others were yelling for him to get in with them. Had the side door of the SUV open."

And?

"He didn't want to get in. Quando. I could tell. He didn't want to."

"So he just got in with you?"

"There was some…They were yelling. One of them showed a pistol. I still had the other guy's gun in my hand."

Oh, lord.

"I just—I showed them the gun."

I raised an eyebrow. "You would have shot them?"

Brick's look registered the seriousness of the question. "Maybe."

"You didn't even know the kid."

"I know others like him."

I breathed. "What happened?"

"They closed the door and took off."

"Without Quando."

"Yeah. You know that kid just got in with me like it was nothing."

"It wasn't nothing."

"Not even close."

"You didn't say anything to him about it?"

"We haven't talked about it. Not then, and not since. I drove home, we got out, and he's just stayed. He's sleeping in the back room. I bought him some stuff."

"And you haven't told anyone? Not the…police or anybody?"

"Nobody knows."

I leaned against the car. "That's weird."

"It's really weird."

"It seems like you ought to talk to the kid."

"It seems like a lot of things. I haven't figured it out yet."

Some stars twinkled above me. I had another question. "How does a kid fall in with people like that?"

"Someone introduces him. Mom or dad. Or a brother or sister. Someone in the neighborhood or at school."

"So anywhere?"

"If you're vulnerable. They can get to you."

"I don't remember seeing those kinds of things when I was growing up."

Brick's eyes focused somewhere far off. "You had a home. A mom and dad. Stability. You didn't have exposure. You didn't see it, but it was there. For others."

I didn't have to think about it to know that Brick was right. White privilege. It was an insulting factor. But something didn't fit. "How do you know so much about all this?"

Brick's focus stayed in that far-off place. "The Marines were my way out."

I remembered that in high school Brick had lived with only his mother. "I thought you were pretty solid growing up."

"My older brother."

"I don't remember you having an older brother."

He looked at me.

Oh. Because he wasn't there. Some kind of trouble.

"Quando needs a chance."

Sure. "There's got to be a way to get him someplace…I don't know. Into foster care? Someplace else?"

"I can't think of anything right now that's better than letting him stay with me. If he puts his head up, he's going to catch trouble. Either from those guys or the police. Or both."

"Maybe."

"Kid doesn't know how to stay out of trouble yet. It's been the only thing constant for him." Then Brick reached for his phone. "I can try texting somebody. Bring jumper cables out."

That meant we were done talking about Quando. Brick sent the text.

Several minutes later he hadn't gotten an answer. I said, "What about J'Leah?"

"You don't want to bother her now. Trust me."

I raised the hood and looked at the solenoid again. "Wait a minute." I took out my pocket knife and opened the two blades that folded across from each other so the whole thing made a U. Then I lined the tips of the blades up with the nuts that secured the cables on the sides on the starter solenoid.

Brick looked in. "That's a really bad idea."

"Little trick my daddy taught me."

"He taught you with screwdrivers."

"Yeah."

"Lot more metal in a screwdriver."

"Might be enough here if I can get something for insulation."

"Jackson, you are a little dangerous."

"It hasn't killed me yet."

"This might."

I took off my t-shirt and awkwardly tried to wrap the knife handle with it.

Brick stopped me. "That's your heirloom Schoenling shirt."

"My daddy gave it to me."

"Mine is already trashed." He took off his ripped shirt and tore the bottom half away, then folded that over several times and wrapped it around the handle of the knife. "Bad idea," he said, but he handed the pocket knife back to me.

Then Brick got in the car and turned the key and I set the tip of one blade against one nut on the solenoid, then lowered the other blade to the second nut.

There were sparks and a crackle and the sound of the starter trying to turn, and then the pocket knife was gone. The car didn't start.

Brick came out and looked. "What happened?"

"The knife's gone."

"Gone?"

I shrugged. "Gone."

We looked around and found the pocket knife on the ground several feet away. One tip was burnt black, and the other was blown off. Brick laughed. "Hot damn, ol' Wilma packs a punch. Is that how your daddy taught you to do it?"

"Just get back in."

"For what? It's not gonna work."

I re-wrapped the strip of shirt around the knife handle.

"It almost worked. Get in."

It took him a beat to decide. "Hold it tighter. And keep your head out of the way."

"I've thought of that."

When Brick had the circuit open again I pressed the broken blade tight against one nut, turned my head as far as I could and still see, and ground the second blade down onto the other nut and held tight.

The starter caught and groaned, turned, and Wilma rumbled to life.

Brick came out and looked at the solenoid. I held up the pocket knife. One blade was half gone and the other was missing a chunk from the blackened end.

The mangled blades wouldn't close. I forced them down and slipped the knife into my pocket.

"You're going to keep that?"

"Why not? Perfectly good half-a-knife right there."

"Jackson, you are a little weird."

"Hasn't killed me yet."

He shook his head. "It's going to."

"Hee-haw and merry Christmas."

Brick closed the hood. "It's a wonderful life. Get in."

On the drive back I said, "All that trouble and it didn't even get us much of anywhere finding the guy."

"You found the club patch at Dorado's. Fewer than six degrees of separation now. Maybe only one."

"That much closer to Kevin Bacon."

"If that's the way you want to look at it."

"And another thing. I learned how to blow up a pocket knife with a Shelby."

"Probably won't use that twice in one lifetime."

"You never know."

Then we listened to AM radio, which as it turned out isn't too bad if that's all you've got.

Wilma delivered us to Brick's. I drove home.

There was enough light inside the house that from the porch I could make out the shape of someone sleeping on the couch.

Marzi woke when I sat on the edge of the couch next to her. She looked at me with groggy eyes. "I didn't mean to fall asleep."

"I'm glad you're here."

She looked closer. "What did you do to your hair?"

"My what?"

Her hand went up to my head over my ear. "It's all matted."

"Oh. I had a little thing. I thought I'd cleaned that up."

"A little thing?"

I shrugged.

"You fell?"

"Not exactly."

Marzi pulled herself up straighter. "So then you what, exactly?"

"Little bit of a tussle."

"It looks like more than a tussle."

"Things didn't go quite as we planned. There was a pool cue and a beer bottle."

She twisted my chin with her hand to get a better look. "And a fist?"

"Like I said, not quite as we planned."

Her hand came away from my face. "Was it worth it?"

I didn't understand the question.

"Did it get you what you needed?"

"Not exactly."

The displeasure was clear on Marzi's face. "I expected you back sooner."

"I did too."

"And I didn't think you'd be beaten up."

"Not beaten up exactly. You should see the other guy."

"You think this is funny?"

Well, no. I guess not. I reached a hand for her leg. "It's not that bad."

Marzi brushed my hand away. "I'm going to go."

"It's almost two in the morning. I'm here now. You should stay."

"I really should go home." She folded the afghan that had been covering her and draped it carefully over the back of the couch.

"I'm fine. It's just a few scratches."

Marzi shook her head. "It's not fine. And I'm not ready for this." And she went home.

17

I WOKE WITH A DROWSY FEELING that something was gnawing at me. Probably this case, going around in circles, and bothering me in my sleep. But the feeling was so distinct I thought I could actually hear the sounds of gnawing.

I reached for my ribs, grabbed my side, sleepily trying to slap at what was biting me. That woke me enough to roll over and see Mrs. Jenkins sitting on the floor beside my bed, casually chewing a mouse.

Good morning to you, too.

I picked her up and with her came the gray furry mass in her maw. "You know the rules," I said, then slid the window screen up, set Mrs. Jenkins on the sill, and not-so-gently urged her out. "You find it outside, you keep it outside."

While the coffee was brewing I wondered where Marzi was at that moment. At home with her own coffee brewing, probably. That was another thing to gnaw at me. Where was this thing with her going?

Before the coffee was done, I had my running shoes on and laced. That itch in my head that had convinced me I was being eaten had to be scratched. A run might help sort it out.

I cut a route through the sleepy village that I didn't usually take, hoping the change of scenery would help shake something loose in my head. Past the public garden plots in the park, tomatoes and zucchini hanging heavy on the vines. Zig-zagging through the grid of houses and alleys, then across the state route and into the south end of town.

The jumble of this case washed around in my head like jigsaw puzzle pieces, trying to find edges to hang onto. I wanted them to fit neatly together into one image, but I suspected that the pieces weren't all from the same puzzle.

There was the Leewold house. Aunt Ida. The fire ring at Massies Creek. The sleeping bag in Angelita's house. The estate cleaning service. The bikers. Angelita's father's stories. The dog and the frisbee.

The dog was a red herring.

Focus. What was the next step? I changed direction and ran toward the Riding Centre and the horse barn there. Go back to Dorado's for a second attempt? How would I play that, after last night?

Or hope for the guy in the coma to come out of it? Would I be able to get to him if he did?

Maybe Bronigan could help in some way?

What was I missing?

Or maybe give up on the whole thing. Maybe Angelita would be ready to call it quits.

I reached the covered bridge over the bike path and took the steps up. It was as far as I could get from home and still be in the village.

My phone bleeped.

I slowed and looked. Text from Angelita. *I just found my father. Call from the prison. They said he's dead.*

That put the brakes on.

I hadn't even gotten my thumbs down on the screen to reply to Angelita when my phone bleeped again with a text from J'Leah. *I think we've turned up the sleeper. Stills from last night.*

Attached were two images of a figure in the dark outside of Angelita's house. The face in the images was clear. A young man, twenties, with a backpack on his shoulders. Maybe the guy who owned the sleeping bag that had been left at Angelita's.

So this thing was twisting in new directions again. What next?

By the time I got back home, Cali had already cooked and eaten. She sat at the table and looked up from her phone when I came in and pointed to the counter. "I left a plate for you."

I wandered over. "What if I'd already eaten?"

"Would that stop you?"

"No." I tried the potatoes. They were spicy with paprika and garlic and just like potatoes should be. I tried the eggs and kissed my fingers from my lips. "Perfection."

"You're just saying that so I'll keep cooking for you."

"That's not the only reason."

"Oh, what else is there because—Dad, what happened to your face?"

I reached up to my bruised chin. "This?"

"Yes, that."

"Nothing. Little dustup."

She frowned. "Dustup? What is a dustup? Nobody calls it that."

"Little tussle. Minor disagreement." Tussle? Isn't that what I called it with Marzi the night before? And look where that had gotten me.

"Were you going to tell me?"

"Tell you what? I'd already forgotten about it."

Cali squinted. "That's a huge…I can see—knuckles."

I turned away. She could?

"And what is that in your hair? What happened?"

I set the potatoes and eggs aside. "OK. Listen, it was a little bit of a bar fight."

"A bar fight?"

"Little bit."

"You don't just forget about a bar fight. Let me see." She pinched back the matted hair over the cut on my head. "How do you get this in a bar fight?"

"You should see the other guys."

"Guys? Dad, what the actual fuck?"

I'd never heard Cali use that word before. She recognized the breach and pulled away.

"Honey, you know there are some risks involved in my work. I've always been careful."

"You call a bar fight being careful?"

"That's not what we set out to do. Things just got a little out of hand."

"A little—*we*?"

"Brick was there. It was fine. Nobody really got hurt."

"Brick? He's supposed to keep you *out* of trouble."

"What makes you think that?"

"It's what he told me."

"Brick told you he'd try to keep me out of trouble?"

"Yes."

"Why would he do that?"

"Because I asked him to."

"Wait—You asked Brick to look out for me?"

Cali crossed her arms.

"Don't you think that's a little…?"

"I already lost mom. I can't…" A tiny tear leaked from one eye. "Did he?"

"Did who? What?"

"Did Brick look out for you?"

"You mean last night?"

"Of course last night."

It dawned on me. "He did. A couple of bikers aren't going to—"

"Bikers!?"

"Listen—"

"You got into a bar fight with bikers?"

I sighed. "That's not—"

"You said that. What's Marzi going to say?"

My long pause gave something away.

"She already knows."

"She does. Marzi was here last night when I got home."

Cali looked around. "Where is she now?"

I glanced at the clock on the stove. "She's probably at work by now."

"So it didn't even bother her?"

Another long pause gave away even more.

"What happened?"

"Marzi was a little—uncomfortable with the situation."

Cali released a shriek I didn't know she was capable of. "Dad, I cannot live with you if you're going to be like this."

I put a hand up. "Whoa."

"I just don't even…"

"Cali."

"You're ruining it."

"Ruining what?"

Cali's lip quivered. "Marzi." And she turned and ran to her bedroom and shut the door.

So this was new. I'd thought that Cali and I were healing and moving forward, and here was this giant bubble of teenage angst that burst before I'd even seen it coming. I wondered what else was lurking.

I was smart enough to give Cali some room. I stayed in the kitchen and cleaned up the breakfast dishes.

She came out about twenty minutes later and leaned casually against the kitchen entryway. "I'm leaving. I have school planning to do with the girls."

"So the girls like Jenny and Asia?"

"And Nadia."

"OK."

"You might have noticed that there are only three weekdays left before school starts."

"So you need to get supplies? Catch up on your summer reading lists?"

"No."

So the bad humor was a poor choice again. I was going to have to think about this teenage thing.

"Clothes. We're going shopping."

I flipped the dishtowel I'd been holding over a shoulder. "You need anything?"

"No. You've already given me what I need." Then she spun and left.

Oh, right. The credit card. At least I was still good for something.

I went out onto the porch and watched Cali walk away until she disappeared around the corner at the end of the street.

Then I went back to work. I called J'Leah. My first question was simple. "Does Angelita know you got video of another visitor?"

"Yes. I sent her the stills. She doesn't recognize the guy."

"Has she freaked out?"

"She didn't shoot him."

"That's something." Next step. "Did you hear about her father?"

"Angelita's father? What about him?"

"He's…" How to put this? "Dead." Very tactful, Jackson.

"Dead?"

As a doornail. "Yes."

"What do you know?"

"Nothing yet. He died in prison."

"She didn't tell me."

"She just found out."

"That seems…abrupt?"

"I can't think of a better word."

"And weird timing."

"That too."

J'Leah took a breath. "So what now?"

"You have any more photos of the guy who might be the sleeper? Something closer?"

"I'll send some. One you'll really like. He looks right at the camera like he knew it was there."

"Did he?"

"Did he what?"

"Know there was a camera?"

"How would he know?"

"I don't know. You just said it was like he knew."

"It's an expression. It doesn't mean he knows. It means I chose very good positions for the cameras."

Of course that's what it meant. "I didn't mean to imply that—"

"You didn't."

Change direction. "Did he try to get into the house?"

"No."

"You're sure?"

"I'm sure. The guy walks around the house. There's some light coming from inside. Through the front window, through the kitchen window. Dim, like nightlights. Or maybe a light left on under the cabinets. He doesn't try a door. He looks in the front window, then the kitchen window, then he leaves."

"He doesn't come back?"

"No."

"You're sure?"

"No one comes back, not even Bambi. The place is dead quiet the rest of the night."

As a doornail. Focus, Jackson. "And Angelita didn't know he was there? Until you told her this morning?"

"She didn't know."

Think. "Can you run facial recognition or something? Do something like how you found the bikers' patch at Dorado's?"

J'Leah released an unladylike snort. "No. I'm not on the inside anymore."

"Inside of what?"

"You know."

I did. Special ops. What she and Brick never talked about. "Is any of that real, anyway? The military using satellites to recognize people on the street by their faces and things like that?"

"It's best that you don't know."

"I think you're teasing."

"I could be."

"I'm hanging up now."

"Old people's terminology. There's nothing to hang—"

I ended the call.

My next call to Angelita was oddly subdued. I had expected her to be more…animated?

"What did they tell you?"

"Nothing. They just said my father had died."

"Who called?"

"A woman from the prison. She was a—something. It was her job to make calls like that."

"And when did this happen? When did your father pass?"

"Yesterday. No—some time during the night. So I guess really it was very early today."

"And how did it happen? What was the cause?"

"The woman said he'd been sick for a long time. It wasn't unexpected."

"Any details?"

"Congestive heart failure."

I knew that could be brought on or complicated by blocked arteries, high blood pressure, drug abuse, all sorts of things. I also knew that whatever the causes, congestive heart failure wasn't usually quick or pretty.

"You didn't know? That he had heart problems?"

"I didn't. I didn't know much of anything about my father."

I slowed things down. The questions made me feel like Joe Friday. Just the facts was fine for Friday and the LAPD, but there was more to Angelita than just the facts. And just the facts wasn't getting me answers on this case.

I asked the thing that had been gnawing at me. "If you didn't know anything about your father or even where he was in prison, how did they find you to tell you he had died?"

A long breath passed through the connection. "I was surprised too."

"So?"

"They Googled me."

"Googled?"

"It seems not much is secret anymore. They had my name on record. The woman said they found my inheritance and that led them to the lawyer's office that handled the will. They got my number there."

OK, that was plausible. Another victory for the Google.

I switched gears again to sympathy. "I'm sorry about your father."

"Yeah."

"If there's anything…"

"I'll let you know."

"I wish we hadn't left you alone at the house last night."

"It's not your job to watch over me."

She was right, but it didn't make me feel any better. "Then here's what I'm going to do. I'm going to try to find this guy from last night. I think I know where to start looking."

"Where?"

"It's a hunch."

"Is that how detectives usually do it?"

"It is if you believe what you see on TV."

I didn't believe everything I saw on TV. But the facts were taking me on a twisted path to nowhere. A hunch couldn't do much worse. And if I was wrong it wouldn't cost me much.

I drove to the Dunders' house next door to Angelita. The hunch still felt good when I got there, but I knew right away my timing was off. It was too early in the day.

There was a good place nearby to burn some time. And if I back-tracked and took a circuitous and scenic route, I could pass by two covered bridges on the way. Good thing I wasn't being paid by the hour.

Cedarville is a little burg with a solid university, a lot of Native American history, and a great coffee shop on the corner. I came out of Beans-n-Cream with an iced coffee and a sandwich that I tucked into the utility pocket of my shorts.

Then I went to the Indian Mound Reserve, walked through the woods past the two-thousand-year-old Hopewell earthworks, crossed Massies Creek, and climbed the Adena mound.

The mound was steep and high but not quite tall enough to reach above the top of the tree line. It was still a nice spot in the sun and offered a good perch above the old glacial melt valley below. I unfolded my floppy sun hat from my pocket. Then I held a paperback book in one hand and my phone in the other, trying to decide between print and Kindle. Men, one foot in sea, and one on shore. To one thing constant never.

I shook the bard out of my head and went for the paperback and Alex McKnight chasing villains across the Upper Peninsula.

I was absorbed when a young guy with a dog following him ran up the mound and circled me in the little space. He looked at the book in my hand, seemed perplexed by it, and pulled a handful of frisbees from his backpack. He jettisoned the discs over the open expanse below, which greatly excited the dog, and then they sprinted down the mound to retrieve the flown objects.

I returned to the book and the excitement in the U.P.

A couple of chapters later a thin man with a large-brimmed hat and carrying a lot of equipment made his way quizzically up the mound. He squatted beside me and looked out over the vista. "I thought you'd be able to see farther."

I put a thumb on my page. "Tall trees."

"Yeah."

The man took a small device mounted on a little tripod from his pack and began performing some sort of work. It took him a few minutes, then he walked around the top of the mound scraping his feet in the weeds. "It's supposed to be here somewhere."

I looked over.

"Have you seen the USGS marker up here?"

"USGS?"

"The geodetic survey marker. Little round metal cap—" He formed his middle fingers and thumbs into a circle. "With some writing on it."

I shook my head. He kept looking.

Several minutes later he said, "Do you mind if I look where you're sitting? I can't seem to find it."

"Sure." I tucked Alex McKnight back into my pocket and stood up.

The man pushed his foot through the dirt where I'd been sitting. "There it is." He cleared an area with his hands and uncovered a metal cap in the ground. The man couldn't have looked more proud if he'd been Brick showing off the Shelby. When the Shelby wasn't dead in a parking lot in the middle of the night.

Then the man unpacked a thin laptop, worked at it for a moment, and pronounced that the survey data was off by some number of inches of elevation that didn't stick with me.

I said, "Thanks for letting me know."

He closed the laptop. "No problem. Y'all have a nice day now."

I promised to, and he gathered his things and scampered down the mound.

Huh. Two thousand years. I wondered what the mound builders would think of their creation now. Sacrilege, or pleased to see that the site had survived and people still found it interesting?

I read another chapter. The sandwich was gone. The sun was high and it was getting hot. Time to follow up on that hunch.

I checked my notes, looking for two names I knew I'd recorded. Were they in my little notebook or on my phone? One foot in sea, and one on shore. One day maybe I'd decide if I would put both feet in the same place.

I drove back to the Dunders'. A whoop and a splash perforated the trees. The hunch tingled in the back of my brain. I walked down the long gravel driveway, circled the house in a wide berth, and called out, "Hello the pool."

A boy who looked about fourteen stood on the pool deck, dripping wet.

"Are you Mark?"

"What does hello the pool mean?"

"It's just to let you know that someone is coming so I don't surprise you."

He flipped his hair. Water scattered in the sunlight. "That's weird."

"It's usually hello the house, but you're here at the pool so I improvised."

"Hello the house. Oh, that's kind of cool."

Good. My repertoire with young men this age was limited. I hoped I could do as well when the time came for Cali to bring one home. "I talked with your mother a couple of days ago about the woman next door. We can call your mom out here, or your dad, if you want to…"

He was already shaking his head no. "I've seen you. I saw you talking to my mom."

"Do you know what we were talking about?"

"Some of it. I know it's about the lady who lived next door." He pointed a thumb toward the Leewold house.

"It is. And her grand-niece who has moved in now."

"Grand-niece?"

"I think that's what they call it. Two generations down."

"OK."

"Did you know Ida Leewold?"

"Not really. She was old. I said hi to her a couple of times. She mostly kept to herself." He looked down as if thinking about what else he should say. "She seemed nice. When I did talk to her, if that's what you mean."

It wasn't, but it was kind of the kid to say.

Then Mark Dunders pointed to the bruise on my jaw.

I touched it gingerly with a finger. "I'm not proud of that."

"I saw you go back to the swimming hole. We're not in trouble, are we?"

"You mean for swimming back there?"

His eyes told me he knew he'd given that away before I'd asked. I shook my head. "Not with me. As for the woman who lives there now, you'll have to sort that out with her. Her name is Angelita Rojas Flores."

He looked like talking with her was the last thing he planned to do.

"Do your mom and dad know you swim back there?"

"They do. She doesn't like it, but dad says that's part of the fun of living here."

"Your mom wants you to be safe."

"I guess."

Every fourteen-year-old boy is invincible. This one included. "Does anyone else swim back there? Or go back there for other things?"

His eyes moved around. Probably thinking what I was thinking. The fire ring, the beer bottles. What else went on back there. He said, "You've seen it."

"I have. Listen, let me tell you why I'm here. We can still call your mother out if you want to."

"No, it's fine."

"I'm trying to find this guy." I held out my phone with a picture of the guy J'Leah had captured from the video the night before.

Mark Dunders leaned in and dripped a little but got a better look. I swiped to another picture.

Mark stepped back. "I've seen him."

"At the house next door?"

"Yeah. And he hangs out in town."

"In Cedarville?"

"Yellow Springs."

Interesting. "You know Yellow Springs?"

"Of course. Everyone does. We go there a lot."

"Uh-huh."

"I've got friends who live there. They used to live down the street, but they moved into Yellow Springs last year."

"And you've seen this guy there?"

"Yeah."

"You know his name?"

"Uh-uh. I see him sometimes sitting on the benches."

"On the sidewalks? Which benches?"

His shoulders went up and down. "Downtown. Anywhere."

So right under my nose. Maybe even right down on the street below my office window. "He's there a lot?"

"Seems to be. People do that."

They did. It was a groovy place to be. But it also drew its share of hangers-on.

I tucked the phone back into my pocket. "Mark, you've been real helpful. I appreciate that. And I'd like to tell your mother that I talked to you, just so she'll know."

"I can tell her."

"Sure you can. But I'd like to tell her too."

"If you want to." Then he turned and jumped into the pool.

I walked around the house and knocked on the front door.

Stephanie Dunders answered. She looked at my chin. The bruise again. "You want another glass of tea? Or maybe some ice for that bruise?"

"No ma'am. Though that was a mighty fine glass of tea."

"Stephanie. My mother was a ma'am, and I don't want to be one."

"Fair enough. I want to let you know that I just talked to your son Mark a little about the Leewold house next door and whether he's seen anything that might be useful. Regarding what we talked about the other day."

"You talked to Mark?"

"Yes, m—"

She smiled. Not a ma'am. Then Stephanie Dunders flipped her head back. "Well? Was he helpful?"

"Yes m—I think he was."

18

MARK DUNDERS HAD MADE IT SEEM LIKE all I had to do was show up downtown and I'd find the guy sitting on a bench. Bench-sitting was a thing in Yellow Springs, but I knew from experience that even people who weren't trying not to be found could be hard to find. And if your day-to-day rhythms involved rotating where you slept, that made it even more difficult.

Like vultures perched on my shoulder waiting to tell me *I told you so*, doubts about the hunch crept in.

The first stop was my office above the village. The chill vibe of a weekday afternoon percolated from the street up to my window. Smatterings of people dotted the sidewalks. A lone busker endlessly tuned a guitar next to the patio at the Trail Tavern. Shoppers toting rope-handled paper bags strolled the brick walks of King's Yard. A group of four locals hunched together in close conversation outside of the Emporium. I guess that made it a tête-a-tête-a-tête-a-tête.

The sidewalk benches that I could see from my window were sparsely populated. Not much help. I descended to make the rounds.

I meandered through the benched downtown. Past the train station that was the visitors' center and the bathrooms. The skate park. The bike path behind the Brewery. Past the Green Canteen and the Corner Cone. I looked into the Highlander laundromat. Walked past the post office.

Down to the library, through the Antioch College campus, down the bike path again.

No one looked like the guy from the stills.

I circled again for round two.

I had resigned myself to round three when I spotted the guy sitting on a low brick wall in King's Yard, surrounded by hostas and flowering plants.

I stopped and said, "Mind if I sit here?"

It was weird because he was alone and there were lots of other places to sit that weren't right next to him. He saw the bruises on my face and it got weirder. He looked away.

The guy didn't say anything, so I sat on the low wall. "How's it going?"

"Another day in paradise."

He could have been serious or joking, I couldn't tell. Guys like that, it could go either way. No troubles or lots of them. I didn't pursue it. He seemed happy enough.

I wiped my brow. "Hot. Good day for a swim."

"I guess so."

"I know a woman who just moved into a place with a good swimming hole in the back. Down on Massies Creek."

He fidgeted.

"Some things got taken out of there, by mistake. I'm trying to find out if anyone knows where to look for them."

The fidgeting racheted up to a leg bob and a knee bounce.

"I think you know the place?"

That put him over the top. He pressed his hands onto the bricks and raised up. "Bro, I ain't done nothing wrong. There was nobody living there."

I raised up beside him. "Hang on. I don't think you did anything wrong. I think you might be able to help."

He didn't run away. That was good. I didn't want to chase him. There was no way that could look good.

The man flicked some hair from his face. "How'd you find me?"

"The neighbor kids have seen you. They said you might be here in town."

"Neighbor kids?"

"Next door. The swimming pool." Dragging them into it now. I'd rather have avoided that.

"I've seen 'em."

"Good kids." I'd only met one, and I was speaking with very little evidence. But hey, it kept the conversation going.

"Why do they swim in the creek? They got a good swimming pool right there at the house."

It was a good question, one that I hadn't considered. "I guess they do both. Why do kids do anything they can hide from their parents?"

A look of recognition crossed the man's face.

"So look, I'm just trying to help out a friend. The woman who moved into that house. She's trying to find out if anybody else has been around. Someone who might know where they took some of the things that were inside."

He looked at me for a long time.

"Maybe that was your sleeping bag in there?" I sat back on the bricks. "No problem. I just thought maybe you'd want to help out. I think somebody else has been coming around there."

He watched me for a time. "You don't care if I slept there?"

"No."

"And you don't think I took anything?"

"I don't."

"Why not?"

It was another good question. "Well? Did you take anything from the house?"

"No, man. I'm not like that."

"I didn't think so." It felt true. By the P.I. book I should have suspected him, but the hunch was whispering not to. And I couldn't in my head connect the dots between this guy and the bikers who showed up at Angelita's house. I leaned back on my palms. "How did you find the place?"

He waved an arm. "People know it. They swim out there. Some people."

"Yeah. You parked at the road? Walk in?"

"Nah. I ain't got a car. I get rides. Used to live out that way. Swam in the creek when I was..." He held a hand out waist high.

So a local guy. "How'd you know the place was empty?"

"Somebody said she died. I figured I could crash there for a while."

"Do me a favor? There's a young woman living there now. She may be worried if you go back and try to—"

His hands went up in a stop sign. "Hey. I don't want to harsh nobody's buzz. I'm cool with that. I ain't going back."

Surfer dude style. Cool. Aloof. No problem here, bro. Like that.

I tipped a finger in his direction. "I appreciate that."

"But one thing? Could you get my sleeping bag back for me?"

"Sorry, dude. I think that's gone." Funny how I'd slipped into the lingo. Sorry, dude. "But how about a ten spot? Get yourself a new blanket?"

He held a hand out. "Right on. But a new sleeping bag will cost more than that."

I pushed a couple of bills into his palm.

"There was some other things. Cans of food and stuff."

There was. I gave him a couple more bills.

He folded the money into his pocket. "Righteous, brother." He hung out a fist and I bumped it.

"You know about the dude in the car?"

I raised an eyebrow.

"Used to come by. Park out front, walk back to the house like he was looking for something."

I widened my eyes encouragingly.

The guy shook his head. "I didn't like him. Used to hide in the woods until he left."

"What'd the guy do?"

"I don't know. I heard him in there. I don't think he ever saw me."

But he would have known someone was sleeping there. He would have seen this guy's bag. "When was this?"

"You know, just—" He waggled a hand. "Recently."

"You ever see his car?"

He got a little animated. "Big black thing. Had these tinted windows." Pleased with himself. Happy to have made a contribution.

"Thanks. That helps. Anything else you can tell me about the car or the guy?"

"No, dude. That's it."

It was. The guy turned and walked away. I realized I hadn't even gotten his name. I hoped it didn't matter. The hunch was whispering in my ear again.

I drove back down the narrow, tree-lined byways to the ancient Leewold house. If it hadn't been for the paved roads, the electric lines, and my truck, I could have imaged myself back in the time when the cabin was a refuge for the former slave family who built it. But I wasn't trying to travel back in time. I was looking for something much more modern.

I idled slowly up and down the road, looking for a wire, a glint of sunlight on glass, a mounting bracket on a tree or a gate or a pole. Anything that would tell me if one of the neighbors might have a camera mounted somewhere that could catch the road, and maybe a big black vehicle that had lurked outside Angelita's place.

It was a long shot that I would find a camera. A longer shot that it had captured an image of the vehicle, and a longer shot still that the owner of that video would share it with me. And asking to get a clear view of a license plate number was a fool's bet.

But I didn't mind chasing long shots. And I had a back-up hunch in case I needed it.

Having idled up and down the road for the better part of forty minutes looking conspicuous, I went to the back-up hunch.

That put me at the Dunders' again. I parked at the road and peered through the trees. The pool was empty, the place was quiet, and the front door was closed.

Ten minutes later a dirt brown pickup truck more dinged than mine slowed and turned into the drive. When the truck reached the house, a tall man wearing a cowboy hat stepped out and looked back at me sitting in the truck.

I stepped out beside the truck and raised an arm. "Hello the house!"

The man I suspected was Duke Dunders didn't wave me off or extract a long gun from his truck's rear window. That was good. I walked down the drive.

The man watched me the whole way, and when I stood in front of him he said, "I saw you at the road."

"Yup."

"My grandaddy used to say that. Hello the house."

Ah, good. A way in. "Mine said *How do there*." I gave it the same emphasis my grandfather had, eliding most of the sounds into almost a single word.

The man took his cowboy hat off. It was weathered and sweat-stained and he slapped it against his leg as if there was dust on it he needed to knock off. "So?"

I extended a hand. "Jackson Flint. I've been here a couple of times and talked to Stephanie Dunders, who I assume may be your wife?"

He took my hand and we shook firmly once. "She is. I am. Duke."

"I'm doing some work for the grand-niece of Ida Leewold. She's inherited the house next door and we're trying to clean some things up."

"Steph told me. I wish you would."

"You wish I would...?"

"Clean things up. What's been going on over there?" Duke cracked his neck as if he'd been waiting all day to do just that. "All the cops there in the middle of the night. We heard the shots."

Oh, that.

"And the moving trucks made sense after Ida passed, but that late at night? Driving around in the dark?"

My hunch tapped me on the shoulder. Long shot, you say? I smiled at Duke. "Trucks?"

"Well maybe just the one, but it seemed odd. People in and out for days. Seemed like they were trying to be quiet about it, but they snuck around like a teenager raiding the refrigerator at midnight."

Duke said it like he knew that sound first-hand. I guess he did.

"How much has Stephanie told you about what I'm doing for Angelita?"

"Angelita?"

"Ida's niece." I pointed to the Leewold house.

"A little. Said you were looking for some family items, if you could find them."

That didn't explain everything, and Duke looked like he knew it. I lifted my ball cap and ran a hand over my head. "Do you have a few minutes?"

"If you don't mind me having a beer. It's been a long day."

I didn't. Duke went inside and came back with two cans of Pabst. He held one out to me without asking if I wanted it, and we pulled the tabs and drank.

Duke set his cowboy hat carefully on the hood of the truck and gave me his full attention.

I ran through the whole thing.

Duke whistled. "That is a crazy-ass story, for sure."

Well, it was.

"So you have no idea who these guys are? Sounds like a pack of them messing around over there."

I shook my head no. "Wish I did."

Duke leaned a hip against a fender of his truck and tipped his can of beer back to finish it. "Well, is there some reason you're here again?"

"I'd really like to find that black vehicle. I wondered if maybe you'd seen it, or maybe one of your kids or their friends? With phones and pictures and video everywhere now, maybe somebody picked up an image of it in the background."

Duke crushed his can and set it gently on the hood of the truck beside his hat. "And they wouldn't even know they had it."

"That's what I'm thinking. Maybe one of your kids. With phones and selfies and everything, them or one of their friends got something in the background while they were in the pool."

Duke leaned back on an elbow. "That sounds like something of a long shot, don't you think?"

Ouch. So he could see I was grasping at straws.

"What would you do with it if you found a picture of that vehicle?"

I took out my P.I. license and showed it to Duke, as if that would answer his question. We both knew it didn't. He glanced at the license and waved it back to me.

I slipped the license back into my wallet. "I sure would like to just talk to whoever owns that vehicle. Might clear up some things for Angelita, Ida's niece. Bit of a shock to her to see everything cleaned out of the house like that."

"I suppose it would be."

"I don't expect to find anything. Just following up might help her come to a little closure."

"It does seem like a bit of an odd situation over there. What did you say you'd do with a picture of that car if you could get it?"

Duke was sharp. I hadn't really said. "Just some polite conversation. If I could find the driver. Shot of the license plate sure would be useful."

I knew Duke was sizing me up. Duke knew that I knew he was doing it. He said, "Be real handy if one of the neighbors had a camera."

"It would. Do you know if anyone does?"

Duke stretched his arms out, relaxing. The beer doing its work. "I do."

I waited. Duke waited. I said, "Which neighbor?"

"Me."

"You have cameras?"

"One. Thirty-day recorded memory. Out at the end of the drive by the road."

I would make sure to look at that on the way out. It must have been hidden well. Put there not for deterrence, but to catch someone. I took out my little notebook. "Stephanie didn't mention that."

"She probably forgot. We put it in more than a year ago after there was a bit of trouble."

He didn't offer any details about what the bit of trouble was, and I didn't ask.

"Stephanie never messes with it. I check it sometimes just to see what it picks up."

I tried to be patient. "Are you offering...?"

"I could take a look at it for you."

"I'd appreciate that."

I gave him the descriptions and time frame I got from the squatter who'd been sleeping in Angelita's house. Duke ran a hand over his chin. "Seems like I might'a seen it."

We traded phone numbers, then Duke picked up his hat and beer can from the hood of the truck. He put the hat on his head and launched the crushed can into an open-topped recycle bin beside the garage. "Tonight soon enough for you on the recordings?"

"More than soon enough. Much obliged." I crunched my empty can and arced it into the bin.

Duke looked satisfied. With me or the toss, I couldn't tell.

He turned away. "Happy to if it helps sort things out over there. It's not been as quiet since Ida passed. Best neighbor we ever had."

Sure. Compared to gunshots and sheriff's cars in the middle of the night.

I headed out. Duke had never once mentioned or appeared to even notice the finger-shaped blue marks on my jaw. Much obliged, indeed.

It was a pleasant drive home. Hunches and dumb luck had taken me farther than I had any right to expect. If they held out a little longer, there was a phone call I would make to try to call in a favor I hadn't earned.

19

FIRST THING IN MY MIND the next morning when I woke up: Duke Dunders never called about the surveillance videos.

Second thing: there was a soft, warm female body next to me in the bed. The body was snoring gently.

I reached over and got a handful of long fuzzy hair. It wasn't Marzi's. It amazed me how Mrs. Jenkins' eight hairy pounds could somehow take up half the space of the bed. At least it was just Mrs. Jenkins this time, no mouse and gnashing of teeth.

Third thing: it had been four days since Marzi and I spent the night together. It was a pattern I didn't care for.

Mrs. Jenkins stretched her neck out and I rubbed a finger under her chin. Then I got out of bed. She incomprehensibly expanded to the fill the entire space of the bed. Cats. Everything belongs to them.

I crept from the bedroom. Cali was asleep. The house was quiet.

I made coffee and took it onto the porch with my paperback novel. The Beatles had it right. Who wouldn't want to be a paperback writer?

The sun rose higher. Two crows cawed loudly back and forth. A blue jay scolded them.

I drank coffee and read. A recumbent bicycle with a triangle flag wagging from a long pole curved down the road. In tow was a burley laden with a large red dog, ears up with excitement and tail wagging.

Life was good and I'd forgotten about the troubles and mysteries at the old Leewold home in the woods.

Then my phone woke up and told me that the rest of the world was closer to me than I thought.

Duke Dunders had texted. *Not what I would call a big car, but I think this might be what you're looking for?*

Attached was an image of a black Toyota RAV4. I zoomed in. The image became a little grainy, but I could see pieces of the road, the chain that stretched across the entry to Angelita's. A few dings in the car. And, luck was a lady—a view of the rear license plate.

Another text beeped in. A closer view of the plate. Duke had typed in the numerals and letters below. An Ohio plate.

I sent an emoji wearing a cowboy hat. *The Duke delivers.*

I got back a pair of dancing cowboy boots. *Yee-haw.*

I set the novel down. Time to ask for that favor.

Bronigan and I had traded phone numbers when he responded to Angelita shooting the intruder at her home in the middle of the night. I called Bronigan now and it went to message.

He called back while I was eating breakfast. "Flint."

"Bronigan."

"What is it? I'm on duty."

"I thought you worked nights."

"Nights. Days. Whenever they call. You remember how it was when you started out."

"I do."

There were some muffled sounds and the squawk of his radio. "Hang on. Let me pull farther off the road." Then something that sounded like tires on gravel, which it probably was, and Bronigan was back. "There's probably only one thing you'd be calling about."

Smart guy. But I switched it up. "How's little Henry?"

"Henry's good. Gaining weight like a baby's supposed to."

"Terrific. And Molly?"

"She loves being a mother. Listen, about the shooting. The Rojas Flores woman. I know you're probably still working with her. I'm sorry we can't do more. It's tough enough to have a car drive by there a couple times a day. I'll try to swing by later. Will you tell her that we haven't forgotten her?"

"I will. How's the investigation going?"

"Don't know. Above my pay grade."

I remembered that feeling. The guys with the most time in getting the most interesting work. "What about the guy she shot? Has he woken up?"

"That I do know a very little about. The coma was induced. To get some things stabilized. They said they think they'll be bringing him out soon."

Good. "Any chance I might be able to talk to him?"

"I have no idea. But I won't be able to help you."

"I know—above your pay grade."

"You got that right."

Here was the tricky part. "I've got something that might interest you."

"Shoot."

I let it register. "Was that a pun?"

Bronigan laughed. "No. But that's not bad. I might use it again sometime. What have you got?"

I gave him a brief update, filling him in on the points that led me to the RAV4.

When I finished, the connection went quiet for moment, then Bronigan said, "Fascinating. Have you given this to the investigating officer?"

"No. What would they do with it?"

"That's above my pay grade." He laughed, but there wasn't much in it this time.

"Think you could run the plates on the RAV?"

"I could get it done. I'd like to have a reason."

"If anything turns up that I think you might be able to use, I could give it to you."

"What does that mean? This isn't the movies."

"I was thinking more of TV."

"You mean like you turn up the bad guy and call me to come in and make the arrest? Play the hero?"

"That would be the best case."

"And the worst case is I pass you privileged information, something goes wrong and boom, little Henry's father is without a job."

I didn't remind him that his wife wished he would quit the sheriff's and get something safer.

Bronigan's radio made some noise. I imagined him listening, then he said, "What do you think this might lead to?"

"No idea."

"So that means maybe nothing?"

"Most likely nothing."

"I don't know what I'd do with it if it did lead to something."

"See? There you go." Silence. I tried something else. "Listen, you've got to think about Molly and little Henry here. I was just talking out loud."

A breathy sigh came through the line. "If you can just put me in the loop a little more here."

Maybe I could. "How do you feel about cowboys?"

"How do I what?"

"Never mind. I'm going to make a call. I may have a way to plug you in."

"What are you talking about?"

"I don't know yet."

I called Duke Dunders. He picked up, and a few minutes later it was a done deal.

I texted Bronigan. *The sheriff's office is going to get a call from a guy named Duke Dunders. He's going to ask for you.*

The reply came a minute later. *Very mysterious.*

That left Angelita. See how she was doing about her father. Give her an update. The lead on the RAV4, the guy she shot coming out of the coma in the hospital. See where we were on objectives.

Angelita didn't answer a text or call. I left a message.

Then I drove out to the Leewold house and walked down the lane and looked around. Just to make sure. See for myself that there were no more bodies on the ground. Nobody sleeping in the living room or peering in the windows.

No one was there. Angelita wasn't home. No one was swimming next door at the Dunders'.

I walked back to the swimming hole at Massies Creek. Everything was quiet. It felt like the summer had already ended. I went home for some lunch.

Cali was out with her friends again. The countdown was almost over. School on Monday.

Marzi was at work and I wondered exactly where things were with us. I took a sandwich and my paperback novel out to the porch and whistled for the cat. The Michigan fight song. It started as a joke, but once the cat got used to it I was stuck with it. People in Ohio didn't generally appreciate the Michigan fight song.

Mrs. Jenkins didn't appear. Maybe she'd taken a dislike to the Michigan fight song too. Or maybe she was right beside me hiding under the hostas and didn't want to come out. Or out prowling some remote region of our little piece of the village.

There was one way to find out. I took the first bite of my sandwich and chewed. The plants at the corner of the house rustled. Mrs. Jenkins loudly asked where her bite was. I knew where I rated. Somewhere below a sandwich.

Mrs. Jenkins had a few licks of her share of the sandwich and slinked off. Soy sausage. What was I thinking?

Bronigan called right when the novel was coming to the climax. The bad guys were coming after Alex McKnight on a boat in the middle of Lake Superior. Very thrilling.

I swiped my phone. "Your timing is good."

"How so?"

"I was just getting to a really good part of my novel."

"Your novel?"

"I'm reading."

"I'm familiar with the concept. How does that make my timing good?"

"It doesn't. I was being facetious."

"Well stop it."

"All right. But did you know that facetious has all five vowels, in the order you generally say them? A-e-i-o-u."

"You're a little odd, aren't you?"

"It's been said."

There was a noise like rumpling paper. "Your friend Duke is an interesting character. Had some pretty colorful things to say about what's been going on at the Leewold house next door."

"You think he's colorful on the phone, you should meet him in person."

"Looking forward to it. About that plate number." The rumpling noise came again. "This is privileged information. But in the spirit of working together, and because you have a duly appointed private investigator's license for the state of Ohio, let me share a few things." He cleared his throat. "The plate is registered to Rufus Butterfield. Likes to go by Redbone, like the hound."

"Redbone."

"The vehicle was purchased legally a little over a month ago. Now here's the interesting part. Butterfield was recently released from prison."

"Don't tell me from Florida?"

"Florida. Now here's where it gets even more interesting. Rufus Butterfield was a long-time cellmate of Nicolas Rojas Flores. No *h* in Nicolas."

"Rojas Flores?"

"Uh-huh. Lists among his survivors Angelita Rojas Flores. The same Angelita Rojas Flores who inherited the Leewold home and shot an intruder in her front yard a few days ago."

I whistled. So the name thing—Angelita's mother had simply taken Nicolas' surnames, and they passed those down to Angelita.

"Jackson?"

"Yeah?"

"This makes some connections for you?"

"It does."

"So the sheriff's office doesn't have any real or official reason to look at Butterfield right now, unless the investigating officer puts these pieces together and decides to make an inquiry."

"Is that likely to happen?"

"No idea."

Above his pay grade.

"And it would be a little further than I could go to tell you exactly how to find Butterfield. If something happened, and there was a question of how you got to him…"

"I understand."

"But if you were simply out looking for the vehicle and happened to find it, that would be something else. You have a reason to be looking for it."

"That sounds like a long shot."

"It does. But it could happen. With a little luck."

"That's not much to go on."

"Then let me make a suggestion. Maybe you should get your car washed."

"I drive a truck."

"Whatever. Maybe it needs a wash."

"Is there any particular reason you don't like the way my truck looks?"

"I know a place that does a good car wash. Let me give you the name. And maybe you should get there before five o'clock today."

Oh. "Thanks, Bronigan. I owe you one."

"It's just a car wash. Nothing else. If you get lucky, that's all you."

"Roger that."

I cleaned up my lunch plate and texted Brick. *Got time for some suds?*

The reply came right away. *Little early for beer.*

I was thinking of washing the truck.

You want me to go with you to wash your truck?

I gave my thumbs a break and called Brick to fill him in.

"What do you need me for?"

"Back-up. Diversion. Persuasion. Whatever. Maybe you can just sit there and have a coffee."

"They have coffee at a car wash?"

"I don't know. I'm just riffing here."

He grunted.

"What have you got better to do?"

"I could think of some things. Have you got a picture of this guy?"

"No."

"You've seen him? Know what he looks like?"

"No."

"So you just know his car then?"

"That's it."

There was a moment. "Maybe take the Shelby. Better distraction. This guy's at a car wash, he might be interested in cars."

"You sound like a P.I. Or maybe you just want a reason to show off Wilma again?"

"Name's not Wilma."

"Sure it isn't. Is the solenoid fixed?"

"No. You can't get parts that fast."

"Then it'll have to be the truck."

Brick sighed. "I'll bring the jumpers."

"Might work if you don't park on a slope. We can push her."

"There's nothing cooler than two grown men push-starting an iconic classic car at a suburban car wash. Is this the place where the topless sorority girls dry the car with fluffy towels?"

"That place doesn't exist. Not even in your imagination."

"Oh, it's real in my imagination."

"Keep it there. I think we're getting a little off track here."

"So all I get out of this is a car wash?"

"Use your imagination, you could get a little more."

"Yuck yuck. Hang on a second."

I waited. Brick came back. "Quando wants to come."

"Quando?"

"You say it like you don't know who he is?"

"Look, it's just—maybe not the best idea. I don't really know how this is going to play out."

"I'll tell him another time."

"He just wants to come because he heard you say sorority girls."

"That's probably it."

20

THE SHELBY RUMBLED like a small aircraft engine. Brick shifted up a gear and the rumble smoothed to a purr.

"Wilma's sounding good."

"Name's not Wilma."

"Sure it is. Does this thing have air conditioning?"

"You can roll the window down."

"It is down. You could drive faster."

He did.

There was still no FM radio, so we fell into chit chat. Brick looked at my face. "Bruise is way down."

"I've almost forgotten about it."

"Next time you could avoid the whole thing by not getting in the way of someone else's fist."

I made a motion like I was writing. "Lemme see, should I be taking notes?"

"What did I tell you about trying to be funny?"

"I can never remember."

The wind sang in the open windows. I told Brick about Angelita's father, dead in prison.

"How's she taking it?"

"Hard to know with her. Her family history is such a mess."

"I guess."

Brick tossed a thumb over his shoulder toward the back seat. "Had to roost Quando again. He snuck back there and tried to come along."

"Maybe he needs something to do with his time."

"I've thought of that."

"School will be starting soon."

"I've been thinking about that too."

"Heard anything from his mother?"

"Mother's in prison."

"Right. Foster parents?"

"Not a peep."

"Or from anyone?"

"That boy has been left hanging in the wind."

In more ways than one, I figured. "Any idea what you're going to do?"

"Do? No idea. And I wish I could say that wasn't a problem."

Then Brick took us off the highway and navigated through urban sprawl. Past fast food and retail and professional buildings.

At a street light Wilma drew looks from drivers waiting in queue to turn. Brick revved the engine.

We passed a strip mall and all the fast food and retail wonders it held, and then I saw something I'd never experienced before—a full-service car wash. I scanned the operation. "What *is* this?"

"Haven't you ever had your car washed before?"

"Mother Nature usually does that. Every once in a while I go to the Kiss and Hug." The Yellow Springs car wash. Wash your car, wash your dog, rent the ancient bus and take a wildlife tour. That place was nothing like this.

Brick circled behind the car wash and pointed. "There's the RAV."

I checked the plates, but I already knew it was our car.

"How do you want to play it?" Brick said.

"I think I'm going to buy you a wash."

They were already gawking. I got out and Brick lined the Shelby up with the entry. A guy in a colorful work shirt with arms out ninety degrees motioned Brick to inch the Shelby forward. Inch it. Slow. You don't want to scratch this one.

They let Brick stay in with the motor running. That made things easier.

Someone behind me whistled. "Man, you don't see that every day."

Someone else shouted, "Hey, Redbone! Get in there."

Another man in the same colorful work shirt grabbed a long-handled brush and stepped beside the Shelby as it entered the bay. He was tall and thin and had close-cropped hair, and he lathered the front and sides of the car as it moved into the wash. The man looked maybe forty.

It was that easy. Redbone. Rufus Butterfield, former cellmate of Nicolas Rojas Flores. Rufus who when he was released from prison traveled from Florida to Ohio and lurked outside of Nicolas' ancestral home, which was recently inherited by Angelita. Nicolas who told extravagant tales about a family treasure he had hidden away, waiting for the day he could come back and reclaim it.

It might be all tall tales, but it looked like the dominoes were starting to fall into place one way or another.

When the Shelby exited the cleaning bay, Rufus was there with a towel wiping and drying. The man who had motioned Brick into the tunnel appeared, looked around and located another towel, and joined Rufus.

I didn't even know a car wash could employ that many people, though I suspected it was the Shelby that had brought them all out for this cleaning. They cradled the car with the towels like it was a baby.

Brick came out beaming and I went up to Rufus and palmed a tip into his hand. "Rufus Butterfield?"

His eyes came up.

"You get a break, I'd like to talk to you for a few minutes."

He looked to the RAV. Like he was going to run.

Brick stepped behind Rufus.

Rufus' shoulders went down. "What do you want?"

I held a hand out, palm-up. Non-threatening. Yeah, there's a big guy between you and your car, but we're all friendly here. No need to worry. "Just to talk a little about Nicolas Rojas Flores. And his daughter. Do you know about Angelita?"

"Yeah, I know who Angelita is. Who are you guys?"

I took out my P.I. license and handed it to Rufus. He looked at it, turned it over, and returned it to me with wet fingerprints on the paper.

"In about forty minutes. But call me Redbone, OK?"

"Thanks, Redbone. We'll wait."

Brick parked the Shelby on the lot where there was a good view of Redbone and his RAV.

I peered through the windshield. "Think you're close enough to catch him if he makes a run for it?"

"Shelby will catch him if he makes a run."

"After you get out and jump the solenoid with the cables."

I got a hard look. "They don't know about that." He went to the trunk, came back with jumper cables, and dumped them into the back seat. "He's not gonna run. And if he does, we'll catch him."

I squinted at Redbone working the long brush on another car. Right, and right.

Then Brick laughed.

"What?"

"Their shirts should say *Still doing it by hand*."

"Did you just think of that?"

"I did."

"Maybe you want to keep it to yourself."

"Ha." He jiggled a little in his seat. "You know the song? At the car wash—"

"I know it."

"—yeah."

"I said I know it."

"All right, gloomy Gus. I'm gonna go walk around."

"What if Redbone makes a run for it while you're gone?"

He flipped me the keys. "Cables are right there."

Brick wandered off. I took out my paperback novel.

Redbone washed. I read.

Cars or people occasionally came up and looked at the Shelby. Most took pictures or selfies. I supposed they wished I hadn't been sitting there to ruin the shot.

Some time later I'd finished the book and Brick's head appeared at the driver's window.

"What'd you see?"

He said, "This place is crawling with people. Cars, traffic, noise. Where are they all going?"

"Beats me."

"It's like the opposite of my place in the woods. Somebody shows up there, it's because they're lost."

"And they want to find their way out of the wilderness to get back to all of this."

"I guess." He got in. "Anything happen?"

I put a hand to the paperback I'd tucked back beside the seat. "Finished this. You'll want to read it."

Brick looked at the cover. Read the back. Tucked the book back beside the seat. Checked the time. "Redbone should be getting his break about now. This is too easy."

"I guess I didn't need you."

"At least Wilma got a nice wash."

I cut my eyes over.

"What?"

"You said Wilma."

"I what? Oh, damn."

Then Redbone came over to the car. Brick and I both got out.

Redbone fidgeted. "I was hoping we could do this in the car?"

Brick got the big smile. Dad on prom night. He opened his door and folded the seat back. "Sure."

Redbone didn't get it. "I was hoping I could sit up front?"

I moved to the back. My feet got twisted in the jumper cables. Redbone settled in the passenger seat and ran his hands over the dash, touched the stick, opened the glove box and looked in. "Cool."

I put my face up between the seats. "Redbone. We need to talk."

"I meant can we do this *riding* in the car?"

Brick turned the key.

Then he remembered the solenoid, and Redbone and I got out and I hooked the jumper cable to one side of the solenoid and let Redbone touch the metal to the other side. The Shelby fired up with a rumble through the floorboards. The guys from the car wash looked over. Redbone grinned at them. Then he said, "I've got thirty minutes. Let's go."

Brick eased us out onto the urban strip.

There was traffic noise as we cleared the congestion, then some wind as we moved onto a more open stretch of road. I had to raise my voice from the back seat. "Redbone?"

"Yeah."

"We need to talk now."

"I know. Lemme just enjoy this for a minute, will you?"

Brick made a turn onto a less populated road. There was an open stretch with no cars and he shifted down and the Shelby jetted forward.

When we slowed and Brick turned into a city park, Redbone said, "You don't know how long I've been dreaming about something like this."

Brick said, "Riding in this car?"

"Doing anything that feels this free."

Brick stopped in the shade of a tree next to some kids at soccer practice, or maybe it was a game. At some ages, practice and a game look about the same. A couple of easy-up tents shaded what must have been parents, mostly mothers, watching and standing over coolers of drinks.

We all three got out and stood in the shade.

Redbone said, "You guys probably know I've been in the pokey?"

I nodded. "We do."

"You don't know what it's like to dream every day that you have room to do simple things like this."

And I never wanted to know what it was like.

Redbone leaned against the Shelby like it was his and watched the soccer moms.

I said, "They're probably all married. With kids."

"I know. And I don't care."

"We don't have a lot of time."

A pinched look crossed his face. "I know."

"We need to talk about Nicolas."

Redbone shook his head. "I don't want no more part of that anymore."

"Of what?"

"I know they shot Diggs."

Brick had been watching quietly, but now he uncrossed his arms and stepped closer.

I raised an eyebrow. "Diggs?"

I already knew who that was going to be, but I wanted to hear Redbone say it.

"Johnny Diggs. Nick's daughter shot him at the house."

"I'll tell you what? Why don't we start at the beginning. My associate here—" I gestured to Brick "and I are looking for some things that may have been removed from Nicolas' daughter's house. I know you were hanging around that house, in the black RAV4 parked at the car wash. And I know that until a little while ago you shared a jail cell in Florida with Nicolas."

Redbone's eyes moved back and forth between me and Brick. "You ain't cops. How'd you find me?"

I said, "Cameras."

"Shit. That's what got me into this in the first place."

I didn't ask. There were more important questions. "Who is Johnny Diggs?"

Redbone gave a hard stare. "You're working for Nick's daughter?"

"Yeah. Like I told it."

"Look, I ain't took nothing belongs to her. I ain't took nothing from that house."

"I believe you." Maybe I did, maybe I didn't. But maybe it would get him to talk.

"I told you I don't want no more part of any of it."

Brick re-crossed his arms. "Of what?"

"Nick's stories."

I let out a breath, waited. "You know Nick is dead?"

Redbone didn't. I could see it on his face.

"Two nights ago."

"That's not a surprise. Nick knew he was dying."

A soft wind cut through the summer heat. It felt good. Redbone watched the soccer moms. I watched Redbone. "Now maybe you'd better start at the beginning."

Redbone did. "Nick was a special kind of guy. Always spinning a story. Always talking. Always saying something. Like he couldn't function unless he was talking."

"He told stories about his family? The family home? Something he might have left there?"

Redbone's eyes cut over. "What do you know about that?"

"I know a little. He told stories about a family treasure."

Redbone nodded.

"You believe them?"

"Nobody could believe all of it. Nick told so many. Always changing the story a little. But he was so…Nick made you want to believe in something. That's what got me through. I think it's what got Nick through."

I checked the time. We were going to get Redbone back late. "You think there was some sort of treasure?"

"I think there was something. Something important to Nick."

"Like what?"

"That's the weird part. He wouldn't say, exactly. He had all these crazy stories, but he wouldn't say exactly what he had hidden in that house."

Brick and I exchanged looks. Maybe it was nothing. Just stories.

I went back to Redbone. "But you came up here looking for it anyway? For whatever Nick thought was so important?"

Redbone looked at his shoes. "This is embarrassing."

"Maybe not."

"I needed something. When I got out. I needed somewhere to go, something to do."

"Uh-huh."

"To keep me from…"

"To keep out of trouble."

"To move forward. To put Florida behind me. To think about anything else." Redbone lifted his eyes. "You think it's all bullshit. Nick's stories. And I'm stupid for coming up and finding his family house. All that's probably true, but it got me someplace that wasn't…where I came from. I don't even care if I believe Nick's stories. I'm done with that. I've already got what I needed from Nick."

It was a nice speech. I believed it. But that's not what I was here for. "I think someone believes the stories. Who is Johnny Diggs?"

"Diggs got killed for believing in Nick's stories."

"Diggs isn't dead. Who is he?"

Redbone shrugged, circled a toe in the dirt, then talked. "Diggs found me at Nick's house—Nick's daughter's house."

"Found you."

"Yeah. Found me."

"You were there watching."

He didn't say no.

"How often did you go there?"

"Look, it was something to do, you understand? Before I got the car washing job? Before I had anything to do. It was something."

So Redbone went there a lot.

"And Diggs was…"

"The mover."

Some gears clicked in my head. "J Guy Estate Removal Service."

"I guess. He had a truck."

"It was just Diggs?"

"No, he had another guy with him. But only Diggs was interested. The other guy didn't care. Ignored me. Like I was invisible."

"But you and Diggs…?"

Redbone ran his toe across the dirt again. "Is this going to help the girl somehow? Nick's daughter?"

"It is."

His hands went into his pockets. "Diggs and I talked. He had some beer in the truck. I thought he was—I just thought we were being regular guys, you know? Having a beer in the middle of the day."

"You told him why you were there?"

"I talked to him. We shot the shit. It's what you do after you've been inside for a long time."

It's what any people did. So Redbone had been looking for a friend. Diggs was there and stepped into the role. "Did Diggs take something from the house?"

"Yeah."

Here we go. "You know what he took?"

"No."

"You didn't help him?"

"No."

"Why not?"

"You know. I didn't want any part of it no more. It didn't feel right. Nick…"

I ran through it out loud. "So Nick tells you stories, and you get out and you're passing the time sitting in front of his daughter's house trying to decide what to do about them. Then Diggs shows up with the moving crew that was hired to get the place ready to sell. You and Diggs get a little chummy, drink beer together. You tell him Nick's stories. Diggs gets interested and takes something from the house but you don't know what it was—"

Redbone was shaking his head no.

"What part of it did I get wrong?"

"Diggs didn't take *some things* from the house. He took *everything*. He sent the other guy from the moving crew off, and he came back and packed all of it away."

"Everything?"

Redbone answered with a shrug.

Brick whistled. "This story has a whole lot of crazy in it, and it's gaining speed."

I didn't disagree. The case had more funny turns than a wooden-legged sailor trying to dance the cha-cha. I pinched my fingers into the skin above my forehead. "So Diggs didn't find anything valuable?"

"Not as far as I can tell."

"Where's the stuff from the house?"

"You'll have to ask him."

"He comes out of his coma, I'll do that." Would this thing never end?

Redbone checked the time. "I know it's just a car washing job. It ain't a big deal. But it's something…"

Brick pulled the cables from the back seat and held them out to Redbone. "You want to—"

Redbone already had the cables in hand and was reaching for the hood.

Brick got in. "Don't worry. I'll get you back in time."

21

MY LUCK HELD A LITTLE LONGER. Bronigan called that evening. "Your boy woke up. They brought him out of the coma."

"If this keeps up I might start playing the lottery."

"What does that mean?"

"Nothing. I've just had a bit of a lucky streak."

"Well don't spend it all in one place."

"I already have. Is there any chance you can get me in to talk to Diggs?"

"Diggs?"

"Johnny Diggs?"

"Who's Johnny Diggs?"

"Guy who Angelita Rojas Flores shot at her house? You were there? The guy we were just talking about who came out of the coma?"

"That's not Johnny Diggs. Guy's name is Hector Martin."

"Hector?"

"Yeah."

"Martin?"

"Says right here."

"Then who is Johnny Diggs?"

"Never heard of him. We got Hector Martin's name from the registration for the plates on the motorcycle that was left at Rojas Flores' house. And the hospital confirmed. That's Hector Martin."

That put a crimp in my lottery ticket. "What do you know about Martin?"

"Not much. He hasn't been on the radar. Until now."

"Well, damn."

"Jackson?"

"Yeah?"

"You want to explain?"

I did.

Bronigan listened all the way through without a word and then released a long and loud, "Huuuuuh. Whaddaya make of that?"

"I think talking to Hector Martin might help make sense of it."

"Probably so."

"What are the chances you could get me in to talk to him?"

"None."

"What about just a little push?"

"No chance. Look, I don't know what you're thinking, but you remember how it was. There's procedure for this. I'm not working that case."

"You responded to the call."

"Jackson."

"OK." So no lottery ticket yet. Luck was being fickle. Dangle something, pull it away. Like a dollar on a string. That was my fault for relying on chance instead of something more substantial. "You could call the nurses' desk, as a courtesy. Ask how the guy is doing. Because you were there at the scene and you've been working with a private investigator who's also concerned about Hector."

"That's a stretch."

"OK, *talking* to a private investigator."

"Uh-huh."

"Who's *interested* in Hector…"

"Semantics."

"Sometimes language is everything."

"I don't disagree. But so is my job."

"You're right. My apologies. I'll have to come at this another way. Give my regards to Molly and Henry, will you?" It sounded weird because it was pandering and I didn't really remember Molly and I'd never met Henry, but I was going for something here.

Bronigan said, "I told Molly about you."

"You did?"

"She remembers reading about you when you found that runaway girl."

There had been a lot of news coverage. I was kind of famous to a few people for a few minutes. "Does that mean Molly approves of me?"

"I don't know. It's just something I thought about when you mentioned Molly. I'll talk to you later, Jackson."

I put the phone down. Went to the kitchen and mixed up a foxpossum, that mysterious and elusive drink I had long ago created but not yet mastered. I got down the bottle of herbed gin I'd made. Added lime and bitters. Some cherry liqueur. Lots of ice. Sipped.

It was good like always. But finding exactly the right balance for the drink was now, as always, just a little out of reach. Like a lot of things.

I stood alone in the empty house. I wondered about Cali, out with her friends squeezing the last drops from a long summer of freedom.

I wondered about Marzi, how she was unwinding at the end of her day, and why I wasn't asking her to unwind with me. I wanted to, but inertia was strong and so was the drink.

I wondered about Mrs. Jenkins, whether she would deem me worthy of a visit tonight.

I wondered about Brick and Quando.

I wondered about life and the infinite universe and our role in it.

That was too much, so I refreshed the foxpossum and added more ice, found a new paperback novel to disappear into, and headed for the bedroom.

I was ready to put this case to rest. Very ready.

If my dreams were sweet that night, I didn't know it. In the morning I couldn't remember having dreamt. The foxpossum will do that to you.

I lingered over my coffee. Cali eventually got up and had a slow start, hunching over her phone and breakfast. I was waiting to get a little deeper into visiting hours at Miami Valley Hospital.

Cali finally looked up and said, "Where's Marzi? We haven't seen her for a while."

"It's just been a few days."

"I know. It just—seems longer."

"It feels that way to me too. We've both been really busy."

Cali twirled a loop of hair around a finger, something I hadn't seen her do for a long time. It reminded me of her mother. "I know Marzi fell asleep on the couch the last time she was here."

"Uh-huh?"

"I heard you come in."

I looked up from my coffee. And?

"How come she didn't stay?"

"It was really late. Marzi had to work in the morning."

Another twirl of hair. "You think maybe we'll see her this weekend?"

"Maybe. I hope so."

The finger stopped. Cali had noticed what she was doing and let the loop of hair fall away. "I was just—" Her shoulders went up and down. "Getting used to her."

"I know. Me too."

And then Cali said something that was well beyond her years. "It's like you and Marzi are trying things on for size. To see if it fits. Except I'm stuck in the middle. Like you have to try to fit things together around me. Is that what you did with Mom?"

I felt a big sigh well up and I worked hard to keep it down. "No. That's not what your mom and I did. And you weren't here then to fit anything around."

"I know that. But with mom, it was different?"

"It was different."

Cali waited for a real answer.

"Your mother and I just knew. There was no trying on. There was holding on. It had to fit. We made it fit, no matter what."

Cali's fingers went back to a strand of hair. She took hold but stopped and let the strand go. "So with Marzi it's going to be…?"

"It's going to be trying things on for a fit. Just like you said. We don't know yet."

"But I'm in the middle?"

I gave it some thought. "I don't think middle is the right word. You're in the thick of it."

"Thick?" She made a face.

"Then something more flattering. You're in the midst of it."

She shook that off. "Keep trying."

"The point is that you're in it. All three of us. It's different than with your mother."

"But you like Marzi?"

Now I let the sigh go. Long, slow, loud. "Yes, I like her."

"So do I. Marzi was helping me to forget about Mom. I don't mean Mom the good stuff. I want to remember that. I mean I wasn't thinking so much about Mom not being here anymore."

And that was my daughter. Wise. Hurt. But determined to move forward. Because you had to. Her eyes had gone down a little and I bent to meet them. "And now you're thinking more about Mom again?"

She caught the moisture that was trying to form in the corner of one eye. "A little."

I gave her a little hug. A gentle, you're-a-teenager-now-and-I-won't-make-too-much-of-this hug.

Cali leaned into it. "What do I do?"

"This. And tell me if you need anything else."

The embrace lasted only a little longer and then we pulled away. I said, "Are you all right?"

"Yeah."

"You'll tell me if you aren't? If you need anything?"

"I will. I'm all right."

I wanted to believe her. I did believe her. But you never knew.

Then Cali's face recomposed itself and she reached for her phone. "Is it all right if I text her? Marzi?"

"Sure." I said it without thinking if that was a good idea. But it had to be a better answer than no.

Then Cali was lost on her phone, and I left to make the trip to Dayton.

Miami Valley Hospital was big. It sprawled across a swath of the city by the University of Dayton and Woodlawn Cemetery. I remembered when the hospital was smaller and there was room for a little twenty-four-hour steak-and-eggs restaurant tucked across the street. That place was long gone and now it was hospital all the way down between Apple and Wyoming Street.

It took a while to find Hector Martin. And when I did, the nurse at the station where I was standing didn't seem happy to see me.

"So you're not a relative?"

"No."

"And you're here because…?"

I went through it quickly. The woman was maybe thirty and seemed alert but looked like she'd already worked a long shift. While I talked she peered at a computer screen and flipped pages on a clipboard. I tried to keep her attention. "So if I could just ask Hector a couple of questions very quickly."

"We don't usually do that."

I gave her my most innocent look. "Yes, I understand." I took out my private investigator's license. "You may have gotten a call from someone at the Greene County Sheriff's office? Did someone say that they were in contact with a private investigator about the events that led to this man's hospitalization?"

She squinted at the license for a long look but didn't take it from my hand. Then she flipped some more pages on the clipboard and read from some handwritten notes. "I don't think…?"

I let it hang between us, and she looked again at the notes. Something in her expression ticked up. "You were with Mister Martin when he was shot?"

"Yes, ma'am. I was hired by the woman who shot him."

Her face gathered energy. "I saw it on the news. It's just awful. What people do to each other."

"Yes, ma'am."

"They said he just came right up to her house and was yelling at her and she shot him. In the middle of the night."

"Yes."

Her eyes lingered on me. "Well? What did Mister Martin do that for? What did he want?"

"That's what we're trying to find out. If Hector is available for a few very brief, very quick questions, that could be a big help to a lot of people involved."

It was a little heavy-handed. I knew that. But it wasn't my first rodeo. I smiled carefully, a lot of seriousness behind it.

The nurse looked over her shoulder at a series of doors in the hall-way. "I think he may be awake."

I held the expression on my face. Encouraging. "Uh-huh."

"If he seems to be doing all right, maybe…just a minute?"

"All I need."

"I'd have to come with you. I promise I won't listen. I can stand at the door."

"Yes ma'am."

She took me to a room with a single patient inside. I didn't know if Bronigan had called to grease the wheels for me or not. I didn't want to know. That would be better for Bronigan.

I stepped in and knew right away it was a bad idea.

Hector didn't look good. A breathing tube was taped to his mouth. A big bandage wrapped around his head, and tubes snaked from medical apparatus down to a vein in each arm. He didn't look awake, or like he had been in a long time. Or would be any time soon.

The nurse peered around the door frame. "He might be able to respond if you squeeze his hand. He might be able to squeeze back. Sometimes they can do that."

I stepped closer to Hector.

The nurse ventured into the room. "If he's awake."

"I think maybe I should just let him rest."

Her eyes said she agreed, but her body came farther into the room. "Just take his fingers gently. In your hand like this." She held her four fingers out together, then curved them toward her thumb.

I knew how to hold someone's hand. If she hadn't looked so pleased to help, I would have walked out right then. But I went to Hector's side and scooped up his hand.

Hector didn't seem to notice. I squeezed once, very gently. Nothing.

I leaned in. "I need to know who Johnny Diggs is."

Squeeze? Maybe just a pulse in Hector's fingertips? It didn't matter. It wasn't the kind of question Hector could answer with a squeeze.

I tried again. "Where can I find Johnny Diggs?" It was a worse ques-tion. Hector was going to answer in Morse code?

I needed a yes or no question. "Do you know Johnny Diggs? Once for yes. Twice for no."

Hector lay silently, with no squeeze. I let his hand loose. This was going nowhere.

The nurse looked disappointed. I said, "I'm sorry I put you out. I'll have to come at this another way."

The nurse lingered. "Was he able to tell you anything?"

"I think so, ma'am. Just enough. Thank you for your help."

That seemed to perk her up.

When we reached the door, a tall woman in a close-fitted shirt and with hair squared off at her shoulders stepped into the frame and blocked our exit. I expected trouble from the nurse's supervisor, but the woman in the doorway stepped away to let us through.

The nurse moved into the hallway. "Mrs. Martin?"

Hello. Martin like Hector Martin?

"Yes."

"I think Hector is asleep right now. You can go in and see if you want."

Mrs. Martin looked in at Hector but kept herself in the hallway where she was. The nurse continued back to her station.

I came in front of the woman. "Mrs. Martin? I'm Jackson Flint. A private investigator who has been hired to look into some of the events surrounding Hector's assault." I handed her my license.

Mrs. Martin accepted the card and turned it over in her hands.

"I understand if you want to go in and see Hector. But if you have a few minutes some time, can I buy you a cup of coffee?"

She handed the card back without reading it. "Let's skip the coffee. How about you buy me a sandwich?"

Well. At least she didn't ask for a drink.

We went to the hospital cafeteria. It was between meals and sparsely populated.

Mrs. Martin sauntered through the food choices and settled on the roast beef dinner. "You're buying, right?"

I nodded yes and she added cherry pie and sweet tea. I got coffee, and we sat down. Mrs. Martin forked a bite of potatoes and beef. "I do appreciate your hospitality." She chewed and swallowed. "My name is Lizzie. Two z's and an *i-e* at the end."

Proud of it. In grade school she probably added a heart over the i and dots over the e to make a smiley face. Not now. Grown-up Lizzie looked hardened, lines deepening in her forehead and at her dimples. A sharp look in her eyes.

I set my coffee down. "Lizzie it is."

"You're not eating?"

"Maybe later."

She shrugged and dug for another forkful.

I gave her room to eat. When Lizzie had wrecked the meat and potatoes and started in on the pie, she paused and pointed her fork at me. "What do you want to know about Hector?"

"First, I hope he has a good recovery."

Lizzie rolled her eyes.

"I represent Angelita Rojas Flores."

"The woman who shot Hector."

"Yes ma'am."

"Lizzie."

I gave her a smile. "Lizzie."

"You called it an assault. Say it for what it is. That bitch almost killed Hector."

I held my tongue. I didn't want to, but sometimes discretion is the greater part of getting to information. "Lizzie, do you maybe know why Hector was at Miss Rojas Flores' house? And could there have been someone else with Hector?"

Lizzie put her fork down, took a big drink of sugar-tea. Said nothing.

"I'm not looking to make any more trouble for Hector. He's had more than his share. I'm just trying to find some things out for my client."

Lizzie snorted. "Your client? You know why they was there? They took all that shit. Packed it out of that house after Hector talked to that guy who said he knew the family. Said there was some kind of something valuable hidden in there, in all that shit."

That's where Redbone fit into the picture, sitting in his RAV4 at the street, wondering what to do with his life. The dominoes were falling, making a pattern that held together. Here we go. I tamped down my excitement. "Really?"

Lizzie's unladylike snort erupted again. "And when they found out it was all just shit, they got good and drunk and decided she was holding out on them. You believe that? Them dumbasses thought that woman was hiding something worth a penny or two, and she ain't even been there when they took all that. How could she a done that?"

Angelita couldn't have. "That's a good question. Let me ask you something. So Hector was working for the estate cleaning company?"

Lizzie looked at me with a heavy dose of suspicion, but she talked. "He worked for them."

"And that's how Hector was able to move the things out of the house?"

The suspicion was replaced with something else, more forceful and defensive. "He ain't done nothing wrong. That was all trash. They was supposed to haul it away."

I leaned back with my palms held out. "I don't disagree. I'm just trying to figure some things."

Lizzie glared. "For what?"

"It's what I was hired to do."

"She wants all that shit back?" Lizzie glanced over the remains of her plates, trying to find something worth digging back into. She settled on the last of the pie. "Hector and them done that all the time. They'd take little stuff. It's usually all just junk. They're supposed to dump it. But sometimes they can get a little something out of it. This is the only time he took so much. Whole storage unit full of shit."

I held my reaction again. A whole *what*? "That's something. Whole storage unit." She didn't correct me, so I figured I'd heard it right. "Was one of the men Johnny Diggs?"

Lizzie coughed out a piece of pie crust. "Diggs? That piece of shit."

It was too loud, and a man drinking coffee at a table nearby looked over.

Lizzie ignored him. "It was Johnny and Hector took the stuff. After Hector talked to the man who told the stories about the family money."

"Just Diggs and Hector?"

She gave one quick nod. "Diggs got the storage unit. He was the one pushing Hector. Got him all worked up about nothing. Them boys get to drinking and they can talk each other into about anything."

And it got Hector shot. I ran through some mental notes in my head. Then I said, "Thanks, Lizzie. This has been really helpful. Can you tell me what Diggs looks like? Describe him?"

"I can do better'n that." She reached into her pocket and extracted a phone, swiped, swiped, swiped, and held the phone out with a picture showing on the screen.

I looked. It was a man in a black t-shirt standing next to a pool table, holding up a cue in one hand. Something looked familiar right away. I put a hand out. "May I?"

Lizzie laid the phone on the table between us.

I pinched the picture larger. There was a lumpy tattoo of a heart or a pretzel on the man's neck. The guy who had accused Brick of cheating at nine-ball at Dorado's. The one who'd started the fight. We'd been that close and didn't know the puzzle piece was in front of us.

Lizzie must have caught the look on my face. "You know him?"

"Might've seen him once."

"You never see him again, it'll be the best day of your life."

I didn't comment on the logistics of that reasoning.

"Anyway, we're done. I don't want me or Hector to have anything more to do with Johnny or any of that shit. Ain't worth nothing anyhow. All that talk. Hector getting almost killed for nothing. Drunken bastard."

"Then you won't mind if I ask where the storage unit is? Do you know?"

"Hell, yes, I know. I been there. Looked through all the stuff with them. What I could stand to."

I waited.

Lizzie looked at me with a question on her face, then she got it. "Oh. You wanna know where it is."

"If you don't mind."

She dismissed that with a wave of her hand. "Fine. Get that shit out of my life." She described a place on a rural route. I'd never heard of it, but those self-storage units will pop up anywhere. I wrote down how to get there.

Lizzie sucked on her straw and gurgled the tea in the bottom of her cup. "Unless you want to break in, you'll need the key."

I turned some scenarios over in my head. Angelita could probably make a case for legal access to the storage unit. That might take some time and money, and who knew if it would go Angelita's way in the courts.

B&E wasn't something I was entirely opposed to if the ends justified the means enough. Life or death. Some great value. Something worth risking the consequences for Cali if it went bad. This wasn't one of those situations, but I could suggest someone to Angelita who would do the job.

I tried another tack. I smiled at Lizzie. "I'm listening."

The glint in her eye said she knew I would ask. "It's hanging around Johnny Diggs' neck on a chain."

A what? Like a high school quarterback's ring? "Are you sure. Why would he do that?"

Lizzie's shoulders went up and down. "Beats me. Johnny is one weird motherfucker. Does shit just to mess with people. Showing off."

"You've seen the key there?"

She moved a hand from collarbone to collarbone, making the shape of a necklace. "On a chain. Right here. Under his shirt."

Weird motherfucker, all right. "You know where Diggs lives? How I can find him?"

"I don't know where he lives. Hector does. But Hector ain't talking." She let out a wheezy laugh that sounded pitiful to me and must have come across the same to her, because Lizzie looked embarrassed. She recovered and said, "You heard of Dorado's?"

Uh-huh? "Biker place out by the river?"

"Yup. Where that picture was taken. Johnny is there most nights."

Click. More puzzle pieces lining up. The picture was becoming more clear. But there was one more thing I needed. I held my smile on Lizzie. "You know the number of the storage unit?"

She came forward in her seat. "I'll tell you what. I'll give you that number if you do two things for me."

"What things?"

"You leave me and Hector out of this. We're done. I don't want nothing more to do with any of it."

"Done." It was a promise I might not be able to keep, but I meant it in the moment.

Lizzie pushed her chair back, rose, and came around to put her mouth close to my ear. "And the other thing? You find Johnny Diggs, you fuck him up good for me."

22

"YOU WANT IN?"

"I'm in." Brick leaned against the big workbench that took up most of one side of his barn. "But tell me again how you got here. To this guy at the bar."

"Diggs."

"Right."

I went through it and connected the dots again.

Brick nodded as he followed. "Complex."

"It was slippery."

"You sure you've got this thing figured out?"

"No. But this makes the most sense so far."

He swatted away a fly. "So the plan is to find Diggs at Dorado's, take the key off him, and see what's in the storage unit?"

"That's about it."

"And that will wrap things up."

"I hope so."

"But I get to see this guy again and tell him how I feel about him calling me a cheater?"

"You still worried about that game of nine-ball?"

"Not worried. Just want to remind him."

"That could be part of it."

"Then I'm in. We can take the Shelby."

"You've got the solenoid fixed?"

"No."

"Then we'll take the truck."

Brick looked longingly at the car. "You just gonna go up to the guy and ask him for the key?"

"Assuming it might not be that easy, I have some other ideas."

"Do tell. You think I'll need to take notes?"

"Just try to keep up."

"Been doing fine so far."

True. Brick had been keeping up, and more.

We laid plans for the night. Then Brick changed into black pants and a black t-shirt that said *No sh*t?* on the front and *No sh*t* on the back.

I laughed. "Subtle. But that asterisk isn't going to fool anybody."

Brick flexed a bicep Popeye style. "Not trying to fool anyone."

Then we had a good meal and coffee out at the picnic table behind Brick's cabin. Quando joined us for the food, then just before dark Brick and I set out in the truck for Dorado's.

The night was warm and we rode with the windows down. Brick reached below his seat to my gun safe. He took out my Smith & Wesson M&P40, quickly ejected the magazine and broke the gun down, then even more quickly reassembled it. "You appear to be fully prepared if things get ugly."

"Yes, sir. Lieutenant, sir."

"You don't know much about the military, do you?"

"Is it anything like the police academy?"

"Let's just say you don't."

"OK. I don't."

He tucked my weapon into the holster strapped under my seat. "I earned my commission. The long way."

"And the secrets that go with it."

His eyes cut away. "The secrets was something else."

Yes, sir.

Then he took out his own weapon and went through the same procedure as he had with mine, seemed satisfied, and tucked the gun below the passenger seat. "You know I feel a little naked without this."

I knew. We'd done this before, weighing the risks of carrying the weapons versus not. Brick always came down on the side of carrying. I did sometimes.

I put my right hand down to the Smith & Wesson, felt it where it was supposed to be, slipping into my hand without effort. "Your weapon, your choice."

Brick left his gun beneath the seat. "I've made it."

I shifted down into a turn and something in the back of the truck broke loose and slid across the bed. I glanced in the rearview. A flap of gray tarp had come loose near the tailgate and was blowing in the wind.

I drifted off the road and slowed.

Brick looked through the back window into the bed of the truck. "What've you got back there?"

"Some lumber. Wheelbarrow and bags of concrete."

His brows went up to ask the question.

"Putting in some fencing around the garden. Going to try to feed a little less to the deer next year."

"Good that you didn't unload any of that. Make it easier if we have to chase the bad guys."

"Funny." But he was right, if you took out the sarcasm.

I went to the back of the truck and pulled the edge of the tarp back down and strapped it in with bungees.

Then I climbed back into the cab and switched the lights on.

Brick settled back in his seat. "You do make things interesting."

We would see. Interesting maybe wasn't what we wanted here.

Brick switched the radio on. Johnny Cash serenaded us. He tried another station. Bruce Springsteen. "Does this thing get anything good?"

"Well, it has FM."

Some old-school hip hop came on. Brick listened for a moment, then turned the dial again. *Smokey Joe's Café* broke through. The Robins. A real oldie.

Brick raised an eyebrow. I raised one back. We listened to the Robins. I sang along.

Brick groaned.

I grinned. "FM radio is fantastic. You should try it."

He didn't laugh.

Dorado's looked exactly the same as the last time. Work trucks and small houses on small yards on a street dimly lit by mercury vapor lights. A line of motorcycles in front of the building and more bikes strung out in clumps along the side.

I stopped down the block on a side street, with the nose of the truck forward just enough to give us an angled view of the front of Dorado's. The radio was off. Brick got serious. "OK, phase one. Do your thing."

I wrenched my baseball cap down on my head, shrugged into my vintage black jean jacket that I'd dug out of the back of my closet, turned off the dome light, and slipped out of the truck.

Brick moved over into the driver's seat.

I walked like all I wanted in the world was a beer and a good song on the jukebox. Friday night. Just keeping it loose and easy.

Dorado's was nearly full. A woman tended the bar with steady, fluid movements and her eyes on what was going on around her. The bartender from the last time wasn't there, the guy who'd broken a table with a baseball bat. So far, so good.

It took two seconds to locate Diggs. He was holding court at a pool table, cleaning up a rack and looking like he was enjoying it just a little too much.

I stepped back outside. Texted Brick. *Different bartender. D is in the house.*

Brick texted back a thumb.

Our phones were on vibrate, the brightness down. I stuffed mine into my back pocket. Phase two.

No one came in or out of the bar while I walked the length of bikes out front. No one came while I walked through the clusters of bikes in the side parking lot. No cars passed, no lights came on at the houses, I heard no voices.

But I found what I was looking for. The club patch was painted on three of the Harleys parked at the side of the building.

This was the part we didn't have to do, the thing that might trip us up. But I wanted something for Bronigan. If I could get it.

I checked the street again, looked to the front corner of the building. Empty.

I leaned into one of the bikes and took the weight off the kickstand, snapped the stand back, and dropped the bike as quickly and quietly as I could onto the pavement. I did the same to the two others with the patch, then moved quickly around the back of the building, down a narrow gravel alley, and back onto the street about midway between Dorado's and the truck.

Brick was already out of the cab and starting slowly toward Dorado's behind me.

Phase three. This part might be even more dicey. I went back into Dorado's.

Sauntered to the bar. Hands in my pockets. Casual. Patient. When the bartender cleared what she was doing I stepped forward. "Pabst."

She reached beneath the bar to an ice chest and came up with a bottle.

I laid a five on the bar. "Looks like somebody's bikes have fallen over outside."

Her hand stopped mid-twist taking the top of my bottle. "Are you sure?"

I shrugged. "I'm just saying. Saw it on my way in."

She set the bottle on the bar. "They're not going to like that."

I waited.

She waited.

"I could say something."

She placed both hands on the bar and looked over at the pool players, the groups sitting at tables around the perimeter. "No, I'll do it."

I slipped away into a corner. Kept my cap down and my head low.

The woman came out from behind the bar and went to a guy watching a game of nine-ball. He bent to listen to her. Two others listened in. Then they all three backed away and turned to others, a little animation in their movements.

That wave spread in broken ripples, until several guys set down their beers or pool cues and hustled out the front door.

I followed. I didn't see Brick. But he was there.

One of the guys who'd come out and gotten a good look at the downed bikes spun on a boot heel and dove back into Dorado's, then there was some jockeying of who was going in and who was coming out, and two guys made their way to two of the downed bikes and bent over to inspect them.

One of the guys was Diggs. I maneuvered behind him, pretended to look at something on my phone, and snapped the photo I wanted.

Phase three down. Now if we could pull off the finale.

The bikes were back up on their kickstands and everyone had gone back into Dorado's except three guys who were speculating about how the bikes had gotten knocked over and whose asses they would kick because of it.

Diggs was one of the lingerers. He was short but had wide shoulders and a thick torso and neck. He looked like a guy who would lift weights on a bench in the corner of his garage but he'd let the fat start to build up around the muscle.

The jawing slowed down and the energy looked like it had mostly gone out of it with nobody listening to them and nobody's ass to kick. When the three of them started inside, I moved over to separate one of them.

"Johnny Diggs?"

He turned. "Says who?"

"Your friend Hector Martin said you might be able to help me. Said you could maybe get me a couple things I'm looking for."

"Wha—Hector's in the hospital."

"Yeah. I talked to him this morning."

"Hector can't talk to nobody. And it don't look like he's gonna be able to talk to anybody. Ever."

"OK, you're right. It was Hector's wife I talked to."

"Lizzie? That bitch. She ain't got no reason—"

"Hold on." I put a hand on Diggs' shoulder and turned him toward the back of the building. He resisted, but he hadn't been expecting it and I put a hard push into it and Diggs turned.

The other two guys were already rounding the corner for the front door. I squared on Diggs. His back was up against the wall. Like the song. Redneck mother. Up against the wall. "You recognize me?"

His eyes searched. "Schoenling boy?"

I gave him a grin. "Lizzie asked me to give you this." I stepped forward and drove a right hand very quickly and very hard into Diggs' solar plexus.

He was surprised and then it hit him. His breath went away and he doubled forward.

I caught him with my left hand and reached with my right under the collar of his jacket. The chain was there, just as Lizzie had said. I tugged it out and a key dangled from the end.

Some light came back into Diggs' eyes. I cocked a hand back and swung to take it out again.

A horn went off and Diggs' eyes slid up over my shoulder. A motor whined and there was the sound of tires sliding on gravel and then Brick was yelling. "Get out of there."

I turned to look. I knew it was a mistake as soon as my head moved.

Diggs ducked and pushed, and I went backward.

The tires crunched and slid. There were footsteps coming fast and Brick shouting again. "No. No." I saw his arms waving as he raced across the lot.

Then my truck was there and the door opened and Quando was coming out. His right arm came up, a glint of metal showing.

Oh, fuck.

I blinked.

People spilled out of Dorado's.

I blinked again, hoping it would go away.

Another car fishtailed across the lot, slammed to a stop right next to Quando, and a guy jumped out and took Quando down.

Diggs squirmed under my grip. I locked my elbow and swung my forearm around into his temple.

The woman from behind the bar stood in the back of a pickup and raised the barrels of a shotgun over her head. Someone else was reaching into his jacket.

Four or five bikers in black shirts and jackets closed fast. Brick was at Quando and had him and the guy who'd tackled him on their feet.

A blast from the shotgun ripped the air.

Everything stopped. Except the sound of a man on a porch next door talking fast into his phone. Probably calling 9-1-1.

Everything restarted. The bikers closing the last few steps between them and me and Diggs.

I heard Brick say, "Ah, hell no" and I yanked the key loose from Diggs' neck and came up with my left hand over my head for cover and my right jabbing fast at whatever was closest to me.

I connected, but a barrage of fists came down from straight above onto my head and shoulders. I ducked and tried to roll out, stuck a jab with a left and a right. It was tight quarters and I couldn't get extension. The barrage of hands came down to my torso and someone swept my legs out from under me. I went down.

I kicked, rolled, and covered. Got ahold of a dirty booted leg, grabbed hard, and twisted it under me. There was a crack and a howl.

Then more yelling and more fists and some boots making short kicks into my flank, and something heavy came down onto my back.

Then one of the men disappeared. I moved into the space that opened where he'd been above me and pushed up to my knees.

Another man disappeared. There was sky over me again and I got to my feet. Punches and jabs came at my torso, my neck, my head. Random and loose punches, not doing much damage.

I locked my elbows to my ribs and my fists to my forehead, swept a leg out under another boot in front of me, and popped a jab at the figure.

Then that guy disappeared. Then Brick was there, grabbing me, pulling. "Let's go."

We ran for the truck. Brick pushed us both into the passenger side.

Quando was driving. Oh, shit.

Brick yanked the door closed. "Go."

Quando did. The tires spun free in first gear and the truck skidded and slipped. Quando jerked it into second and the tires crunched and bit and we shot out onto the road.

My left foot was jammed down on the floorboards with Quando's feet, and my right was on the passenger side with Brick. The stick rested high up against my thigh. I tried to squeeze back in the seat. "Third."

Quando pressed the clutch and I shoved the stick away from my thigh. "Where'd you learn to drive like that?"

Quando kept his eyes ahead and his hands tight on the wheel and said nothing.

"Or to drive at all?"

The rpms ran up. Quando glanced over. "Fourth?"

"Skip to five."

He pressed the clutch and I jumped the gears. "Wait. Just stop. Pull over."

Brick was trying to reach beneath his seat but we were too crowded in the cab for him to maneuver.

I tried to reach under the driver's seat but couldn't get there. "Wait. Where's the gun?"

Brick came up with his pistol. In a flash he checked the safety and the load.

"Where's *my gun?*"

Quando moved his hip and I saw my Smith & Wesson underneath. I grabbed it. "Jesus fuck, you could have *shot your ass off.* Stop the truck."

"I'm looking for a place."

"Stop the truck. *Now.*"

Quando slowed.

I wrenched the stick out of gear and stretched my foot across Quando's leg, trying to get to the brake pedal.

The truck swerved.

Brick put a hand on my arm. "Jackson."

I couldn't reach the brake pedal, but the truck slowed. "That was the stupidest, most insane—"

"Jackson."

"You were hiding in the back?"

There was a push on my shoulder from Brick. But there was nowhere to push me. We were packed in like the D train in Manhattan.

"We had it *under control.* And then you—"

Brick jabbed an elbow at my ribs. "Jackson."

"What?"

The truck came to rest. Brick clicked the safety off his pistol.

"What the—"

"They're coming."

A group of motorcycles swarmed behind us, mean white eyes of light screaming toward us in the dark.

I pushed the stick into gear. "Go."

Quando did.

We ran up through the gears, Quando holding the wheel to the road and me working the stick. It was an empty two-lane that ran parallel to the highway. Just us and the bikes. And it didn't take them long to catch us.

Quando white-knuckled it. "What now? What do I do now?"

"Keep it straight."

A big black bike roared up to Quando's open window. He jerked the wheel and the truck swerved and the biker almost went down.

That brought them on us like a hive of bees. Both sides, at the front fender, behind us. Boot heels thunked into the side panels of the truck.

Brick twisted sideways. "This is getting stupid." He raised himself into the open window, turned his back to the wind, and leveled his pistol on the biker inches from his elbow.

The biker immediately fell back.

Brick moved his aim to a biker with his boot out to strike the truck. That one fell back.

Brick twisted back into the cab. A bike screamed forward to Quando's window and its rider wrestled one hand into his jacket.

The genie was out of the bottle. Just like we'd talked about. Once Brick had drawn his weapon, once Quando had come in with a piece, we were locked in. Someone was going to get shot.

I raised the Smith & Wesson and struggled to find room in the tight quarters to turn around. Then a long curve of road opened before us, with a gravel shoulder that canted down into the river.

I pointed to Quando, pointed to the slope, and made a motion for Quando to turn the wheel.

He did, too hard. The truck veered sideways and the wheels skidded, skipped, and then slid loose.

We spun nearly around, the load in the bed of the truck sliding and thumping and jumping. The gray tarp flapped and broke free and filled the view in the mirror. I looked to see the wheelbarrow and lumber and bags of concrete slapping onto the gravelly slope.

Then Quando had the truck righted and we were spinning down to the water.

A bike veered on the road and went down on its side, its driver leaning on top as it threw sparks from the crash bar.

Quando jammed the brakes. "What now?"

"Take her in."

Another biker veered around the downed rider, slipped, and laid his bike onto the road.

Quando started to the water slowly. I reached over and stepped on his foot, and the truck lurched forward.

It was a shallow stretch of river I remembered from my childhood. My father had a canoe when I was in grade school and he would take me and my brother down the river on summer days. In the dry season this was a stretch we might have to portage, lifting the canoe and carrying it by the gunnels until the river narrowed and deepened again.

Tonight there was enough water to float, and we did.

The nose of the truck plowed a neat line of water up and over the cab, then bit in and dived down. The bed rose on the water behind us and the wheels skipped from riverbed to water, riverbed to water.

Moisture seeped in at the bottom of the doors. Quando let the pedal go and the truck idled and drifted sideways. For a brief moment it was quiet and peaceful in the dark, a half-moon winking down on us.

We were near the middle of the river, maybe twenty feet behind us and twenty to the other shore. The front tires bumped the riverbed. The back tires drifted away.

Bikes entered the water behind us.

I elbowed Quando. "Punch it."

He did. The tires spun and water churned and the truck skittered in and out of purchase on the gravel bottom of the river until they found a grip and we jounced up through the waterline on the far side.

I squeezed my shoulders around and looked back. A couple of the bikers had found a shallower passage a couple dozen yards downstream and were picking their way across the river.

Quando saw them too and turned the truck around.

I reached for the wheel. "What are you doing?"

The truck bounced and I lost my grip on the wheel. Quando made a line for the river-crossers. He splashed the grill into the water and raised a jet of water that crashed against the Harleys. One bike toppled from the force. Quando spun the wheel and the tires ground into the riverbed and the back of the truck spun into another bike.

"Quando!"

He turned the wheel again, his foot down on the gas. One of the bikers was stopped with his bike tank-deep in water. He raised an arm and a glint of metal came with it. Quando spun the truck and crashed water and gravel over the biker.

Brick's long, thick arm came over me and snatched the wheel. "Enough. Let's go."

Quando did, grinding the truck up out of the river where we'd entered and back onto the road.

Quando stomped on the gas and we wound the truck up through the gears. The road behind us cleared.

After a couple of miles I put a hand on the gearshift. "Stop."

Quando did. We all got out. Brick holstered his gun under the seat, then put a hand out and took mine away. "I think we all better dial it back down now."

I wanted to be angry at Quando. I wanted to shout. I wanted to put a hole in Quando's grin. But it was just the weirdest and funniest thing I'd ever seen.

I looked over the quiet, moonlit fields. I looked at Quando. "Fucking Bo Duke."

Brick grinned. "Hot damn, them country boys didn't know whether to spit or go blind."

"They what? That is the stupidest thing…"

Brick pointed to his shirt. *No sh*t?*

Then something broke loose in me and a big hyena laugh escaped. Quando joined in the howling.

It passed after a moment and Quando said, "So I'm not in trouble?"

Brick stepped up to Quando. "Nobody said that, son." He pointed to the truck. "Get in. You're in the middle."

We wedged in around Quando and the truck engine caught and spit out water vapor from the exhaust. I turned us around and headed back in the direction we'd come.

Brick leaned around Quando. "Jackson. What are you doing?"

"Soon as those guys are gone, I'm gonna go back and get my lumber."

23

EVERYTHING HURT. Again. Even body parts I thought hadn't been touched the night before. The big toe on my right foot hurt when I walked. Why would that be sore?

Snippets of a conversation from the night before when I dropped off Brick and Quando turned over in my head.

Quando, to me: Brick flattened them guys. You shoulda seen it. He nearly took that guy's head off knocking him off of you.

Brick: It ain't so much to be proud of.

Quando had looked hurt and confused, slapped back by Brick.

Brick, to Quando: We'll talk about it. They're people too. Think about what Jackson is going to look like to his daughter in the morning.

Well, it was morning and I was thinking about that now. The toe was nothing. It didn't even hurt enough to make a limp. The real damage showed up when I looked in the mirror. Cuts and bruises and swelling. But nothing that had required stitches, no broken bones, and no signs of a concussion. Without Brick it would have been a different story.

The truck had a couple of dents in the side panels and I'd lost some concrete and lumber. Quando was unscathed, and Brick showed only a scratch on his forearm. Me and the truck had by far come out the worst for wear on our team.

I made coffee, filled Mrs. Jenkins' food bowl and refreshed her water, downed some aspirin, and waited. There would be no hiding it. Cali was sure to see the damage.

I waited a long time. Then I heard Cali rise, make her way to the bathroom, and shuffle out to the kitchen where I sat at the table.

She poured herself a finger of coffee. Cali was just starting to drink it, and she experimented with tiny portions. After doling out a few careful drops of cream and a sprinkle of sugar, she came to the table and sat across from me. Her eyes came up. "Oh."

I held my mouth in a tight line against the puffiness and a cracked lip. "I'm not going to make a joke this time. I'm going to give it to you straight."

Nothing.

"If that's what you want."

A quick nod.

I gave her the short version. She sat without moving and listened without making a sound. When I got to the end she blinked. "What do you want me to say?"

"You don't have to say anything."

"Can I ask some questions?"

"Of course."

Cali breathed. She breathed again. Her brow squinched and she tilted her head. "I can't believe any of that. I just can't. Brick was supposed to look out for you. And he brought this—kid, and…"

I let her turn it over.

"You didn't really bring Quando, did you?"

I shook my head.

"He sneaked. And it would have been worse without Brick."

"Yes."

"And you were going to go anyway. Because…"

"Because that's what I do. Sometimes it's a little risky."

"But you were supposed to be careful. You said…"

I waited. Cali didn't add anything, so I said simply, "I did."

The corners of her mouth went down. "What are you going to tell Marzi?"

It wasn't a question I'd expected, but I had an answer. "The same thing I'm telling you."

"She's not going to like it."

"Probably not."

"Mom would never put up with this. You wouldn't be doing it if she was here."

"Doing what?"

"Any of it."

"A lot of things would be different if your mother was here."

Cali got up and left.

I stayed at the table. The thing of it was, she was probably right.

But I had to finish it now. Almost there. I shifted some gears in my head. Cleared the domestic and put my mind to finishing the case. This would be over soon, and then I could return to Cali and Marzi.

Angelita had been patient. She'd wanted to go to the storage unit the night before. But it had been a late and difficult night, and I wanted to set something else in place before we went.

I had sent Deputy Bronigan some items last night. Lizzie Martin's name. Her connection to Hector Martin and Johnny Diggs and Angelita shooting Hector in her yard. Diggs' license plate number from his Harley.

It was already making the news. Deputies from the Greene County Sheriff's office, working together with another county, had brought in Jonathan Diggs for questioning as an accomplice in the recent shooting at the Leewold property. Diggs' mug shot was in the news clips, with images and video from the night of the shooting. There was a photo of Hector Martin, with a report that he'd woken from his coma was still in the hospital and remained largely unresponsive. The case looked like a wrap.

I went out to the porch and texted Bronigan. *Was that your handiwork?*

My phone rang. Bronigan. I answered. "It *was* you."

"I assume you've been looking at the news."

"I have. Such fine police work. Why don't I see your picture in the clips?"

"My job is to serve and protect."

"And not to be seen?"

"Not so much."

"So no grandstanding then."

There were voices in the background. Some clacking of a keyboard.

Bronigan said, "There'll be a press conference later this morning. You won't see me in it."

"Above your pay grade."

"Definitely."

"That will be you. Some day."

Bronigan let that hang between us.

I shifted my phone to the other ear. "Will it do you any good at all?"

"Might. The brass knows my name now."

"That's something."

A yawn came loudly through the phone.

"Have you gotten any sleep?"

"Sleep is for the weak."

"And for a family man. I'll bet you've got a wife and newborn calling your name."

"More like I've got a dirty diaper calling my name."

"You do what you have to."

"Thanks for bringing my moment back down to earth."

I laughed. "Any time. Give my regards to Molly and little Henry."

"I will."

"And Bronigan?"

"Yeah?"

"Keep in touch."

He made a clicking sound like pointing a finger as a gun, and signed off.

I drove to the Leewold house. When I arrived I climbed into the passenger seat of Angelita's Toyota pickup and let her drive. This was her show now.

The self-store facility was remote, on a empty stretch of road and surrounded by high chain-link fencing. The place looked old but well maintained. Security cameras watched the front gate. A card reader allowed access through the main gate.

Well, damn.

Angelita hung her head and let out a sigh.

I agreed with the sentiment, but I pointed to a weedy patch of ground out of range of the cameras. "Park there. Let's just have a look around."

I walked the perimeter, Angelita lagging behind. At the back corner a truck was parked at the end of the long metal building. A middle-aged man in work clothes was unloading a lawn mower and weed whacker from the back of the truck. He had dark skin and looked fit and like he was used to working.

The man saw me and I raised a hand. "Hello."

He waved back.

"Do you have second?"

He leaned the weed whacker against the side of the truck and came over.

I hooked a finger through the chain fencing. "Doesn't look like too bad of a job. Not much there to mow." There was only one long, thin strip of grass inside the fence along the back line.

The man swept his arm over the grassy area outside the fence. "Gotta do all that too."

"Then I take it back. Are you the owner?"

He took stock of the cuts and bruises on my face, shifting side to side to get a good look. "Mister, most people would ask if I knew the owner, not if I owned it."

"My apologies if I assumed."

"None needed. What can I do for you?"

Angelita caught up and stood beside me. I introduced her, then stepped back. "I'll let her tell the story."

She did, and held up the key to the storage unit to show him, then asked if he would let us in.

The man took his cap off and wiped the moisture on his head. "I'd like to help, but I can't really advertise this place as secure if I let someone in who's not registered for a unit."

I nodded in agreement. "Listen, Mister...?"

"No mister. Just Ike."

"Ike, can I show you something?" I held up my phone where he could see.

Ike came closer to the fence, and I played a news clip that announced a suspect had been held for questioning in the recent shooting at a home in Greene County. A photo of Johnny Diggs came on the screen.

Ike scratched his chin. "I'll tell you what. It seems like that might be a guy I rented a unit to not too long ago. You let me take that key back and try it on the lock there. If it fits I'll decide if I should let you in."

Angelita passed the key through the fence to Ike and told him the unit number, and he went to check.

Then Angelita dragged her hand across the fence. "What do you think?"

I shrugged. Who knows? We've come this far.

A minute later Ike whistled from way down at the other end of the lot near the entry. He waved us over.

Then Ike returned the key to Angelita, motioned us through the gate, and went to mow the grass.

The storage unit was mid-sized, and Diggs got his money's worth. The place was packed. Bed frames, dressers, mattress, a long line of moving boxes. A couch, chairs, kitchen items. A rack of clothing, coats, bookshelves, books spilled on the floor.

A lot of it was torn up or had been rummaged through. Slits in the mattress and fabric of the chairs, items strewn from boxes, books tossed from the shelves. Angelita ran her fingers over the edge of a bookshelf. "These are Aunt Ida's things."

"I'm sorry they've been treated so poorly."

She picked up a loose book and returned it to a slot on a shelf. "They moved all this stuff…?"

"Butterfield worked for the moving company your realtor hired. J Guy. He would have had to move it all anyway."

"What do they usually do with it?"

"Guy said they give some to Goodwill. Some they take to the dump."

Angelita stepped farther into the unit, bent to look at the remnants in an open box. "So that's what would have happened to all of this."

"Yes. But instead Diggs convinced Hector Martin to pack it all over here because—"

"Because Hector talked to the guy who was my daddy's jailmate, who was lurking around the house."

"Rufus Butterfield. And Hector rode in the same motorcycle club with Diggs, and they convinced themselves that the stories they heard from Butterfield were true."

"And all this happened because…"

"Because your father told a good story."

Angelita looked around the unit. "Incredible."

"I guess. People believe what they want to. Or need to."

She touched a few more things. Picked up a sweater and sniffed it.

I faded back. "You think there's anything worthwhile in here?" It sounded crass when I heard it come out, but Angelita didn't seem to notice. "Maybe something sentimental? Some memories?"

She set the sweater back down. "Definitely."

"There's a chance that Diggs will come back. There might be another key. Or he could bring bolt cutters."

Angelita frowned.

"I don't know how long they can hold him. J Guy has offered to send a truck over. Today. And some guys. They'll take as much of this out of here as you want to. All I have to do is let him know."

Her eyes glistened. "There's so much. All of Aunt Ida's things."

"There is. But if you want anything, we should probably get it now."

She straightened. "All of it. I'll sort through it later."

"I'll call Guy."

Then I went outside to give Angelita some room while we waited for Guy's truck. Ike had finished mowing the strip of grass inside the fence and opened a small service gate in the back to get to the larger patch outside.

I wandered over. "You want a hand?"

Ike looked at me like he was deciding what kind of offer I was making him.

"I'm giving her some room. Give me something to do."

"You wanna whack?"

I did. I worked the fence line inside and out and was ready to give Ike a break from the mowing when a truck rumbled up to the front gate. The driver stepped out and looked through the fencing. J Guy Estate Removal Service was printed on the side of the truck.

I pushed the button to manually open the gate from the inside and ushered the moving truck down to the unit.

Angelita was sitting in front of an old cedar chest that was open and full of papers. She had a brown and brittle packet nestled gently on her lap and she was reading from it. I saw wet at her eyes.

I turned to the moving guys. "Can you give us just a few minutes?"

They had no problem with that and went to the back of the truck with water bottles.

I went in to Angelita. She motioned me to come beside her. "I didn't think my father had anything valuable. It was just stories. He would have told me. Or Aunt Ida would have known. It just didn't make sense."

It was what I'd been thinking all along. "Maybe your father needed something to get him through. Maybe his stories was that something."

"So all of this—those guys moving all of Aunt Ida's things, me shooting that guy, all that work you did to find this…"

"And all that money you spent to have me do that."

"Yes. But I inherited a surprising amount of money from Aunt Ida. I don't know how she had all of that. I thought maybe that was the treasure."

"I think it's however you want to think about it."

She spread her hand across the papers on her lap. "But look at this."

It took me a moment. I'd never seen them before. "Manumission papers?"

"They called them freedom papers. They bought their way out of slavery. Others escaped and ran away to join them up here in the north at Leewold."

She read the look on my face.

"They called the house Leewold. It's here in the notes. This tells the story."

"Those must be very old."

"And very fragile. They were sealed in plastic bags, and those were sealed in a airtight bin." She held up a yellowed bag with more papers and an ancient leather notebook held together with twine.

"Those must be worth—"

The look on her face told me she already knew.

24

WE ENDED THE SUMMER with a Sunday afternoon dip in Massies Creek. Angelita wanted to do some sort of thing her Aunt Ida had done with the family when she was a kid, but Angelita didn't have family anymore. So she asked all of us and said she would explain when we got there.

I went alone. It wasn't what I wanted. I wanted to plan something with Cali for the last weekend before school started, but when I accepted Angelita's invitation and invited her to go along, Cali took the opportunity to remind me that one of us should spend some time with Marzi. If it wasn't going to be me, she would do that.

I talked with Marzi about what was happening. Cali was pitting my work against herself and Marzi. It wasn't something we were going to sort out with the wave of a hand. Marzi decided it was best that she didn't go with me to Angelita's either.

I almost didn't go. But the weekend with Cali was already lost, and it meant a lot to Angelita. Brick and J'Leah were bringing food to make it a picnic. It was the least I could do to partake.

Brick and Quando arrived shortly after me. Brick nosed the Shelby down the lane to the Leewold house and stopped in a sunny spot.

Angelita walked over and whistled. "Nice car."

Brick gave the daughter-at-prom smile. "I told you. And I think I promised you a ride."

Angelita looped her arm through Brick's. "You did. We'll do that a little later." She steered him toward the house. Quando followed, carrying a tray of cheese and veggies and hummus and looking happier than I thought he could.

We laid the food out in the kitchen. There was the sound of another car arriving, and we drifted outside to greet J'Leah.

She backed her Honda in front of the Shelby.

Brick waved her off, pointing to the shade tree.

J'Leah leaned out the window. "I don't want to park under the birds."

Brick laughed. "I know a place with a good car wash."

J'Leah didn't make the connection.

Brick circled a finger. "Then pull in around behind me."

J'Leah did that without asking why.

I snorted.

"What?"

"I see you still haven't gotten the solenoid fixed. You're going to look a lot less cool to Angelita when you have to push start that thing."

Brick leaned over and whispered. "I'm not going to let that stop me from taking her for a ride."

Then we all went inside and added the little sandwich bites that J'Leah had brought to the other food, and Angelita gave everyone the one-minute tour. She'd picked a few items from her aunt's belongings to bring to the house. An old clock that she remembered had been on the mantle. The bookshelves. A chair.

Most of the rest of the things were in another storage unit. Angelita had moved them to protect them from Johnny Diggs or someone else coming back. They were in the same facility, in a different unit.

"What can I say?" Angelita said. "I like Ike."

I groaned. The others looked confused. We left it at that.

Then Angelita showed us the one other thing she had on hand from the items we had recovered. The freedom papers. "Someone is coming tomorrow from the Afro-American Museum in Wilberforce. We're going to find a safe place to keep these."

Angelita picked up one of the plastic bags with a yellowing paper folded inside. "And I'm going to get some copies made. You can see my family's names here. Sometimes who owned them. I'll frame some of the copies and hang them."

Quando bent way forward to look at the letters through the bag. "Owned them?"

I remembered Quando and Angelita sitting in the shade of the tree talking when we'd been here before. It looked like that conversation wasn't finished yet. Good.

When the one-minute tour that had turned into twenty minutes ended, we sat down to eat. J'Leah looked over as I picked up a sandwich. "I don't know how you can chew through all those bruises on your chin."

"Not much choice," I said. "You didn't bring any milkshakes."

We ate. After a while I got Angelita's attention. "Do you feel those papers are safe here until you work out where to keep them?"

"I do. They'll probably end up in the museum at Central State. And I called that lawyer you know. He's going to help me sort out…all of the things that have been happening."

Brick looked at Angelita. "You called Samuel Thomas?"

"You know him?"

"Worked with us on something Jackson had going on earlier in the summer. ST will do you right. I just talked to him."

Now I looked over.

Quando lifted his head. "About me."

I gave Brick and Quando my full attention, but neither of them offered any explanation.

"So one thing," J'Leah said. "There was no…family treasure?"

Angelita set down her sandwich and wiped her fingers on a napkin. "It's something Jackson said. My daddy's not here to tell me, so it's how I decide to interpret his stories. I think the freedom papers are the treasure."

J'Leah and Angelita held eyes on each other for a moment. I didn't pretend to understand the connection that must have been happening between them. The mysterious bonds that Angelita had alluded to bringing us here for seemed to already be happening. J'Leah and Angelita. Brick and Quando. Quando and Angelita's family history.

It made me want Cali and Marzi there with me even more.

Then Angelita went to the bedroom and came back with an old book in her hand. She held the book out. On the cover was an image of a man and woman standing on a wooden porch, looking at the sun in the distance. The title was *Brighter Sun*, by Greene B. Buster.

"I found this in my aunt's things. I remember it from when I was little. Aunt Ida used to want to read it to me. She was trying to tell me that our family story is like this family's story, but I wasn't old enough to listen then."

Quando had his sandwich down and his eyes open. Angelita handed the book to him. "You can read it if you'd like to."

Quando didn't have to say yes.

Once the eating had slowed down, Angelita made an announcement. "So. That thing I asked you to come for. That my aunt used to do. That's why I asked you to bring your bathing suits."

She didn't explain, just told us all to get ready and changed if we needed to and she'd be waiting out back for us.

Brick and I wore swim trunks. He looked like a Greek statue, but with larger, darker muscles. Quando's swimwear was an oversized pair of shorts that I knew would float around him like a raft in the water. Angelita and J'Leah had their swim gear under their clothing.

Angelita walked us back to the bank of Massies Creek, and then she explained. "When I was very little, family would come here and visit my Aunt Ida and the old home. It was mostly old people. My aunt's brothers and sisters, people who are dead now. They swam in the creek."

She pointed to the water. "Right here. It was a binding. A family coming together. It had something to do with the old people. Something they did from way back. But I never really understood. I was too little."

We all looked at the water. J'Leah stepped forward. "So what do we do?"

Angelita lifted her shirt over her head. Underneath was a bathing suit top. "We get in."

Then she and J'Leah both had their shirts and shorts off and were moving toward the water.

The rest of us followed.

It wasn't swimming so much as wading, but the water was deep and slow enough to make it a good place to get in.

When we'd all gotten wet, Angelita said, "Aunt Ida used to say *It's water to bind.* I don't know what she meant exactly, but I hope it's something like what we're doing now."

Brick said, "Isn't that what Mr. Nightlinger said in the John Wayne movie? Water to bind?"

I rolled over in the water. "But wasn't Mr. Nightlinger talking about making pie?"

Brick said, "He was."

Angelita pushed herself through the water. "Maybe we're all kind of like a pie." She looked around the wetted group. "A mixed fruit pie."

J'Leah laughed. "Maybe a mixed nut pie."

That did it. There was splashing and counter-splashing and general water mayhem.

I would have liked this with Cali. I would have liked it even more with both Cali and Marzi there. But Cali needed something we hadn't found yet. Something I didn't know how to give her.

Marzi was a piece of the equation I couldn't balance yet, either for me or for me and Cali. Maybe one day Cali and I would take a dunk together in Massies Creek. Maybe Marzi would join us.

Maybe that wouldn't happen. But some way Cali and I would keep our bond. It wasn't a choice. It was something we had to do.

For now, the group of us swam. We splashed and laughed and had some kind of bonding. We got out and dried. We lingered and talked.

The day grew late and we said our goodbyes.

On the way home, I drove past the house where I'd first met Angelita. The border collie was out front in the fading light, gracefully arching its back as it ran to catch a frisbee that floated over its shoulder.

Thank You and Acknowledgments

The summer after the first Jackson Flint novel, *Fair Game*, came out, my friends Dave Stratton and Toni Laricchiuta invited me to their back yard to join their reading group as they talked about the book. It was during covid, and we sat spaced apart and I enjoyed being even relatively close to more than just my wife and a few close friends for probably the first time since the pandemic had begun.

As the evening wound down, I ended up talking with Chuck Buster, who told me that he thought the novel was color blind—that he had tended to read Jackson Flint as a Black man, naturally making the character more like himself. We talked about how it was interesting that Jackson is actually white in the story, but other characters are Black: Brick is lighter skinned, and J'Leah is darker. After a while, the color of the characters mattered less than that they were human and they interacted in interesting enough ways to just be people.

Then Chuck told me the really interesting thing. His "Uncle Greene" had written a book published in the 1950s about his family's escape from slavery in Kentucky to Greene County, Ohio. Right there where we were living and talking. And Chuck was the legacy of that. Fascinating.

I immediately went about locating and reading a copy of that book: *Brighter Sun*, by Greene B. Buster. I was just starting to think about what the sequel to *Fair Game* would be. After talking with Chuck and reading *Brighter Sun*, I knew that would play a part in the story in this book.

Chuck's family story is one of many similar stories. That legacy is all around us in Greene County, Ohio, and beyond.

Thanks, Chuck. And thanks, Dave and Toni, for inviting that conversation under the stars.

Hi, there.

Thanks for reading. I assume you've read the book because you're at the end. If you haven't read it, maybe I'll see you here again if you do.

Will you indulge me in asking a favor? If there's anything you liked about this book – the characters, plot, mystery, dialogue, setting, how the characters interacted – anything at all, would you write that in a review on Amazon?

That will help me know if people like the books and I should write more.

Thanks again for reading. I deeply appreciate it. The Jackson Flint books are A LOT of fun to write. I hope some of that came through in your reading.

Cheers,
Scott

And hey, if you want more of Jackson Flint, Brick, J'Leah, Cali, Marzi, and the others, look for other novels and short stories in the series at my Amazon page.

Made in the USA
Las Vegas, NV
20 April 2023

70864398R00144